D1647977

FOLLOW THE SUN

FOLLOW THE SUN

LIZ LOCKE

RANDOM HOUSE CANADA

PUBLISHED BY RANDOM HOUSE CANADA

Copyright © 2023 Liz Locke

All rights reserved under International and Pan-American Copyright Conventions. No part of this book may be reproduced in any form or by any electronic or mechanical means, including information storage and retrieval systems, without permission in writing from the publisher, except by a reviewer, who may quote brief passages in a review. Published in 2023 by Random House Canada, a division of Penguin Random House Canada Limited, Toronto. Distributed in Canada and the United States of America by Penguin Random House Canada Limited, Toronto.

www.penguinrandomhouse.ca

Random House Canada and colophon are registered trademarks.

Library and Archives Canada Cataloguing in Publication

Title: Follow the sun / Liz Locke.
Names: Locke, Liz, author.
Identifiers: Canadiana (print) 20220483116 | Canadiana (ebook) 20220483175 |
    ISBN 9781039007178 (softcover) | ISBN 9781039007185 (EPUB)
Classification: LCC PS3612.O27 F65 2023 | DDC 813/.6—dc23

Text design: Talia Abramson
Cover design: Talia Abramson
Image credits: Noel Hendrickson / Getty Images; Peyman Farmani / Unsplash

Printed in the United States of America

10 9 8 7 6 5 4 3 2 1

Penguin
Random House
RANDOM HOUSE CANADA

For Dad, who had faith.

ACAPULCO

September 25th, 1966
Las Brisas Hotel
Acapulco, Mexico

Dear Daddy,

I tried to sing you a song, on the patio overlooking the sea. I tuned my ukulele just as you taught me, listening for the telltale signs of a string kept too loose or too tight; of a note slightly left of center.

But in the end, the music wouldn't come together. Scales went up when they should have gone down, while flats with razor-sharp edges taunted with each staccato:

"Not good enough."

"Who said you could try?"

Maybe it was me, or maybe it was the wind.

Or maybe the melody was hiding in the mistakes.

Love,
Caroline

ONE

LEGS BENT, ARMS extended, I sucked in a breath and pushed from the diving board. Sounds of music and laughter flashed by, muting as my head hit the water. The world above became a shimmering mirage of unfocused light, the icy temperature a shock to my skin. I felt the rush of being young and alive; invincible despite knowing the bottom was far below. Kick hard enough, and you wouldn't drown.

The newspapers called Acapulco the playground of the rich, and oh, how we came to play. Our retreats stretched from the Côte d'Azur to Rio, exotic locales made even more beautiful by the rose-colored filter of luxury. And despite our constant search for the next fashionable backdrop, there was something special about this Mexican seaport that drew us back again and again. Perhaps it was the faint scent of hibiscus drifting through the salt air. Or the cheerful pink hue of umbrellas lining the water, shielding bronzed bodies from the afternoon heat. Or the way the sun made the mansions dotting the hillside shine like diamonds as it crawled across the sky—our only indication time was not standing still.

Resurfacing, I swam to the platform that hovered like a bull's-eye in the middle of the pool. Daphne lay reclined on its edge, breasts straining against the cups of her lemon-yellow bikini. She was the Marilyn to my Jackie, sensuality radiating from every pore. I reached up to tap her shoulder, finding it slick with tanning oil.

"I'm ready for a drink. Wanna join me?"

She glanced at the bar from behind her white-plastic-framed sunglasses. "No, darling, you go ahead. Chat up that actor everyone's going on about."

"Actor? I thought he was in a band. Something about monkeys . . ." I wrinkled my nose at the small man flirting with two fashion models.

"Whatever he is, he's cute. And in high demand, apparently." She raised an eyebrow at his female companions. I took a second look, but before I could form an opinion, my gaze fell on another man a few feet away. He was tall, his eyes shielded by sunglasses, but by the angle of his head, there was no mistaking their focus: me. His hands held a small camera, and my skin prickled with awareness. How long had he been watching?

"Hey, who's that guy standing behind him?"

Daphne lifted her glasses and squinted to see farther. "In the blue shirt? I think he's a magazine photographer. *Time*? *Vogue*? Something like that. Why?"

"He's staring. Like he knows me."

"Maybe he just *wants* to know you."

I made a face, playfully splashing a handful of water onto the platform.

"That's not funny!" she shrieked, her body flinching against the cold drops.

Fearing retaliation, I laughed and swam out of reach.

Daphne and I had been best friends since our Swiss boarding school roomed us together almost a decade ago. I'd been a scared, shy adolescent who'd wanted nothing more than to call my father and demand he come rescue me from my Alpine prison. But when this twelve-year-old girl walked in with all the swagger of a young femme fatale, she took one look at me and said, "We'll make a rebel out of you yet." Instilling confidence where there was none before, she taught me valuable life lessons such as how to smoke Gitanes like Brigitte Bardot, the subtle art of stuffing a bra, and the quickest way to shimmy up a trellis three hours after curfew.

Some of our old schoolmates were already married, while others had gone on to the hallowed halls of Smith and Wellesley. But there was a third path for girls like us, a tiny side door into a world of glamorous adventure. Jets were our magic carpet, delivering us to places where deadlines and decisions didn't exist. We followed the sun, relishing the days before boys and rings would appear to bring us back down to earth. For both Daphne and me, that moment seemed blessedly far off.

After completing a few more laps around the pool, I swam to a ladder and lifted myself onto the concrete deck, arms and legs aching with exhaustion. Twisting the water out of my hair, I still sensed a pair of eyes on me, though I didn't dare turn to look. Not yet.

"Towel, madam?" A club employee greeted me with a stack.

"*Sí, gracias.*" After running the terry cloth over the wild swirls of my Pucci swimsuit, I spread it over a lounge chair before motioning to a passing waiter, who approached to take my drink order.

"*Margarita por favor, y una más para el hombre.*" I pointed to the bar, toward the tall figure, who now had his back to me. Mimicking the action of taking a picture with my hands, I tried to convey that I wanted to send a drink to the photographer, and not the celebrity standing near him. The awkwardness of making the first move was a fair trade for satisfying my curiosity.

Picking up my tattered notebook, I started to jot down some lyrics I'd come up with during the swim. I'd work out an arrangement on the ukulele in my hotel room later, away from eyes and ears and words like *hobby* and *lark* and *isn't that sweet*, and all the other whispered slights that made me sigh with defeat.

Engrossed by a turn of phrase I'd just written, I didn't notice the looming shadow until a drop of water fell from the bottom of a glass and landed on my thigh.

"I believe this one's yours, ma'am?"

Raising my eyes, I sucked in a breath at the sight of the man standing in front of me. He wore a blue polo shirt that matched the cloudless sky above us, contrasting with the leather camera strap slung around his neck. His blond hair was styled clean-cut, and a square jaw framed a mouth of straight white teeth. I hadn't realized from afar just how handsome he was, but up close it was obvious. He was the type usually found on a fifty-foot movie screen, not standing beside a pool in Acapulco, real as the drink he held. The slight bend in the middle of his nose was the one thing preventing him from being too perfect, like the sculptor had looked away for a moment and let the chisel slip. But even this only intrigued me further.

Clearing my suddenly dry throat, I explained, "There must

be some mistake. I ordered two—one for each of us. I hate to drink alone."

"See, that's the thing, ma'am. I try to stay sharp while I'm on the job. But I wanted to thank you just the same." His voice held the Southern twang I missed with every beat of my heart, bringing both sorrow and comfort at the same time. "Didn't mean to interrupt if you're workin' on something. Is that a poem?" He stared curiously at my book.

Quickly, I closed the cover and placed it off to the side. I didn't know which I feared more—condescension or genuine praise.

"I'm twenty-two; that's too young to be called ma'am. Caroline, please," I said, extending a hand.

He shook it, his grip firm and confident. "What a relief—a normal name. Everyone I've met here goes by a funny little nickname. Mimsy or Bobo or Kiki. And that's just the men."

I laughed, charmed. "Well, I'm just plain Caroline. Caroline Kimball. And you are?"

"Jack Fairchild. *Life* magazine sent me down here to do a photo essay. You happened to be in my frame."

"I'll bet. I saw you staring at me from the bar. I decided to be bold and introduce myself."

He sat down, handing over my margarita. "It's part of the job, I guess, watching people. You caught my eye when you went into the water. All that long dark hair, flyin' out behind you. And then I couldn't help but wish I'd been sent here to take pictures of you instead of the cliff divers."

His words warmed me like a shot of tequila snaking through my blood. Was it a sin to indulge in a little harmless flirtation?

"So, Jack Fairchild of *Life* magazine. Where do you hail from?"

"Oh, a little town near Midland, Texas. My folks are in the ranching business. I shot straight out of there the day I turned eighteen and never looked back. I've lived in New York for goin' on eight years now. Still can't shake the accent, unfortunately. People tell me it comes and goes."

"Don't apologize; I like it. It reminds me of my father. He came from a family of Houston oilmen." Lord, I hadn't thought about Texas, or my stern-faced relatives, in forever. After Daddy's funeral, they'd cut off all contact with Mother and me. As though we were the hangman's noose instead of collateral damage.

"Houston, huh? I bet you went to one of them fancy finishing schools. I never would've known you had some Texan in you."

"Only trace amounts, I'm afraid. I'm more a citizen of the world now."

"One of the beautiful people?" He smirked, like the concept was something laughable. The tabloids hadn't helped us in that regard. To the general public, members of the jet set appeared elitist and out of touch. Socialites with too much money and time, our crises belittled by pithy headlines and sensationalist reporting. But what the papers always got wrong was that underneath the expensive clothes, behind the makeup and jewels, there was often just an ordinary person with ordinary problems. Problems that couldn't be solved in a thousand hotel rooms or villas, much as one might try.

"You seem to be adapting well," I pointed out, letting his assumption slide. "Sitting by a pool in Acapulco, taking pictures of girls in bikinis. Nice gig, if you can get it."

"Sure beats muckin' out horse stalls on the ranch."

I took another sip of my drink and studied him. Despite his almost unbearably handsome face, his lack of pretension put me at ease. Even more remarkable, he hadn't reacted to hearing my name. For once, I wasn't David Kimball's tragic daughter, or Emanuela Leoni's look-alike progeny. I reveled in the anonymity.

"So, after you finish in Acapulco, are you off on another magazine assignment?"

"Back to New York first, then who knows?" He raised a shoulder in casual acceptance. "I'll just be glad to get another job, no matter where it is. How about you? What's next?"

"Not sure yet," I confessed. "I hate to plan too far in advance. I guess I'll be off to some other city or town where the sun's still shining and the drinks are still cold. Though a warm café au lait in Paris is always tempting, even in the rain."

"No work or responsibilities? Doesn't that get boring?"

I bristled at his judgmental tone. "Tell me—does developing pictures in a darkroom day after day ever get boring? Some people spend their whole lives in a job like that, right?"

"Yeah, and if I hadn't gotten a magazine editor interested in my photos, I might still be one of them."

"So put yourself back in the lab. If someone gave you a million dollars and said you could travel anywhere you wanted, for as long as you wanted, wouldn't you do it in a heartbeat?"

He considered the question. "Maybe for a little while, but after that? I'd get restless. Probably start to worry I was wastin' precious time. There are too many things I want to do before the clock ticks down."

"Luckily Pan Am makes it possible to outrun those worries. And for the record, poolside margaritas are never a waste of time." It was a joke, meant to take the sting out of his words, but I still felt the cut. With one sentence, he'd slashed through the thick shield I wore around my insecurities. The secret fear that, despite all my daydreams and notebooks filled with words, I'd already missed my chance. The chance to know what it felt like to stand before an audience, split my chest open, and hand them my heart.

He shrugged, shaking his head. I didn't know which of us I wanted to convince, but I couldn't let him walk away thinking my life was trivial or dull. Once that seed was planted, it had the potential to grow and fester and turn into something more dangerous. Something that would make me run faster, play harder.

"I wonder—are you free for dinner tonight? You can join our party for an evening, then tell me if you still think I'm *wastin' precious time.*"

He hesitated before flashing a crooked grin. Challenge accepted. "Okay, just plain Caroline. You're on. Where and when?"

"The bar at Las Brisas, eight o'clock. Prepare for a lengthy cocktail hour."

Jack tilted his head. "And just how many drinks you plannin' to squeeze in?"

"Enough to make me forget you called me ma'am. Twice." I smiled and winked, just as he raised his camera to snap a quick photo. Though it would be weeks before that film was developed, I already felt exposed.

TWO

THE SCENT OF orange blossoms filled the air as I scrubbed my skin under the warm spray of the hotel shower. A pink Jeep had driven me back the moment the sun started to sink behind the hills, and I'd dashed inside to rinse off before dinner. I hummed the beginnings of a tune, the rudimentary lyrics echoing off the tiles:

> *Sunbeams reaching down, down, down*
> *Below the surface*
> *As we drown, drown, drown*
>
> *Grab my hand*
> *Pull me up*
> *Take me to another town*

Eventually the water ran cold, forcing me to turn off the faucets. Stepping out, I could hear Daphne's angry voice from the bedroom.

"I told you a thousand times, I'm not coming. After Acapulco, Mother and I are going to Paris for the new collections, and then I'm spending the holidays in Gstaad like always." She paused. I gathered she was on the phone with her father.

"Yes, I know London is just across the Channel, but if you think I'm going to sit at a table next to your child bride and pretend she's not a home-wrecking whore, you are mistaken!" Daphne yelled. Taking a second to hear his retort, she fired back, "Then go ahead and freeze my trust fund; see if I care. Spend it on a new pram so you can take the missus out on the town!" She slammed down the receiver.

"Wow, everything all right?" I called, grabbing a fluffy towel from the rack.

"Oh, it's just my stupid father and that tart he married. They want to parade me around like we're all one big, happy family. What a joke."

I shook my head, familiar with the game they played. Daphne would rail against him, threatening to cut all ties, then in a week she'd declare that she just *had* to go to London to meet Brian Jones or someone who knew someone who knew Paul McCartney, and while there she might as well see her bastard of a father and attend one of his society events. At which point he would ignore her, she'd cause a scandal to get his attention, and their whole toxic merry-go-round would begin again.

"What are you wearing tonight?" I asked, moving into the bedroom. It wasn't worth pointing out that at least she still had a father to argue with. Some of us weren't so lucky.

Daphne smiled and leaped toward the closet. "I've been waiting all week to debut my Dior. The time has come, darling." She held up a short yellow beaded dress with long sheer sleeves. I nodded, knowing the design would draw attention to her legs.

"By the way, I told that photographer from the pool to join us. But now I don't know what I was thinking. He acted like traveling with my friends was some sort of crime."

"I know exactly what you were thinking. You were thinking he's cute, and something different. And god, isn't anything different just *wonderful* at this point? All the men we travel with are so *dull*."

I shrugged, her words hitting the same nerve Jack had earlier. "He said something I can't seem to shake—that I'm just wasting time."

She frowned. "Cheeky bastard. He doesn't even know you!"

"No, but look at it through his eyes. He meets a girl without any real home, who can afford to stay at a place like this and spend her days lying next to a pool. And when he asks what my future plans are, I tell him sipping coffee in Paris." I shake my head, realizing how utterly ridiculous I must have sounded.

"But he knows nothing about your life. He doesn't understand what it's like to be told that because you're a girl, your only options are marriage or working twice as hard to claim whatever scraps of a career the men in charge will deign to hand out. People make the mistake of assuming that being young and rich and beautiful is a blessing, but try being told you'll never be more than a pretty face. Watch those words harden into a shell you put around yourself to stop it from hurting each time you reach for more and come up empty."

A shadow swept across Daphne's face, and I knew she wasn't just defending me, but herself too. Where my pipe dream was music, my friend's was acting. In the past two years she'd managed to get some tiny parts in low-budget European productions, but true Hollywood stardom was a slippery target. I'd watched her shake off harrowing casting calls, skimpy costumes, and terrible parts in terrible movies, knowing the wounds cut deeper than she'd ever let on.

"I know. You're right—we just met, so how could he understand anything about me? The weird thing is, I *wanted* him to understand." If only so he could explain it to me, perhaps. Tell me why I couldn't stop running from a future I didn't desire, while simultaneously hiding from the one I did.

Daphne bit her lip, hesitating. "I hate to bring it up, but are you nervous about inviting him to dinner because you're worried what Henry would say? Because if that's the case, darling, he's never come right out and made any promises to you, has he?"

Henry, whose memory was a tiny flickering flame in my consciousness. Heir to one of the biggest art fortunes in the world, as handsome as he was personable, Henry Halliday was supposed to be the love of my life. Behind closed doors, it wasn't that simple.

"No, he hasn't. I guess I don't know what he's doing on his end. Or what he thinks I'm doing on mine."

Daphne's mouth puckered. "A romance for the ages." Turning back to the closet, she said, "I think that aqua number your mother sent is just the thing for tonight." Ticking off items on her fingers, she continued, "Pale lips, silver shoes, and we'll do something special with your hair. Ooh, and your diamond earrings. Can't forget those."

"You don't think diamonds are a bit much?" After all, it was just another dinner with the same people we saw all the time. *With one intriguing new addition.*

"Absolutely not. Diamonds are never too much."

Arriving at the hotel bar later that evening, we were met by the sounds of Latin jazz and hushed conversation. Well-dressed men and women clustered in small groups, sipping drinks and discussing the day's news. Our hostess, the Duchess of Staffordshire (or Taffy, as she was known to most), held court at a seating area on the opposite side of the room, next to Billy Lloyd, my close friend and jet set hair stylist du jour. It was a badge of honor to snag his exclusive services, for it told everyone that not only could you afford a remarkable talent but you had the means to fly him all over the world.

Most of his clients considered Billy a fantastic keeper of secrets, but it was his own secrets he held most tightly. Born Bartholomew Lipschitz, he'd worked his way up from shampoo boy to stylist in a famous New York salon before snagging the attention of a prominent member of the Vanderbilt family. She'd hired him to accompany her to Palm Beach for the season, and from then on, Billy Lloyd was part of the scene. He'd found an unconventional home among the "try-sexuals" of the jet set, meaning "try anything once." But whereas Daphne's exploits with men would be whispered about beside the pool the next morning, Billy's remained in the shadows.

"Caroline, darling, you look ravishing!" Taffy exclaimed, waving me over. I bent to give her a kiss against both cheeks, inhaling her perfume. Shalimar. "You caught a bit of sun today; your skin is glowing."

"It's this place! You were so kind to invite me on holiday."

She silenced me with a raise of her hand. "Nonsense. It's having young people like you around that stops me from feeling old. We've got a musical guest later I hope you'll like. I flew him in this morning—a folk singer by the name of Leitch. Donovan Leitch. Princess Margaret just raved about him."

I smiled politely, already familiar with Britain's answer to Bob Dylan. But deep inside, my guts churned with indignation that this man got to sing his songs without anybody looking askance, whereas if I tried the same thing, I'd probably be laughed off the stage. "I look forward to it," I said, realizing my jealousy wasn't her fault. The duchess didn't make our society's rules, any more than I did. "And I hope it's not a problem, but I met a photographer today and invited him to join us for dinner. His name's Jack Fairchild."

Billy's face lit up with curiosity. "Really? The International Ice Princess has a date? What's dear old Henry have to say about that?"

I scowled at him, wishing he'd stop using that ridiculous nickname. I'd had the occasional dalliance, same as anyone else, but just because I didn't parade them around like Daphne, that didn't make me frigid. And as for Henry, well . . . that was a discussion for another time.

"Jack is just a friendly acquaintance. Barely even that. It's not a date."

"We'll see, dear Caroline," Taffy said with a tiny smile. "Though I wish my own daughter were half as sensible as you. But you know what London is like nowadays—just no morals anymore."

"Yes, things certainly have changed." I didn't want to tell her it had nothing to do with "swinging London" and everything to do with the fact that the duchess's daughter craved sexual attention wherever she could get it.

Suddenly, I felt a nudge behind me as Daphne whispered into my ear, "Tall drink of tequila, seven o'clock."

I twisted and saw Jack sauntering into the bar, searching among the crowd. He locked eyes with me and smiled. I turned back to Taffy and Billy.

"If you'll excuse me, my guest just arrived."

"Be sure to introduce us; I'd love to hear more about his work," Taffy said, waving me off. Billy merely winked over the top of his martini glass.

I leaned closer to Daphne and tilted my head toward the bar. "Want to join us for cocktails?"

"No, darling, the viscount just got here too. I'll find you later." I watched her slink toward a striking man with tan skin and salt-and-pepper hair, and knew I wouldn't see her again until morning.

Walking over to where Jack waited, my hands twitched with nerves. In my world, I was used to meeting new people, knowing whatever connection we shared came with a time limit. So why did it feel different tonight?

"You're here!" I greeted, kissing his cheek.

His gaze traveled the length of my body, taking in my aqua chiffon dress and subtle diamond earrings. "You look . . . Wow," he said, at a loss for words. "I'm underdressed." He wore tan pants and a navy sports coat of indeterminate label. Korvettes, most likely.

"I'll let you in on a secret: my mother's a fashion designer. Maybe you've heard of her—Emanuela Leoni? She sends me pieces so I'll wear them and get other women interested. Lucky for me, she's talented."

"Sorry, I don't know too much about fashion," he admitted. "But I know what I like, and I like that on you. Though I'll bet just about anything would look pretty if you were the one wearing it."

His compliment traveled straight to my belly, ending in a delicious twist. "Do you want a drink?"

"Sure. I was going to order you one but didn't know what you'd like."

I turned to the nearest server. "Gin martini, please. And how about you, Tex? Are you still on the clock?"

"No, I'm off for the night. Whiskey, please," he ordered. Turning to me, he asked, "Tex? Is that my new nickname?"

"Yep. As you've pointed out, we've all got one. Everyone except me, that is."

"I'll bet I can come up with something." He started to count out some pesos for the bartender, but I waved him away.

"First rule of the jet set: we never pay for our own drinks."

He looked confused. "Well, somebody must be covering them."

"That would be Taffy. See the woman with the white hair cut like an artichoke, sitting in the corner? That's the Duchess of Staffordshire. She organized this trip, inviting several friends to join her at this hotel for a couple of weeks. When she hosts a dinner, as she is tonight, the bill goes to her."

He laughed. "That's ridiculous! Some lady I've never met is gonna buy me a meal and drinks? Why?"

"Because it makes her happy," I explained. "She likes having young people around to spice up the conversation. She's the queen of this kingdom tonight, and we're all the court jesters."

Tex shook his head, unable to reconcile our habits with his old-fashioned masculinity. "How'd you get mixed up with this crowd anyway?"

"My father was a painter, and Mother always designed for celebrities, even before her company took off. They were both the life of the party, and that party moved all over the world. Once I got old enough to tag along, I did. Mother and I rarely travel together anymore, but it's still the same people. They became a sort of family to us after Daddy died. Not in the traditional way, like in a Norman Rockwell scene, but they anchored us, at least. And besides, nobody has that kind of family anymore, do they?"

He shook his head. "Not me, that's for sure. Sometimes I think the phrase 'mean drunk' must've been invented in West Texas. Specifically in my parents' living room."

I stared at him, wondering who this cowboy really was. He was nothing like all the other men I'd grown used to, consumed by image and status. I didn't realize until that moment how badly I'd been craving something else.

"Where are you staying while you're here?" I asked, changing the subject.

"Oh, I'm down at the Mirador. It's next to the spot where the divers take their plunge. Saves on taxi fare."

"That's a good hotel. But I like it here because of the private pools next to the rooms. Daphne and I can swim any time we want."

"Daphne?"

I pointed across the room. "The girl in the yellow dress, talking to the man with the silver hair." Most men would do a double take upon seeing my bombshell friend, but Tex surprised me by giving her just a glance.

Turning back to me, he declared, "She looks like trouble."

"That's because she is. Definitely." I laughed.

"So when you aren't at a cocktail party or hangin' out beside swimming pools, what do you like to do? What's your passion?"

It'd been a long time since anyone had asked me that question. A long time since anyone had considered there might be more to me than a pretty smile and a well-worn passport.

"Oh, this and that. I write poems, and I play the ukulele sometimes." Embarrassed to be revealing this part of myself, I took a large sip of my drink.

"You blush like there's something wrong with that."

"No, I . . . it's just not something I talk about that often. I'm not a real musician or anything; I just like making up songs, jotting down lyrics about the places I've been."

"Maybe someday you'll play me one," he pressed. "When you've got the time."

All at once the space was too warm. His blue eyes searched mine, and I forced myself to look away. I hadn't considered the possibility that there might be more in store for us than just tonight. Turning toward the balcony, I pointed out at the moonlit water.

"Would you like to see the view over the cliffs? I should introduce you to Taffy too." I touched his elbow to escort him.

"Followin' you," he said in his amiable Southern drawl.

Although technically I was the one acting as tour guide, part of me felt like it was the other way around. He'd shown me how good I'd gotten at pretending I didn't want more for my life, content to stay trapped in purgatory. But standing in front of that beautiful vista, it was painfully obvious—desire had finally come knocking.

Over a candlelit meal of fresh-caught snapper and citrus salad, Tex charmed my friends, recounting how he went from a skinny kid with a camera to darkroom assistant to freelance photographer for some of the top New York publications. Even though some of us were gun-shy around members of the press, his artistic background appealed to our collective vanity. It was his job to capture beauty, and as he'd already pointed out, we were the beautiful people.

"Caroline, darling, your friend is just marvelous," Taffy said across the detritus of half-eaten desserts. "Young man—how would you like to continue taking photos of us? I mean, even after this trip."

Tex smiled. "That's awful kind of you, ma'am, but I just go where the job is. Y'all are fascinating, don't get me wrong. But I've gotta stick to the places I'm assigned."

"What if it were part of a magazine story? 'The Jet Set Takes Off!'" Taffy spread her hands, visualizing the headline. "Would you take the pictures, then?"

He looked to me for guidance. I shrugged my shoulders, enjoying watching him squirm.

"Do you think readers would be interested in a story like that?"

"Of course they would! Those gossip columnists make a mint off us. Wouldn't it be nice if for once a respectable publication printed the truth?" She extinguished her cigarette, taking another sip of wine. "Leave it to me; I have friends in the business. I'll give Diana a call and see what we can do."

"Diana?" he whispered to me.

"Diana Vreeland, editor of *Vogue*," I explained. "Another rule of the jet set: first names only."

"Good luck getting this one in front of a camera, though," Billy said across the table, pointing at me. "She hates being the center of attention."

Tex looked at me, his eyes daring. "That won't be a problem. I was always a good tracker back on the ranch. She won't even see me comin'."

He was right—I definitely hadn't.

Later, as we swayed to a slow rumba beat on the makeshift dance floor, Tex said, "So there's something I've been meanin' to ask you since this afternoon."

"What's that?"

"How come a clever girl who writes songs next to swimming pools, and can make friends with just about anyone, and has a face that could start a thousand wars—how come she also has the saddest eyes I've ever seen?"

I flushed at the realization that someone had seen behind the screen of couture and makeup, meant to hide the fact that without my father, I was nothing special. With his death, he'd taken all the magic out of my life, leaving only useless props behind.

"Maybe it's because I understand that whatever I do, or whatever I want, doesn't actually matter," I finally said. "My fate was decided a long time ago: become the wife of a wealthy man, mother of a spoiled child, and maybe if I'm lucky one day, I'll end up like Taffy over there. Paying the bill for young people more interesting than me. It's a first-class, nonstop flight to the future, and boarding begins any minute."

He shook his head. "Planes can get diverted, if the weather's bad enough."

"Or crash . . ."

Stepping closer to him, I felt the solid muscles of his chest press against me. Steady hands clutched my waist through gossamer fabric, and I leaned my head against his shoulder, exhaling. Unsettled by his words, I was wary of showing him any more of myself—he'd already seen too much.

The music ended, and the room clapped politely. A thin man with a button nose stepped onto the small stage, holding a guitar. As he began to play a melancholy song about catching the wind, the poet in me listened with rapturous ears, while the jealous girl inside seethed with longing. I wanted it to be my words, my song. I wanted to be that brave.

I turned to Tex. "It's getting late. Would you mind walking me back to my room?"

"Be glad to."

Outside, Jeeps waited to take tired guests back down the hill. Tex held my hand as I climbed in, and never released it during the short drive. Scents of tropical plants mixed with the humid air, sweeping across our faces as we descended. Too soon, we reached my suite, and I fished the key out of my evening bag, feeling his eyes on me.

"I guess this is good night." The reluctance in my voice was obvious as I wrestled with the temptation to invite him in.

He leaned casually against the doorjamb. "I guess it is. One quick question, though, before I go."

"Yes?"

"Why'd you invite me here tonight?"

Something I'd been asking myself too. "Because you made me curious," I confessed. "Like talking to you might lead me down a rabbit hole. I wanted to see where it went."

"And yet, I feel like I'm the one who just visited Wonderland. Like I'm gonna wake up tomorrow and realize this was all some crazy dream or magic spell."

"If you dreamed it, odds are I probably did too. Do you think we should meet again and compare notes?" My heart pounded as I waited for his answer.

"That's probably a smart idea. Just to make sure I'm not crackin' up, imagining duchesses and diamonds and one very boozy tea party." He smiled as relief flooded over me. So this wasn't the end of our road; not yet.

"Call me tomorrow, then. You know where to find me." I pointed to my room number. "I . . . I'd better get inside."

"Yep, you'd better. G'night, Alice." He plucked a hibiscus flower from a nearby plant and brought it closer. Tucking it into the side of my hair, his fingers brushed the skin of my ear, and I shivered, pretending it was the ocean breeze giving me chills.

"'Night, Tex." With one last smile, I turned and went inside to collapse on the bed, finally exhaling. Staring at the cracked plaster ceiling, pulse racing, I touched the fragrant bloom nestled tight against my scalp.

Magic.

September 26th, 1966
Las Brisas Hotel
Acapulco, Mexico

Dear Daddy,

Did you ever feel like you were on the cusp of something big? Like with one chance meeting, your whole life was about to change? Was it like that when you met Mother?

Maybe it's silly or romantic, but I can't help thinking I was meant to cross paths with this tall Texan whose job it is to see people. Really see them.

I wonder what he sees in me . . .

Take a picture
Keep it in the dark
A little time
A little light
Could this be the start?

Love,
Caroline

THREE

YAWNING, I SHUT my notebook and stretched my arms against the pillows. I'd had a hard time falling asleep last night, and an even harder time staying that way. Daphne's bed was still empty, indicating things had gone well with the viscount. Reaching for the phone on the nightstand, I rang for room service and ordered my usual breakfast, adding an extra serving for when she finally returned. Then I tossed on a robe and picked up my ukulele, wandering outside to sit by the pool.

Gazing at the hillside and ocean below, I thought not for the first time that Las Brisas had to be one of the most beautiful properties on Earth. Trekking to the club at La Concha almost seemed silly when I had this at my fingertips. It was always the same tired gossip down there about who had snuck off with whom the night before, who had created a scandal at one of the nearby discos, and where the next group destination would be. Marbella or Mustique; it had all started to blur together.

Gradually, I started to strum while my other hand pressed

down chords. I could still remember Daddy laughing in frustration when my tiny fingers couldn't stretch as far as his. Even though his fame had been achieved through painting, he'd enjoyed making music too—plucking out nursery rhymes and folk songs for me to sing along with him. When he saw I was itching to play, we'd tried first with the guitar before settling on the ukulele. It had a simple, sweet sound, *just like his princess*, he'd said. Even though I was probably more than capable of handling an acoustic guitar now, I couldn't say goodbye to this smaller version yet. It was one of the few things I had left of us.

Just as I opened my mouth to sing, the patio door opened and Daphne stepped gingerly onto the slate tile, last night's shoes in her hand. My hands stilled on the strings.

"Look who I bumped into!" She instructed the young waiter trailing her to put the breakfast tray on an umbrella-shaded table by the pool. "*Muchas gracias*, Miguel." She kissed him on both cheeks in lieu of a tip. He stumbled back inside, a bashful smile on his face.

"She lives," I said wryly, going back to strumming.

"Oh, you know how it is. One minute you're sitting having drinks, listening to the viscount ramble on about his country house in Provence, and the next you're in his room discovering delicious new uses for a necktie."

I rolled my eyes and set the ukulele down, rising to pour myself a cup of coffee. "He's a bit old for you, though, no?"

"Age is just a number. It's what you do that matters." She raised her brow to emphasize the point. "And believe me, he can do it all." While she went back inside to change out of her dress from the night before, I basked in the warm sunshine, the surrounding silence a perk of the lifestyle—the richer you were, the quieter your world.

Daphne re-emerged in a colorful Pucci silk caftan, hair piled on top of her head. "Thanks for ordering breakfast, by the way. You're a doll," she said, blowing me a kiss.

I caught it, pretending to put it in my pocket.

"So, don't keep me in suspense. What happened with that photographer? Billy said he saw you leave together."

"Nothing." I shrugged, taking another sip of coffee. "He was a perfect gentleman. He rode down here with me, walked me to the door, then said good night." Blushing at the memory, I recalled how the simple sweep of his finger against my ear had made me tremble all over.

"That's *all*?! You didn't even invite him inside?"

"No. It . . . it just wasn't like that." How to tell her that I'd desperately wanted to, but the fear of turning him into a forgettable one-night stand had stopped me? She wouldn't understand the feeling of wanting more, of relishing the electric current of anticipation.

"Oh dear, is he gay? At least Billy will be happy about that. You know how he likes the tall ones."

"I can promise you he isn't gay!" I replied, indignant. "We definitely flirted. He said he wants to see me again."

"Well! Now we're getting somewhere. Did you make a date?"

"No, I told him to call me here. We left it casual."

Daphne sighed, frustrated my story wasn't more interesting. "You know, darling," she said, picking up a sweet roll, "I'm beginning to sour on La Concha. Far too crowded. Would you be disappointed if we stayed here today?"

"Fine with me." Secretly, I wanted to stay near the phone. "I'm sure Miguel would be happy to bring you cocktails."

"Now you're talking!"

※

Later that morning, after a swim turned into sunbathing and a game of backgammon, the telephone rang from the bedroom. Nervous but elated, I set my dice down and skipped across the warm pavement.

Taking a calming breath, I answered, "Hello?"

"Caroline—it's Henry." My insides deflated a bit at the sound of a blue-blood accent on the other end of the line. I could picture him sitting in his office, shirtsleeves rolled up, hair freshly trimmed, earnest smile on his face like a young Montgomery Clift.

"Oh, hi!" I tried to keep my voice upbeat. After all, he was nice enough to call, to make the effort in keeping our long-distance relationship afloat. By contrast, I'd let our boat fill with water, never even trying to plug the leaks. "I can't believe you found me. The trip was so last-minute."

"I rang the apartment in Paris and your mother gave me your hotel information. Isn't it the rainy season down there?"

I laughed. "As if a cloud would dare pass over us. Taffy wouldn't hear of it." I twisted the cord around my finger, leaning against the edge of the desk. I couldn't help but wonder if someone else was getting a busy signal right this second.

Henry hesitated a moment before continuing. "Well, listen, the reason I'm calling is because I've had an offer on *Ojos Verdes*. I wouldn't be doing my job if I didn't at least tell you."

I frowned, crossing my free arm around my midsection. As a

partner in his father's art gallery and the longtime steward of my father's work, I knew he had to ask, even if we both knew what my answer would be. "Out of curiosity, what am I turning down this time?"

"Forty thousand. From a Japanese buyer who wants it for his daughter. I think he'd go higher, if it makes a difference."

"It doesn't. But I appreciate you checking anyway. *Ojos Verdes* isn't for sale, now or ever." The portrait my father had painted of me when I was nine had become a constant bone of contention. Mother had urged me to sell it when we auctioned the rest of Daddy's work in '62, but I'd refused. No one would ever be able to recognize the face in the mass of abstract shapes on the canvas, but those emerald slashes in the middle were *my* eyes. And his. That painting could never hang on a stranger's wall, not for all the money in the world.

"I really am sorry to have to call you about this. Father insisted, and you know how he gets." Henry sighed. "I'd much rather talk about what you're listening to and reading these days than business."

"Simon & Garfunkel, and *Valley of the Dolls*."

He laughed. "That trashy Jacqueline Susann book? Really? You must have borrowed it from Daphne."

"Billy, actually." I smirked. "Why, what's on your nightstand?"

"Carnegie's *How to Win Friends & Influence People*."

I giggled. It was so Henry. "Oh yeah? How's that working out for you? Win any friends yet? Besides me, of course."

"And here I thought I was only trying to influence you. Guess I missed the mark."

I smiled. It had always been like this between us—easy. In a way,

Henry was as close a friend as Daphne, for he'd known me just as long and understood the dynamics of my family better than anyone else. But somehow, as we got older, our friendship became less about the past and more about the future. A future complicated by the fact that we were both too afraid to say what we wanted it to look like. Or maybe we'd never stopped to think about it.

"So, will I see you in Paris this fall? I'll probably be there before we go to Switzerland for the holidays." A trip I already dreaded, but there was no getting out of it. Not with Mother doing the planning.

"Probably not." He sounded disappointed. "Things aren't going well with the new installation in New York, so Father wants me here to supervise. Then we're spending Thanksgiving and Christmas at the Newport house with everyone. Mimi's already got her staff turning down the beds." I'd only met his grandmother once, but she was a pistol. How she'd managed to spawn Henry's expressionless waif of a mother, I'd never know.

"If I can get away, I'll try to come see you," Henry promised. "But until then, there's always the phone. And airmail."

"And carrier pigeons! We haven't tried those yet. I've got a line on a gray-headed one with a white belly. I'm told he has a keen sense of direction."

He laughed. "All right—I've got to go. Enjoy the rest of your trip, and don't sit out too long. You don't want to burn."

Oh, if he only knew how much I'd burned last night, long after the moon had replaced the sun.

"Bye, then, and thanks for calling." I returned the phone to its cradle, but before I could take even one step away, it rang again.

"Lemme guess," I said, smiling into the handset. "You think a message in a bottle is more efficient than carrier pigeons."

"I don't know about that, Alice. I'm pretty partial to telephones." Jack's low Southern drawl caressed me from the other end. I was grateful he couldn't see my cheeks turning red with embarrassment.

"Tex? Is that you? Sorry, that was meant for someone else. We were talking about—Never mind. Hello."

He laughed. "So you're stickin' with the nickname, then. Fair's fair, I guess."

"Hey, at least you're not a character in a children's story. I could have gone with Beanstalk," I said, trying to play it cool. "Did you make it back to your hotel last night?"

"Oh, sure. I think the taxi driver tried to set me up with his niece, but my Spanish isn't so great. I either told him I was shy or pregnant. Whatever my excuse was, he stopped talkin' and got me there awful quick."

I laughed, picturing it. "Are you working today?"

"Yep, that's why I called. I have a meeting with the divers soon. I'm going with them to the top of the cliff to take photos, then more shots as they jump off. After that, I'm free as a bird. You feel like catchin' the one o'clock show? There's a viewing platform at the Mirador."

I'd seen the divers before, but it was always a fascinating spectacle. "Sure, that sounds nice. Maybe afterward we could go to the beach. There's a good one not too far from your hotel."

"Great! Listen, after the show, go to the outdoor bar, La Perla. I'll meet you there when I'm able to climb down."

"You mean you're not going to jump too?" I joked.

"Nah, the camera's not waterproof. See ya later, Al."

"Later, Tex."

By that time, Daphne had come inside and was lying on the bed, eavesdropping.

"Someone looks quite pleased," she remarked once I'd hung up the phone.

"He's funny. And nice."

"You conveniently left out the word *sexy*," Daphne persisted.

"And he called me Al."

"Al?" Her forehead wrinkled in confusion.

"Short for Alice. Forget it; it's just a silly joke." I moved to the closet to choose an outfit.

"Are we still going to pretend you're not interested? Your whole face lights up when you talk to him."

I shook my head. "It's complicated. You know that better than anyone. My lifestyle—it just doesn't make sense to bring someone like him into it. Plus, there's Henry to think about."

"Oh, are we thinking about him now? I'd assumed you'd forgotten. Or wanted to. Maybe that was just me." Her lips formed into a pout.

"Henry's good and decent. And very well respected," I said on my way to the bathroom. I didn't feel like telling her I'd just gotten off the phone with him before Tex called. She and Henry had never been fans of one another; I think a part of her resented that he knew me in ways she didn't.

"Yes, he is all those things. And also unfathomably *boring*! Now, a photographer on the other hand . . ."

"Tex and I are just friends. Maybe not even that. I just met him yesterday!"

Daphne sighed. "You really can't blame me. I'm a sucker for forbidden love."

I threw a towel at her. "Then go back to your dime-store novels. I have to get ready."

※

After the taxi dropped me off at the Mirador, I meandered through the neighboring square toward the promenade. The day was sunny and warm, the ocean shimmering below the cliffs. Yachts bobbed over their anchors, waiting for the show to begin. Seeing them reminded me of the first time I'd witnessed the famous Acapulco divers.

It had been a few months after Daddy's suicide when Mother accepted an offer from a Greek shipping magnate to host us on his boat for a lengthy cruise around Mexico and Central America. He'd been eager to pursue an affair with the notoriously desirable Emanuela Leoni, and it was his poor luck that she came with a grieving teenager in tow. I spent most of the trip sulking in my stateroom, but there was one particular afternoon when Mother surprised me by taking my hand and leading me to the ship's stern. She told me to hold on to the white railing as she stood behind me. Pointing toward the cliffs of La Quebrada, she whispered in my ear, "Just wait, *piccola mia*. When the man leaps from the top, don't take your eyes away. You will witness true bravery. It is a very rare thing in this world." We stared rapt as the tiny dot of a man plummeted to certain death, then miraculously reappeared in the water below. His courage made me believe I might resurface someday too. It was a memory I came back to when tensions rose ever higher between Mother and me. It helped to recall that, once upon a time, she had been the parent I needed.

On the viewing platform now, families crowded around the

edge in small groups. The wind whipped the silk scarf tied around my hair, and I stood next to a father holding his small daughter, sheltering her from the strongest gusts. Squinting against the midday sun, I could just make out Tex at the top of La Quebrada, his lanky form in sharp contrast to the compact bodies of the divers. I checked my watch—a minute to one o'clock. The men on the cliff began to take their positions as a hush fell over the crowd at the Mirador, all of us waiting in suspended animation. At last, a diver raised his arms above his head and leaped silently over the edge, falling, falling, until slicing like a sharp knife through the water, leaving only a tiny ripple in his wake. The tourists applauded, delighted by the spectacle. *True bravery*, my mother's voice echoed in my mind.

Others made the dive, gleaming copper forms descending 125 feet into the sea below. Elegant in its simplicity, the show was a thrilling interaction between man and nature. Once it was over, and the applause of the crowd had dissipated, I climbed back up the winding trail to the hotel bar where I'd agreed to meet Tex. I selected a seat overlooking the water and ordered a gin and tonic from a smiling waiter.

Down in the ocean, yachts began moving back out to sea, ferrying their passengers toward the next luxurious port of call. Couples around me checked maps and itineraries, their conversations white noise against the unexpected melancholy settling over me. It happened often, during those moments I found myself alone yet surrounded by strangers. I liked to think I'd dealt with the loss of my father, but seeing that man on the platform with his little girl had shaken me. I still thought of Daddy constantly. The way a cigarette rested casually between his long, paint-smeared fingers. The smell of his hair tonic, and the way it shined in the sunlight. The way the skin around his eyes crinkled in happiness as soon as I entered the room, even if he and Mother had been arguing just a second before. It had been five years since that horrible day he left us, but it still felt like yesterday.

"That's too serious a face for Acapulco. It's better suited to someplace cold and rainy."

I looked up to find Tex next to my shoulder, a Leica camera clutched in his hands. I didn't know how much time had passed since I'd first sat down.

"Mother says I always look like this when no one's watching. But now that you're here, you can chase the clouds away."

Tex lowered himself into the chair next to me and motioned to my drink, by now half-empty. "I forgot, happy hour starts early with you folks."

"Does it ever end?"

He laughed, staring out at the view beside us. "Did you catch the show?"

"Yes, it was wonderful. I saw you at the top, with the divers. You stick out like a sore thumb next to them."

"You mean I can't pass for a short, muscle-bound Mexican? Al, you wound me," he winced, hands over his chest.

"They sure know how to fill out a bathing suit."

"So, that's your type? Beefcake studs with a death wish?"

I shook my head at the question. "I don't have a type. But bravery is an admirable quality in anyone."

"You know, I was expecting them to be quaking with fear, but they weren't. They stood stock-still until the water was just right for the jump. I don't know how they knew, but they did."

"Did you get the photos you needed?"

"I think so." He nodded. "The diving, plus lots of shots near their prayer altar. It'll humanize the spread, show they're real people, not just some gimmick in an Elvis movie."

I smiled, impressed.

"They said the night show is spectacular, with the flaming torches," he continued. "But it'd be harder to shoot. I'd have to bring all kinds of equipment with me." He waved off the idea. "At that point, it'd feel too staged."

"When does it come out in the magazine? I'll probably be in Europe, but I should be able to find a copy."

"Second to last week in December. They want to show a warm, tropical paradise while New Yorkers are shivering in the slush."

"Poor bastards." I raised my glass. "To sunny afternoons in Mexico."

He grinned and pulled his camera up to capture my face, all signs of tragedy wiped away.

A short while later, I stretched my legs out on the soft sand, taking in the scenery. Gentle waves kissed the shore of Playa La Angosta, and just beyond the break, turquoise water glistened in the afternoon light. Tex lay next to me, his left arm beneath his head, staring at the sky from behind his sunglasses.

"What do you see up there?" I asked.

"The exact same sky we had over Midland. And the same one over New York, though the buildings try hard to block it out."

"Night skies are a whole different ball game," I mused. "In cities you hardly see the stars, but in the desert outside Palm Springs, or anywhere on Formentera, it's like the whole universe is lit up just for you. But I guess I don't have to tell you that, coming from West Texas."

"Formentera? Never heard of that place. Where is it?"

"It's a tiny island in the Mediterranean, off the coast of Spain. We have a house there; more of an artist's retreat, really. I used to visit during summer breaks from boarding school." I smiled at the memory. I hadn't been back in years, and I didn't know if Mother ever went. After what had happened there, I doubted it. "It's beautiful, all rocky and weather-beaten. Daddy and I would ride bicycles all around the shoreline."

"Formentera," he said, testing out the name. "Hmm. Might just have to go someday."

"You should! It's hard to get to, but worth it once you're there. The surrounding sea isn't just blue, it's sapphire. And the grass underneath the water—like Poseidon's fields. You can almost imagine him down there, protecting this tiny corner of Atlantis."

Tex laughed. "To hear you tell it like that? Yeah, I can imagine it."

"Daddy always said words can paint pictures too, sometimes even better than a brush." I didn't say it aloud, but that's what I tried to do with my songs. Paint a picture of my life the only way I knew how.

"So, your father. He wouldn't by any chance be David Kimball, would he?"

I sat up, surprised. "You know his work?" I didn't know why I was so shocked; Daddy's paintings were exhibited all over the world. Maybe I'd just hoped for a clean slate with Tex, to not feel the disappointment that came with meeting someone who assumed they knew your life after reading one newspaper article.

He pushed up to his elbows to look at me. "I saw one of his pieces at the Museum of Modern Art. Hell of a talent."

I nodded, relieved he hadn't said more. "It helps to know he'll never truly be gone; his work is still here, and people think it's important. For better or worse, he'll never fade away completely."

Standing up, I said, "Come on, I feel like a walk."

We shook the sand from our clothes and skin, and I strolled to the shoreline, letting the water sneak up over my toes as he fell in step beside me.

"I still write letters to him," I admitted. For some reason, I wanted to share this part of myself with Tex. Like maybe he was the one person who would understand and not judge me for such a silly habit. "You asked me last night what I write, and that's part of it. The letters in my notebook are a way for me to tell him what's happening in my life since he's not here to see for himself."

"And your music? Is that for him too?"

I bit my lip. "Not *just* for him, but he's probably the only one who'll get to hear it. Mother thinks the whole idea of me wanting to be a singer is ridiculous. *Tacky* is the word she uses. And I see her point; it's not like there are a lot of wayward heiresses out there busking on street corners. Oh sure, I've known girls in my crowd who could sing, and even some who could play an instrument, but it's more of a party trick than a career option. Just something to do before the husband and kids make you forget yourself and the things you once dreamed of. But Daddy never made me feel like that. He always told me music would be the thing that makes me fly higher than all the rest. Up to the stars, if I wanted."

"How old were you when it happened? When you lost him, I mean."

"Seventeen. Old enough to understand the meaning of the word *suicide*, but still not old enough to *really* understand. But I suppose it's not the kind of thing that would ever make sense, no matter how old you are."

Tex shook his head. "Did he leave a letter or any kind of explanation?"

I swallowed down the thickness in my throat that always came when I talked about this. "Not really. Just his guitar, and a little slip of paper that said: *For Caroline, when she's grown.* Guess I'm still not grown enough, because I haven't let myself graduate from the ukulele."

He smiled. "I can picture it. Like Audrey Hepburn in *Breakfast at Tiffany's*, only a hotel balcony instead of a crummy fire escape."

My insides lightened at that. "You got me. I play saccharine Johnny Mercer songs to a cat with no name. While wearing Givenchy."

"And you're a real phony with everyone you meet, except the friendly male prostitute upstairs. You tell *all* your secrets to him."

I smiled. "Yeah, like this nosy photographer I met in Mexico. I barely knew him, but he still got me talking about all kinds of private things. So what's that say about you, huh?"

"Not my fault if women want to spill their guts to me." He raised his hands in defense.

"You sound like Billy."

"You mean that guy at dinner last night? The one who does hair?"

"That's him." I nodded. "You wouldn't believe some of the things people tell him when he's working. Things he then passes on to me and Daphne because we're his closest friends."

"Phew, that's a relief. I thought you were gonna break my heart and tell me he was more than a friend." When I didn't respond, Tex stopped walking and turned to me. "What is it?" he asked.

I knew I had to tell him about Henry. I stared at the water as a strong breeze twisted my skirt around my legs.

"Look, Tex. There's something I haven't mentioned yet. I'm . . . You see, there is someone. A sort of boyfriend, and everyone assumes we're headed toward marriage. His father was my father's art dealer, and as kids, the two of us were thrown together. No matter how crazy things got with my parents, he was always there for me, as a friend. But now that we're older, expectations have arisen, and things are . . . different." I knew I wasn't making much sense, probably because for the last few years I'd struggled to define my relationship with Henry.

Tex nodded, taking a breath. After some time he said, "Well, darlin', can't say I'm surprised. You're too gorgeous to be single. Gotta say, he's one lucky sonofabitch. I hope he knows it."

"Sometimes I have no idea what Henry knows and doesn't know. I think I've revealed more to you about myself in twenty-four hours than I have in over a decade with him. I guess the difference is, you asked."

"This is maybe one time when I wish I hadn't."

I took his hand, forcing him to look at me. "I'm a little ashamed I didn't tell you sooner. It's just that I like being with you so much. You're not pretentious, and you didn't come to me with an idea already formed about who I am. Sometimes it's easier to open up to a stranger than to the people who have known you your whole life. And easier still when it's someone you might never see again. Less chance of your words coming back to haunt you."

He stood facing me, his thumb rubbing tiny circles against my knuckles. I wanted to say more, and it looked like maybe he did too, but we were unable to find the courage. After a beat, we started heading back to where the taxi had dropped us off, the moment lost.

"When do you go back to New York?" I asked.

"I fly out tomorrow morning. The *Life* editors are chompin' at the bit to go to press. Now that I've got my photos, I'll need to find another assignment."

Before I could stop it, a reckless thought formed. Somehow I knew—this was my moment. The water was just right.

"I'm attending a party tonight at Dolores del Río's estate. Afterward, Daphne's going out to the Tequila a Go Gó. I can skip the disco and head back to the hotel if you want to meet at my room." The words tumbled out before common sense could take over.

"Are you sure that's a good idea?"

"No. But I'm finding it harder and harder to care about what's a good idea these days."

He was silent, until at last he nodded. I knew in that moment we were both ensnared by the same web of temptation.

"What time?"

FOUR

SWIPING A CHILLED shot of tequila off a waiter's tray, I squeezed a lime wedge into my mouth and tilted the glass back. Bitter acid mingled with the earthiness of the spirit, burning a path down my throat.

In the outdoor living room of the gorgeous villa, party guests perched on sofa arms and mingled near the pool, passing joints back and forth. A Brazilian jazz record played on the hi-fi, while flickering candlelight illuminated the bronze skin and white teeth of a privileged class. It was the type of party the jet set lived for. This magnificent estate was a lingering testament to Hollywood's Golden Age, a place where faded icons could share stories of studio bosses, production codes, and all the sordid details of the backlot. Their box office power may have disappeared, but here, under the starry skies of Mexico, their lights would never dim.

In Acapulco, you were nobody unless you'd been to one of Dolores's parties. My standing invitation stemmed from her friendship with Mother, who had first met the aging actress when my father painted her portrait. I was pleased to see it still hanging in the entryway, all sharp angles and colorful distortion. Mother had designed many gowns for her over the years, though tonight she wore a traditional Mexican tunic layered with turquoise jewelry and a signature flower in her hair. Even in her sixties, she was stunning.

Daphne, my faithful plus-one, had jumped at the chance to attend tonight's gathering, hoping to meet somebody, anybody, who could introduce her to a director or producer. The ultimate goal: Bond girl. I had to admit, she certainly looked the part. With her teased blond hair, smoky eyes, and low-cut beaded dress, she made me feel almost dowdy by comparison. I'd have minded being so thoroughly upstaged if I wasn't preoccupied by my impending rendezvous with Tex.

As the numbing effects of the tequila settled over me, I turned to her and whispered, "I wonder how late this thing is supposed to go; they haven't even passed the hors d'oeuvres yet."

"What's the rush, darling? You know the disco doesn't get fun until at least midnight."

"Actually, I'm not going with you. I made other plans."

Her eyes widened with surprise. "Oh really? Do tell."

"Don't read too much into it, but I'm meeting Tex. He's leaving tomorrow, and I just wasn't ready to say goodbye this afternoon." I didn't tell Daphne he was coming to our hotel room; that was a decision I wasn't ready to explain, to her or myself.

She smiled with mischief. "You won't get any judgment from me. I say play the field while we're still young and gorgeous. You know I love a secret affair."

"It's not a secret anything. I'm telling you, aren't I?" I pointed out. "And let's not make this into something it's not. Tex is just a person I enjoy spending time with. He knows about Henry; I told him this afternoon."

"How'd he take it?"

"Sufficiently disappointed." I couldn't help the tiny grin on my lips.

"Well, whatever happens, just remember—you're fantastic, and he's lucky you noticed him at all. No need to be nervous."

I hugged her tight, grateful for the pep talk.

"Careful, darling, I think I just lost a few beads." Daphne playfully covered her bosom as we dissolved into a fit of laughter. James Mason wandered by, eyeing us with curiosity. She made a face behind his back, causing us to erupt all over again.

"Bloody grass, turns everybody into teenyboppers," he muttered to his date.

I left Daphne and tried to focus on the glitterati surrounding me, making polite conversation about the unpredictable weather of Lake Tahoe, the skiing in St. Moritz versus Cortina, and my mother's latest collection. One of Dolores's more lecherous friends stroked my arm as he told me stories of his villa in Positano, and my skin crawled in response. It was always the same at these parties. A young, pretty ingénue was like catnip to these men. I'd been lucky that it usually went no further than suggestive looks and light petting, but I was careful to never stray far from the group. If a girl went unaccompanied down a dim hallway, she never knew what, or whom, she might meet at the end. It could be a maid, or it could be a snake in Pierre Cardin. Nothing of the frightening sort had ever happened to me, but I'd heard plenty of stories. Being a woman, even a rich one, came with a lifetime of caution.

Perhaps that was one of the many things that drew me to Tex—
he didn't trigger any alarm bells. He didn't make me feel like a
cheap prize in a box of Cracker Jack, something to be used for
a brief time then tossed away. As my mind swam with Dolores's
expensive tequila, I pictured Tex's sharp blue eyes and the way
they saw straight through me. The music got louder, the guests
more and more intoxicated, and staying suddenly seemed impossible. There was only one person I wanted to talk to, and it wasn't
anybody in this scene of beautiful pretenders.

I begged a late-arriving guest's chauffeur to run me back to the
hotel, and we sped through the night, the surrounding hillsides
a blur. Deposited at the entrance to my suite, I fumbled in my
purse for the key. Crickets chirped in the distance, but they barely
registered over the ringing in my ears. Checking the time, I saw
it was still early enough for room service to bring me an iced tea
and sandwich. The tequila had jumbled my head, and not in a
good way.

I changed into a bikini, ordered my snack, then headed to the
pool. Lowering myself down the ladder, the shock of the cold
water sobered me up in an instant. I performed a gentle breast-
stroke to warm my blood, careful not to get my hair wet.

Saying goodbye to Las Brisas would be hard. This time next
week, I'd most likely be back in Paris, staying at Mother's pied-à-
terre in the 8th arrondissement. There would be winter attire to
purchase, perhaps ski equipment for Christmas in Gstaad. Though
I dreaded the holidays in Switzerland, I almost looked forward to
the train ride from France. Airplanes were convenient, but there

was something much more romantic about rail travel. The fine white linens of the dining car, the hours of solitude in a first-class cabin, and the world whizzing by through a window—like a step back in time.

I was startled by a waiter's timid knock on the patio gate, his tray visible under the outdoor light. I motioned him forward, and he set my order on the table next to my lounger. I thanked him in Spanish, and he shook his head, smiling at the silly girl in the pool ordering a meal so late at night. Once he was gone, I pushed out of the water, quickly wrapping up in a towel. I hadn't had anything to eat since the sweet rolls at breakfast, and my stomach grumbled at the sight of food.

Picking up the sandwich with one hand, I walked back to the bedroom for my ukulele, taking big bites along the way. Hunger finally satiated, I settled onto a chaise and brought the instrument to my lap, strumming softly at first, then louder. I closed my eyes and began to sing Brian Wilson's "In My Room." Such a sad song, but strangely comforting. Like maybe someone else understood what it was like to wish the world would go away, leaving you alone with your dreams and schemes.

Just as I finished the final verse, I heard movement from behind me. I jumped up, clutching the ukulele like a shield.

"I knocked, but you must not have heard me," Tex explained, stepping out onto the patio. "The gate was unlocked, so I just came in. You don't have to stop on my account. Please, keep singing."

Heart racing, I took a deep breath. "I'm glad it was you." I pulled the towel tighter around my chest. "I guess I lost track of time. I'd planned to change before you got here."

"I took a chance you'd get done with your party sooner rather than later. Figured I'd hang out at the bar here if you weren't back yet." He spoke slowly, almost distractedly, while he stared at me like he didn't recognize the person in front of him.

"What is it?" I asked.

Tex shook his head, as if to clear it. "Sorry. It's just . . . that song. Damn, Al, I don't think I've ever heard anything like it."

"The Beach Boys? You've never heard the Beach Boys?"

"No, of course I've heard the song before. But the way you sang it—like a siren. And I'm the sailor about to sink his ship. Look, I've got goose bumps." He held out his arm to me, and I ran my fingers across it. Touching him did funny things to my insides, and I quickly drew my hand back.

Clearing my throat, I willed my skin to cool, knowing it was seven different shades of pink at the moment. I didn't usually let people hear me sing.

"The party wasn't all that great. That's why I'm back early. At least Dolores serves excellent tequila; otherwise, it would have been a total waste."

Tex grinned, taking a closer look at me. "You mean to tell me you're a little drunk right now, Al?"

I shrugged. "Maybe, maybe not. The swim helped. Speaking of which, I need to either get back in the water to warm up or change into something dry."

He glanced at the pool, then at me. "Nice night for a dip."

"Do . . . do you want to get in?" I didn't know whether to be terrified or thrilled by the notion that he'd say yes.

"I didn't bring my swim trunks. But if you promise not to peek . . ." He trailed off, smiling at me.

I bit my lip, considering the idea. I was already playing with fire tonight—what was one more piece of kindling?

Slowly, I lowered my instrument and dropped the towel. In the dim light, his mouth formed a tiny O, his expression becoming heated. Stepping back, I held his gaze while I climbed down the ladder. My thighs met water, and I plunged all the way under, swimming to the opposite ledge. I surfaced and stared out over the hills of Acapulco, glowing silvery purple under the nearly full moon.

Behind me, there was a clink of metal from Tex's belt, followed by the swish of trousers hitting cement. After several agonizing moments, a gentle splash told me he'd slipped into the pool. My heart pounded as I waited, my body daring him to approach.

Suddenly the water rippled around me. He was close; so close that if I wanted to, I could reach back and touch him. But I knew that one touch would turn into two, or three, or four, and stopping would be impossible.

I turned around. "You must think I'm an awful tease."

"Not awful." He shook his head. "Confusin', maybe."

"How so?" I backed up a bit, the heel of my foot hitting the wall of the pool.

Locking eyes with me, he said, "It doesn't make sense why you'd hide that voice. You let yourself become part of the flock, but your daddy was right—you were born to fly above 'em all."

He moved even closer, and his knee bumped against mine. I trembled, my body on high alert.

"Are you cold?"

"No," I whispered, tilting my chin up. His lids grew heavy as he stared at my mouth.

"Tell me more about the guy you mentioned earlier. Henry. How come I'm here with you, and he's not?" He reached his hand around me to grip the pool ledge, partly caging me in. It should have felt dangerous, but it didn't, not even a little.

"Henry and I don't have that kind of relationship. Possessive, I mean." It felt wrong to talk about this with another man, especially one who made my body respond in a way Henry never had. "His family has galleries all over, plus he travels to meet with artists. I suppose we're engaged to be engaged, but we've never officially said the words. Everyone just expects us to get married because that's how it works in my world. A girl doesn't have any true worth until she finds a husband. A rich husband, to be precise."

"Is that really your world?"

I nodded.

"Then I'm sorry for you, because you're worth a whole damn lot, even without a rock on your finger. Don't you know that yet?"

I looked away, absorbing his words. God, how I longed to believe them. To believe in the freedom they implied.

Tex turned my face back to him. "Does Henry ever kiss you?"

"Yes," I admitted. Sweet, chaste pecks like something from an old Andy Hardy picture, but still affectionate.

"Well?"

"Well, what?"

"Does he kiss you *well*?" he clarified, his voice impatient.

"I guess I'm not sure what I should compare it to."

In a flash he was on me, firm lips moving slickly across my own. I opened my mouth as his tongue began stroking me, claiming me. His body pressed closer, and the thin fabric of his underwear brushed against my upper thighs. Fingers traveled higher, resting against my jaw, positioning me in a way that told me I was his, if only for one glorious moment. Water lapped against our heated skin, and my toes strained to keep purchase on the cement. If death came by drowning, I'd happily die like this.

As if sensing I'd lost the ability to conceal the truth, Tex pulled his lips away and looked down into my eyes. "I'm gonna ask you again—does Henry ever kiss you? *Really* kiss you?"

"No," I replied, shaking my head in fervent denial. Jack Fairchild had just made every previous lip-lock null and void.

"Just as I thought. He wouldn't be your sort-of boyfriend if he had." He leaned in and touched his nose to mine, our breaths mingling.

"I don't want you to think badly of me," I whispered against him. "Despite what it may seem like, I'm not the kind of girl who gives her heart away to a different man every night."

"I wouldn't think that for a second. And I don't believe you've given your heart away to anybody. Yet."

Once more, he pulled me to him, and our mouths resumed their delicious dance. The heat rose inside me, begging and insistent. I couldn't get enough of him, this handsome stranger who didn't feel like a stranger at all. I released a whimper as his kiss traveled down my neck, his hand grazing the side of my breast. It was then that I heard it—the sound of voices talking and laughing, coming closer.

"The pool's just out here, darlings," Daphne said, before gasping in surprise. Tex's lips stilled, and I pulled back a few inches. My best friend stood in the doorway, framed by the bedroom light. "Caroline? Is that you?" she asked, squinting into the darkness.

I moved farther away from Tex, my cheeks hot with embarrassment. "Yes, it's me. We just came out for a swim. I didn't think you'd be back this early," I called over his shoulder.

"Unfortunately, there was a bit of a scandal at the club. Jayne Mansfield showed up in a dress that almost made her tits pop out on the dance floor, and suddenly the room turned square. There was a scuffle, and she was asked to leave, but by then all the fun had gone out of the place. So we moved the party here. I thought you'd be out. I *am* sorry, darling," Daphne explained. "And, my apologies to you as well, Mr. Fairchild." She smirked, knowing exactly what we'd been up to in the pool.

Tex turned to Daphne. "Don't you worry about it. It's probably about time we got out anyway. Caroline's shiverin'."

I was indeed shaking, but not from the cold. As we stared at each other, silent words passing between us, people started to file out onto the patio. Someone produced a radio and tuned it to a station playing American rock 'n' roll. "96 Tears" burst through the static, and the scent of marijuana filled the air. Long legs attached to miniskirts began to bob and weave, the revelers too self-absorbed to care about what they'd just walked in on.

Tex guided us to the nearby ladder and helped me climb out. I hurried to my chair to get a towel for him, knowing his underwear wouldn't conceal much when wet. Handing it off, I carefully avoided looking down.

"I'll get a robe. You can change in the bathroom if you'd like," I offered. He gathered his clothes and shoes, then followed me inside. His naked torso was long and lean over the towel he clutched to his waist, and my hands twitched at the memory of its ridges and planes. He disappeared into the bathroom, and I took a deep breath, my emotions all jumbled up. I knew I should be relieved we'd been interrupted before going too far, but disappointment weighed more heavily.

While he changed, I took a short robe from the closet and went to the mirror over the dressing table. Tucking damp hair behind my ears, I noticed that the makeup so carefully applied earlier had mostly washed off, save for some lingering mascara. I wiped at the dark streaks under my eyes and touched my lips, still raw from his kisses. Staring at this unrecognizable version of myself, I felt my breath hitch when Tex finally appeared behind me.

"Everything all right, then?" I asked through a stiff smile.

He slicked back the wet strands of hair that had fallen across his forehead. As I turned to face him, he took both my hands in his. "Caroline, I—"

I silenced him with a shake of my head. "No. If you're about to apologize, please don't. I don't regret what happened. Not for a second."

"I wasn't going to apologize."

"You weren't?"

"No. Nothing to be sorry for. We're just two people who got caught up in moonlight and Acapulco and swimmin' pools." He smiled and shrugged, but I could tell he didn't really believe his own words. Something important had just happened, to both of us.

He continued, "I know your life is crazy, but you think you still got room in it for a friend?"

Friends. "Of course." My chin sank a little bit, the word like a sad consolation prize.

He threaded our fingers together. "I guess this is the end of the road for us, huh? I go back to New York, and you go on to . . . somewhere?"

"Paris, I've decided. In a few days."

"Paris," he repeated, like it was an inevitability. "Will you do something for me?"

"Of course. What?"

"Send me a postcard. From Paris or wherever else you jet off to. I'd like to know there's a girl like you out there in the world, makin' it all the more beautiful when she sings. And that maybe sometimes she still thinks about the friend she made in Mexico."

I nodded, a sharp lump in my throat. Then suddenly I was tugged against his body, my head colliding with his chest as his arms closed around me. I clung to him as though he were the only person in the world who could rescue me from this life. Before tonight, I never realized I needed saving.

After silent seconds, he finally released me. I heard the faint notes of music outside, and the laughter of young people without a care in the world. He looked down at my face and subtly shook his head. Was his heart breaking too?

"Don't forget, now. Send postcards, care of *Life*. The address is in each issue. I've got a friend in payroll who'll know where I am and get 'em to me."

"I will," I promised. We stood like that for a minute more, then he leaned in and pressed his lips to my forehead.

"Bye, Al. You take care of yourself."

"Goodbye. And thanks, Tex. For everything."

He smiled sadly, his mouth crinkling at the corners, before he turned and walked out into the night.

GSTAAD

December 20th, 1966
Geneva Airport, Switzerland

Dear Daddy,

You'd think I'd be used to Christmas without
you by now, but sadness hit me like a freight train
the second I heard my first jingle bell.

In an instant, I pictured snowflakes falling on
your hat and coat, shimmering like tiny crystals
under the streetlamps of Paris. Then in a flash you
were in New York, bellowing off-key carols at the
shopkeepers and taxi drivers. I guess I should be
grateful I've got no memories of you on a ski slope;
it makes Gstaad just a little more tolerable.

There's something I want very badly this year;
however, I know it won't be waiting under
Mother's tree. A person is a tall order, especially
when it's a tall person.

Joyeux Noël,
Caroline

FIVE

THE SOUND OF the whirring blades pulsed through my ear protection like a spastic heartbeat as we soared over Swiss mountaintops. Mother sat beside me, tapping manicured fingers on her knee. She'd insisted we take this helicopter from Geneva, a gift from a wealthy client. He needed it over the holidays in Gstaad, so it might as well carry us instead of fly empty. I would've been happier on the train, but as usual, Mother preferred to make an entrance.

Maria was already at our rented chalet, erecting the foil Christmas tree and putting away provisions she'd bought from the market in town. It was a role she'd been performing for the last thirty years, having served as Mother's companion and maid in Florence until the outbreak of war forced them to flee the country together in 1940. Arriving in New York City by ship, the two women had lived together in a small flat until Mother met Daddy at a bond rally. He'd been awestruck by the glamorous Emanuela Leoni, self-proclaimed descendant of Italian nobility, and begged her to marry him after only one week. She'd agreed, but only if she could still pursue her dream of fashion design and keep Maria on as part of the household. Hopelessly smitten, he gave in to her demands without hesitation.

Although Mother had quietly and steadily grown her list of clients while Daddy was coming up in the art world, it wasn't until after his suicide that the House of Leoni became known outside our rarefied circle. They say no publicity is bad publicity, and in the case of my father's untimely death, that theory proved true. Suddenly, everyone from Miami to Madrid wanted her version of the Little Black Dress, so elegantly modeled by the artist's grieving widow in all the newspapers. When orders flooded in, she appointed Maria to act as business manager, traded New York for Paris, and took her first steps out from Daddy's shadow. But even though Maria now played a substantial role in the company, she'd never stopped being Mother's closest friend and confidante. She wasn't just an employee—she was family.

As we neared the town, dense clusters of chalets began to dot the hillside. Skiers perched on the mountaintop near the Eagle Ski Club lift, their bright snowsuits like sprinkles on a bowl of ice cream. In the distance I spied the Gstaad Palace hotel, a turreted castle rising out of the valley. The helicopter began its descent about a mile past town, on a flat stretch of land where the snow had been cleared.

My stomach dropped as we got lower and lower, finally landing with a soft thud. A mechanic on the ground slid open the door, helping us out under the still-churning blades. Hunched down, we ran to the snowy edge of the pad, clutching our makeup cases and overnight bags. Maria had taken most of our clothes in advance so everything would be steamed and hung before we arrived, but Mother and I agreed that a woman must never be caught without her essentials. The helicopter could crash in a remote corner of the Alps, but we would be rescued with flawless complexions and petal-pink lips.

A short distance away, Maria waited next to a car, waving to get our attention. Mother walked briskly over, stopping for a kiss on both cheeks. "*Ciao, amica*," she said with a rare smile.

Maria grinned, then looked past her to me, reaching out her hands. "*Buon Natale!*" she greeted me, taking my cold fingers in hers. "Another visit to the North Pole, eh?" Her English was heavily accented, but enthusiastic. She took our small bags and loaded them into the trunk of the car. "Come, we go!" Mother got in the front, and I settled onto the seat behind her. I glanced back at the helicopter, its blades still spinning, and for a split second considered running back and begging the pilot to take me anywhere but here.

Once we began the journey down the twisty roads to our chalet, Maria asked, "So, how was the trip, ladies?"

"Dreadful! That pilot must have been fresh out of flight school," Mother scoffed. "I was almost ill."

"We could have taken the train. As I suggested." A headache had already begun to form behind my eyes, and I couldn't resist an "I told you so."

"Why take the train when we have a helicopter at our disposal? Now we have plenty of time to get ready for the party at Chalet Ariel tonight," she reasoned.

I sighed, knowing that arguing was pointless.

"I think you will be pleased with your room, Caroline," Maria said brightly. "You have a wonderful view of the valley and sunshine in the morning. The fresh mountain air will do you good."

Since my return to Paris, my daily routine had involved hot, speed-fueled nights in the underground clubs, sleeping until noon, and extravagant shopping sprees. I wasn't dumb; I recognized I was trying to fill a void. After Acapulco, my old life didn't fit anymore. And despite knowing all the vitamin shots and dancing in the world wouldn't make it the right size, a temporary fix proved easier than altering the seams.

"I'm sure it's fine," I replied, knowing my sour attitude wasn't Maria's fault. I hoped she didn't take my lack of enthusiasm personally.

"I set the Christmas tree up in the living room," she continued. "It's so modern and festive at night, with the colors on the wheel spinning beside it."

"Once again, we would be lost without you," Mother said. "How you managed to wrangle this rental property out from under Gunter I will never know."

"He is, shall we say, distracted with his new bride." She spoke of Brigitte Bardot, who had recently married Gstaad playboy Gunter Sachs.

"From what I hear, they've both got several *distractions* on the side," Mother murmured, ever the gossip. "He'll be lucky if she stays until New Year's."

"Oh, you are so bad, Ema," Maria laughed, shaking her head.

With a frown, I laid down in the back seat. The gray sky outside the window made me wonder what it looked like above a certain photographer whom I hadn't managed to erase from my mind. It had been three months, but I still remembered how his lips felt against mine.

"Ack, so dramatic," Mother lamented, glancing back at me. "I'm beginning to think we should have left her back in Paris."

I didn't disagree.

※

When we arrived at our chalet, Maria helped carry our things inside as I followed Mother through the front door.

"Fabulous! Just fabulous!" she exclaimed.

I stepped through the foyer and took in our surroundings. Shag carpeting covered the living area under low sofas upholstered in white twill. Traditional Swiss blankets were laid across their backs, while wool pillows added pops of color. Stylish books had been artfully stacked on a coffee table, lit by a giant gold arc lamp. Beyond the living room was the dining area, and up above, a loft with wooden railings. The exposed beams of the ceiling towered over us, and on the far back wall, floor-to-ceiling windows offered gorgeous views of the mountains. It was impressive and luxurious; Mother demanded nothing less.

Maria had set up a silver tree in the corner of the living room, scattering a few beautifully wrapped packages beneath. We usually had a sparse gift exchange Christmas morning, swapping sentimental trinkets picked up on our travels, rather than opulent or expensive presents. I was no longer the six-year-old girl excited by all the toys my father lavished upon me. I was a twenty-two-year-old adult, capable of buying whatever I needed or wanted, anywhere in the world. But lately, I didn't even know what that was.

"I'd like to get settled in and take a bath. Is my room upstairs, Maria?" I asked.

"*Sì, principessa.* Up the stairs, last door on the right. I already put your things away. Your ukulele is in the closet."

"Thanks. The place looks great, by the way." I knew she'd worked hard at making it a home for us, however temporary it might be. I left her and Mother downstairs to sort out their plans for the coming week.

In the closet of my room, there were, indeed, a dozen gowns from the Leoni winter collection hanging up, the familiar lion logo stitched into the linings. I had to hand it to Mother: she had enormous talent. Running my fingertips across the sequins and fine-knit cashmere, fondling its cool softness, I decided that if wealth were a fabric, this would be it. I glanced at my ukulele case on the floor and sighed. Lately I'd had a hard time focusing on writing new songs, as if all my inspiration had fled through the door of a Mexican hotel room, right along with Tex. How could I write ballads about love when I wasn't even sure what the word meant now? Was it the desperate beat of a heart under flushed and tingling skin, or the empty ache of loneliness after that heartbeat finally slowed? Perhaps it was neither, and I was a fool to try to put a name to my feelings.

Walking into the bathroom, I turned on the water over a large claw-foot tub. A picture window revealed the gray afternoon, snow still falling all around us. The alpine scenery was majestic but cold, as though I were looking at someone else's view, someone else's idea of a relaxing retreat. Not even a speck of turquoise water or bright-pink fabric to lift my mood.

I removed my clothes and slipped into a robe before going back to the bedroom to peruse the magazines Maria had left out. On the nightstand, under copies of *Vogue* and *Mademoiselle*, sat the current issue of *Life*. My breath hitched as I spied the teaser headline on the cover: "Travels in Sunny Acapulco!"

With twitching hands, I flipped through until my attention was snagged by the glossy color photos about twenty pages in: dreamlike images of the cliff divers, the pink and white stripes of the pool umbrellas at La Concha, waiters carrying trays of fruity cocktails, and the beach where we'd walked that sunny afternoon. There were no pictures of me, and though I knew it was irrational, I felt disappointed. It wasn't so much about vanity as it was a need for some sort of proof that our time together had been real. That it had actually happened, and that it was special to Tex. Without tangible evidence, my mind had managed to turn it round and round until I feared I was just a brief diversion to him. Perhaps what he should have been for me.

With the bath nearly full, I set the magazine on a chair and took off my robe. Sinking into the warm water, I felt the tension in my muscles ease as his images replayed across the backs of my eyelids like a slideshow. The contrasting tones of the cliffs and sea, the tan skin of the sunbathers, the condensation on the margarita glasses—it all brought me straight back to that paradise. Did he still have the photo he'd taken of me next to the pool the day we met? Had I blinked and ruined it? Was it languishing as an undeveloped negative, or had he made a print? Questions that would probably never be answered.

A knock on the door, a turn of the knob, and Mother entered the bathroom, full-length caftan brushing the floor. She held two glasses of wine.

"I thought you might like a drink while you relax. I certainly needed it after that helicopter. A very nice Riesling—Maria picked it up at a shop near Von Siebenthal." Handing me the chilled glass, Mother pushed the copy of *Life* onto the floor and took a seat next to the tub. I almost cried out, warning her to be careful with the magazine, but I held my tongue. It wasn't worth explaining; not to her.

"The party at Chalet Ariel begins at seven o'clock. There will be light cocktails, then a seated dinner to follow. You should plan to be ready by six thirty. Do you need Maria to fix your hair? The beige dress with an orange shawl will suit you well."

I sighed, taking a sip of my wine. "I don't think I'm going with you tonight. I'm just not feeling up to it."

"Don't be silly, of course you're going. It's Liz and Dick; one does not turn down an invitation like this. Besides, I want her to see the dress; it would look divine in her new picture. The one she's making with Brando."

"Can't you wear it?"

"Of course, but it's better on you. A bit simple for my taste." She pinched her lips together.

"Gee, thanks."

"Caroline, you know I don't ask much of you. I let you traipse all over the world, spending your inheritance, wearing my beautiful clothes. In return, I implore you to go to one party, and suddenly you can't be bothered. You would rather sit in a bathroom and do god knows what. Read magazines?"

I groaned inwardly. I wasn't up for a fight with her; not tonight, when I already felt so glum. "First of all, Daddy left me that money, and I can spend it however I like. And second, I thought you *wanted* me to be seen all over the world, wearing your designs, pretending life is just one big glamorous party in a Leoni gown."

"What's to pretend? Your life *is* a glamorous party!" She threw her hands up in frustration. "But that's not the point. You're only twenty-two, and you should have a little fun before you marry and face real responsibilities. I wish I'd had that chance at your age. The war took it away from me. I have no problem with you traveling and enjoying yourself, but now, when your mother asks you to do one favor, it is as though the world is ending. What is the matter with you?"

I exhaled, knowing she wouldn't understand, no matter how hard I tried to explain. "It's nothing. I'm just tired. We only arrived today, and I was hoping to relax this evening."

Mother shook her head. "No, it's not just tonight. You've been acting strange for weeks. I've seen you, wandering the flat, coming in at all hours glistening with sweat and reeking of marijuana. Is there a problem with Henry? Is that it?"

I was surprised she'd noticed my recent spiral. True, she'd waited until it affected her directly before bringing it up, but maybe this was her misguided way of showing she actually cared.

"No, things are fine there. Boring, but fine. We still write letters and speak on the phone sometimes."

"Do you wish he were here in person? Is that it?" she pressed.

"No. I can assure you, geography is not my problem with Henry." I glanced at the discarded copy of *Life* on the floor. Last month in Paris, I'd sent Tex a postcard at the address I'd found on the magazine's masthead, just as he'd asked me to. On the front of the card was a picture of the Tuileries Garden, and on the back, I'd written, "*O Tiger-lily . . . I wish you could talk.*"—*Al*

Hesitating, I decided to ask the question that had been plaguing me since Mexico. "When you met Daddy, did you ever consider all you'd have to give up if you married him? Did you ever wish you could have done more before you became a wife or a mother?"

"What a question!" She looked mystified. "Your father and I always had a strong partnership. You know that. Just because my name wasn't splashed across the pages of *Harper's Bazaar* didn't mean I wasn't already making clothes for important people. I was fortunate to be able to fulfill my creativity within the shelter of his world. Not many women are so lucky."

"But what if . . ." I pushed past my nerves. "Say it was something else. Like singing, for example. Something that might have taken you away from home more often, or put you under a spotlight. A spotlight that was maybe brighter than your husband's. Do you think you could have pursued something like that and still had a family?"

Her lips settled into a frown. "Ah. So this is the trouble, then. I always told your father it was a mistake to encourage your fascination with music. And here you are, conflicted over a choice that does not even exist. I don't say this to be cruel, but I don't think you need to worry about having to 'give up' anything to get married. It assumes a demand for your work that just isn't there, my darling."

In other words, I'd never make it as a singer, so I may as well take what I could get as a wife. I closed my eyes and sank back into the water, letting my chin sit on top of the bubbles. I was well past done with this conversation.

After a moment of silence, Mother finally stood. "*Allora*, I can see you will not be good company tonight. I'll wear the dress myself and bring Maria. She's a better saleswoman than either of us, anyway."

She reached down to pick up the magazine she'd pushed off the chair. Examining the cover, she said, "Acapulco. Weren't you just there?"

I nodded. "It was lovely," I replied mournfully. "Really lovely."

"You see, my darling, lovely, uncomplicated days are not so bad. Many people never know such blessings. You'd do well to remember that."

With a quiet click of the door, Mother left me alone with my uncertainty. She didn't understand, and it was becoming more and more clear that she just didn't want to. I sipped the wine and closed my eyes, letting my mind leave this tomb of melancholy. Letting it float away toward hibiscus flowers and mariachi music and, somewhere out there, a man with a camera.

SIX

"WAKEY, WAKEY, DARLING," a soft voice trilled in my ear. "Time to rise and shine."

My heavy eyelids opened, revealing a bedroom in the valley of the Alps and the golden-blond streak of Daphne's ponytail. She sat on the edge of my bed, lightly tapping my shoulder.

"Daphne?" I mumbled, my voice still thick with sleep. "What are you doing here?"

"It's Christmas, darling, where else would I be but Gstaad? Your mother rang me at the hotel and told me you were still a bit blue. I decided to pop by and tell you that you absolutely *must* come with me to a picnic on the mountain today. Champagne, lots of yummy food, chocolate—doesn't that sound marvelous?" She was working hard to be cheery, although we both knew it was the same old party with the same old people.

"Tired . . . You should go, though." I pulled the covers back over my shoulder, burrowing deeper into my pillow.

"No, I will not accept defeat." She yanked the blankets back and stood over me. "You've been acting funny since Mexico. Out at Régine's club every night, spending a fortune on shoes during the day, having drinks with that letch Roger Vadim; darling, that's just not you. Every other girl I know, yes. But not you. You're getting up, you'll swallow one of my little black beauties, and you're going up that mountain."

I sighed, heaving my body up. "Fine. And you can keep your pills. Coffee would be nice, though."

"I'll get some from Maria. You"—she pointed at me—"shower and put your face on. Dress warm. It may be sunny, but it's bloody cold."

"Here we go!" Daphne shouted as we jumped from the lift. Our boots landed on thick white powder, crunching through the snow on our approach toward the crowd at the top of the mountain. Collapsible chairs had been set up, their bright colors dazzling in the intense light. A helicopter sat off to the side—the delivery system for lunch at high altitude. Behind my mirrored sunglasses, my eyes throbbed with the pulse of caffeine. I was awake, but it was an empty high.

"How long are we staying again?" I asked, glancing at the clusters of skiers.

"Don't be like that; we just got here. Come, a glass of champagne and raclette are just what the doctor ordered." Daphne and I dropped our skis before she tugged me toward the buffet.

"Is that Caroline?" an excited voice behind me called. Turning, I saw Vivienne Eldridge-Peters approaching.

"Oh god, it's Horse Face," Daphne muttered in my ear.

"Hush, now," I whispered back. "Vivi! What a small world!" Seeing my old schoolmate brought an unexpected smile to my face as we exchanged air-kisses. Vivi had been in the same class as Daphne and me at boarding school, and she'd been as studious as Daphne was rebellious. She was unfailingly kind, inviting me out to dinner with her family when they visited, and offering me a quiet room to play my music when things got crazy. Sadly, there had always been an undercurrent of desperation about her. More than anything, Vivi craved a place at the popular table—a place Daphne enjoyed dangling just out of reach.

"And Daphne DeVossier—you haven't changed a bit!"

"Viv, how nice." Daphne smiled politely.

"Isn't this wonderful, all of us together again! But of course, it *is* Gstaad, right? Anyone who's anyone is here now."

"As are you, apparently," Daphne said under her breath. "Caroline, darling, I need a drink. I'll get you one too."

Secretly, I wondered if Daphne's subtle digs were a result of jealousy. After all, Vivienne came from one of the few happy homes in our circle, while my best friend had grown up in the opposite.

"Thanks, Daph."

Vivi and I claimed a couple of canvas chairs, covering our laps with plaid woolen blankets.

"So, tell me everything!" she began. "Are you here with your mother?"

"Yes, and Maria, of course. They went to dinner at Liz and Dick's last night."

"Ooh, I heard all about that party this morning. David Niven had everyone in stitches. And what about you? Did you spend the evening with Henry?"

"No, he's in Newport with his grandparents. He's so busy meeting with artists and organizing shows for the new gallery that he's become hard to pin down."

"You must make such an attractive pair when you're lucky enough to be in the same place at the same time. I can't think of two nicer people to end up together. I really mean that," Vivi said graciously.

Just then Daphne arrived with a bottle of champagne and three glasses. She handed them out, pulling up a chair. "I figured we might as well settle in. They're just now slicing the prime rib."

Popping the cork, she filled the glasses, and we toasted. I could grudgingly admit to being glad I'd left the house, even if it meant answering questions about Henry. I couldn't run from him forever, much as I wanted to.

"What about you, Viv?" I asked. "How's your love life?"

She smiled and blushed. "Well, as a matter of fact . . ." She set her glass down in the snow to remove her glove. Beneath it lay a perfect princess-cut diamond. "I'm engaged! To Tom Kipling. We've been seeing each other for a year, and he finally popped the question last month. We're planning a summer wedding."

Everyone knew Kipling's Gin. Their spirits weren't entirely on par with Tanqueray or Beefeater, but nonetheless sold well among those with limited means. One assumed the Kiplings didn't drink their own product.

"Cheers, darling, well done!" Daphne acknowledged, clinking her glass with Vivi's. "By the size of that rock, gin is in."

Vivi started laughing uncontrollably. "Gin is in! Oh, that's good, Daphne. You should be in advertising!"

"She's too busy trying to be an actress," I reminded her.

"That's right, I forgot! Had any luck, Daph?"

"Yes, as a matter of fact. I had a small role in the new Antonioni film, *Blow-Up*," she replied smugly.

"Antonioni? I don't think I know him. Is it a good picture?" Vivi asked.

"Critics are calling it a masterpiece. I'll be traveling with Michelangelo to Cannes this spring to support it. I suppose it's probably not your cup of tea, though, Viv. Quite intellectual."

"I can't wait to see it," I said, trying to keep the peace. "And I'm sure you're great."

"Caroline, darling, you're a dear. I know *you*, in particular, will love it." She winked. "But what I'm desperate for now is a meeting with Cubby Broccoli. I'd be perfect in a Bond film."

"Ooh, do you know who I heard he's meeting with? Bardot!" Vivi whispered theatrically. "But of course she's got Gunter to think about now. Egads, those two. The only time they come up for air is to flirt with other people. I have no idea why she agreed to marry him."

"Well, what would you do if someone dumped a thousand roses on your backyard from a helicopter? How does anyone say no to that?" Daphne countered. "Not that I'm big on the marriage game, but there are some proposals a girl just can't refuse."

"Maybe," I acknowledged. "But shouldn't Gunter and Brigitte be a lesson to us all? To not rush into something without thinking it through? Maybe she'd have been happier as a single girl in Saint-Tropez."

"I can't speak for Brigitte, but I for one can't wait to walk down the aisle. Especially with a man as great as my Tom," Vivi said with a dreamy look on her face.

I took another sip of champagne and watched all the laughing families and couples around me. Would I ever feel that way next to Henry? Smiling with our rosy-cheeked children, in matching ski outfits, clutching hands? It was a beautiful picture, though slightly out of focus.

"Daph, this champagne has gone to my head. I'm going to get a bite to eat." I peeled back my blanket to stand.

"Good idea. Excuse us, Vivi," she apologized, rising to join me.

"It's all right, I need to head back down the mountain. I assume I'll see you both at the Palace party?"

I grimaced. Yet another New Year's spent in the ballroom of the lavish hotel, drowning my boredom in alcohol.

"Yes, I'm sure we'll be there," I replied. "Bye for now, sweetie." I leaned over to touch my cheek to hers. "And congratulations to you and Tom. He's a lucky man."

Vivi smiled. "I'm the lucky one. *Ciao!*" she called, waving back to us.

Daphne started in as soon as we got to the buffet table. "God, Horse Face hasn't changed one iota. Marrying into that awful Kipling family—their gin is truly the worst. You couldn't pay me to drink that rotgut."

"Oh, stop. Tom's not so bad. I think he and Vivi are well suited."

"I'm not saying he's not nice." Daphne placed a small amount of meat on her plate. "I'm just saying his family obviously knows nothing about quality."

I chose a roll and some fresh cheese, realizing I finally had my appetite back. "She seems happy. You certainly have to envy her that."

"I envy nothing. Besides, I plan on finding my own happiness later, with a boy from Le Rosey." She slid her eyes toward a group of young men clustered nearby.

"God, Daph, they're barely eighteen!"

"Yes, isn't it wonderful? They'll be ever so grateful."

I laughed and shook my head, knowing we'd be eighty years old and she'd still find ways to be shocking.

As we rode the lift back down into the valley, a strong shiver raced through me. After three hours outside, and a few clumsy runs down one of the easier slopes, I could barely feel my toes and fingers.

"Buck up, darling, my hotel has a fabulous indoor heated pool. You'll be warm in no time," Daphne reassured me, her nose and cheeks pink from the cold. "I talked to Billy this morning. He's in town with Taffy. She's hired him out for the holidays," she continued.

"Oh, lucky us!" We never knew where he might show up next, such was the demand for his services.

"Yes, and he said he has a surprise. I don't know what it is; he wouldn't spill. Just said it was something that had to be given in person."

"Maybe he's showing off a new boyfriend?"

"Don't be daft, you know he'd never do that." She shook her head. "'Out of sight, out of mind,' he always says. Everyone knows he dates men, but old ladies like Taffy don't want to be reminded of it."

"Maybe it's diamonds, then," I joked.

"With his sense of humor, it's more likely to be plastic tiaras from the five-and-dime."

At the bottom of the mountain, we trudged through the snow to the ski club's lounge. Inside, hot toddies warmed frozen hands, while those too lazy to make it up the mountain in the first place sipped a third or fourth glass of mulled wine. A faint cloud of cigarette smoke hung over the room, making the star on the top of the Christmas tree glow hazily.

"Do you want to stay here?" I asked. "I can find us a comfy spot."

"No, I already told Billy we'd meet him at my hotel. So long, ski pants; hello, swimwear."

After a short ride in her little Peugeot ("A loaner, darling"), I found myself floating in the pool at Daphne's resort, our glasses of brut champagne resting on the edge next to us. The gentle heat of the water was a salve to my tired leg muscles. I'd borrowed the rare conservative suit in my friend's collection, a low-cut candy-apple-red one-piece. Daphne wore a black bikini, topped off by the diamond earrings her father had given her on her last birthday. When I asked if she was worried about losing them in the water, she said, "Not really. In fact, I've got five other pairs in my mother's safe in Paris. Besides, if you've got 'em, flaunt 'em!"

"Isn't that what you say about breasts too?"

"Absolutely!" We dissolved into laughter, clinking our glasses together.

"Watch out, children—drunk ladies in the pool!" a voice bellowed.

I turned to see Billy walking toward us, decked out in a fur-lined parka and dark-purple velvet trousers. A small group trailed him; a few faces I recognized, but some I didn't.

"There you are, you devil!" Daphne exclaimed, wading through the water with her glass held high. "Caroline and I have been waiting for ages. I was just about to give up and go back to the room."

"As if I'd believe that. I knew I'd still find you here as long as the champagne didn't run out. And I see it hasn't." He swiped the glass from her and emptied it into his mouth.

I lifted mine and raised it to him from across the pool. "Merry Christmas, Billy! And cheers to the only man in the world I want to spend the holidays with."

"Gosh, that better not be true. Otherwise, my surprise isn't as fabulous as I'd hoped."

I frowned, just as the group of people behind him parted and I spotted a familiar tall figure with a crooked nose. He held a camera up to his grinning face and pointed it at me. As the shutter clicked, I couldn't hide my stunned delight.

"Tex!" Daphne cried, waving him over. "Oh, Billy, what a wonderful treat! Just when we thought this would be another dull holiday filled with handsy trust fund boys. Caroline, isn't it fantastic?"

I nodded, still staring as he walked toward us. My heart was pounding so hard, I almost expected it to cause a ripple in the water.

Knowing he was watching made me incredibly self-conscious.

I swam to the ledge as he kneeled down. "What are you doing here?" I asked, looking up into his glittering blue eyes.

"You know me, always chasin' after pretty girls in swimming pools." He shrugged. "Well, maybe just one pretty girl."

"He's here to shoot for *Vogue*!" Billy explained. "Taffy called Diana and arranged it all. He's taking the pictures, and there's another reporter here to write the story about us. It's that blond woman in the corner over there." He pointed to a girl in glasses, clutching a notepad like it was her security blanket.

"Why would anyone want to read a story about *us*?" Daphne asked. "I can't think of anything more boring."

"That's because you grew up surrounded by all this," Billy scoffed. "To the secretaries eating lunch at their desks, or teenage girls in Des Moines, our life is exciting. Christmas in Gstaad, Valentine's in Nassau, Easter in Palm Beach—people eat it up."

"Is that true?" I asked Tex. "You're photographing us for *Vogue*?"

"Yes, but don't worry; you won't be in the magazine if you don't want to be."

"No, it's not that. I'm just surprised you came all this way, especially over the holidays. Don't you want to be with your friends in New York?"

"Diana gave us a list of people we should cover. Your mother was on it. Figured if she's here, there was a good chance you'd be with her." Then he added quietly, "I got your postcard, Al. Reckon I'm here for that talk."

I blushed as muscles deep within me clenched.

Gstaad had just become a whole lot more exciting.

December 23rd, 1966
Gstaad, Switzerland

Dear Daddy,

I've started writing again—tell me what you think:

Snowflakes falling
Children calling
Were we ever so free
So free . . .

You make an angel
And I'll make a man
Give him buttons for eyes
And sticks for hands

We'll shiver and shake
Leaving footprints in our wake
Could we be so free
So free . . .

Love,
Caroline

SEVEN

LIKE THE LYRICS of an infectious pop song, thoughts of Tex became a constant refrain in my mind for the next two days. I searched for him across every crowded room, my ears straining to hear the deep cadence of his voice or the click of a camera. Knowing he was here, so close to me, was comforting and terrifying at the same time. His work assignment for *Vogue* kept him frustratingly busy, and I longed for time alone as we'd had in Mexico. Did he ever think about that kiss we'd shared in the pool? And had he fantasized about another one as often as I had?

Our paths finally crossed again two days before Christmas, at the Eagle Ski Club's restaurant. I had just settled into a chair next to Billy on the veranda, blanket over my legs and a mug of tea in my hands, when Tex walked through the glass doors. He towered over the other people who'd come in early from skiing, his jeans and insulated canvas jacket a contrast to the Burberry and Bogner surrounding us. Billy turned to see what had snagged my attention.

"Well, well, look who it is . . . Should I make myself scarce?"

I wanted to yell *"Yesss!!!"* but merely shrugged. "That's not necessary. He's probably too busy working to spend time with me right now."

Billy rolled his eyes. "Oh, please." He waved to Tex, whose face erupted into a huge smile when he spotted us. I quickly smoothed down my hair and rose to greet him.

"Well, if it isn't the elusive Caroline Kimball. I was beginning to think you were ignorin' me."

"I could say the same of you. I've seen you around with your camera, but I didn't want to interrupt. I know you're here for a job."

"Among other things," he admitted, tilting his head.

Billy stood, offering his seat to Tex. "Say, would you do me a favor and keep her company? I need to make a phone call."

"I think I can handle that."

I could've kissed Billy at that moment.

Tex removed his gloves as he sat, giving me his full attention. "I'm sorry I haven't had time to talk. Taffy's had me on a short leash. She wants to make sure her daughter ends up in the magazine, so she keeps askin' me to tag along wherever they go." He leaned in and lowered his voice. "That girl's a real piece of work. Tried to feel me up in the back seat of a car."

A stab of jealousy rocketed through me, followed by the image of a disfiguring accident on the slopes. "I hear she can be a handful."

"More like an armful. Don't worry: I let her down gently."

I shrugged my shoulders. "I wasn't worried." *Right . . .* "So, where else have you been hiding this week?"

"Oh, there were a couple of dinner parties. Some get-togethers on the mountain. Cocktails at the Palace. Tell me if I'm missin' something, because from my end, it seems like a repeat of Mexico, only colder."

"No, you've got it pegged. Trust me, I'd rather be sunbathing than trying not to ski into a tree."

"So why stay? You could go anywhere, do whatever you want. Why are you here?"

Somehow, I didn't think he was talking about just Gstaad.

"There's the million-dollar question." The one I'd been asking myself ever since we'd said goodbye in Acapulco.

"You don't have an answer?"

"I have an answer for today: because Mother is the only real family I've got left, and she wanted to spend Christmas in Switzerland. As to the rest of it, well, it might just be inertia."

He frowned, as if sensing there was more I wasn't saying, but accepting that this was all he'd get for now.

"Speaking of your mother, I'd like to arrange a time to meet her and set up a shoot. Miss Vreeland wants her in the magazine spread."

"She's having a small Christmas Eve celebration with a few friends tomorrow night," I offered. "You should come—if Taffy can spare you, that is."

"Do you want me there?"

"I wouldn't have invited you if I didn't."

Tex smiled. "Then I'll be there."

"Good. So where's your camera? It's odd to see you with empty hands."

"They wouldn't let me in here with it. The Eagle has a strict no-photos policy, even for journalists," he explained. "Taffy had to pull strings just to get me temporary access. And even then, I can't come back more than three times this season. Thank goodness you were here, or I would have wasted one of my visas."

I laughed. "We *are* awful, aren't we? Private clubs and all that. I swear I only hang around here because it's quiet. And Mother made such an effort to get us memberships that I feel like one of us should actually use it."

"She doesn't come herself?"

"No, she prefers gowns to skiwear. Most of her networking is done at night, not on the mountain. Gstaad is a good business opportunity at the holidays, even if it isn't the first choice for either of us."

"And where would you spend Christmas if you could be anywhere in the world?" Tex sat back in his chair, studying me.

"Hmm . . . I don't even know anymore," I admitted. "Maybe it's not the place that's important, but the people. Isn't that what they say about Christmas? It's about being with the ones you love?"

He nodded, his gaze steady as he leaned in and placed his hand over mine on the table. "It is, Al."

Before I could react, the girl who'd been with Tex at Daphne's hotel chose that moment to approach our table.

"Jack, there you are. I've got what I needed. Are you ready to go?" She looked out of place and anxious to leave.

"Uh, yeah, I suppose so," he said, releasing me. "Let me introduce you two—Jennifer Beardsley, this is Caroline Kimball. Caroline and I met when I was shooting a piece on Acapulco," Tex explained, before turning back to me. "Jennifer is the reporter assigned to my pictures."

"Pleasure," I said, extending my hand. She shook it firmly, a tight smile on her face. I already hated and envied the time she got to spend with him.

"Nice to meet you, Miss Kimball. Jack? Ready?" She pointed at her watch.

He stood up, looking apologetic. "We've gotta skedaddle. But I'll see you tomorrow night?"

"Yes, I'll call you later with directions to our chalet. Where are you staying?"

"The Hotel Olden. Room 15. If I'm not there when you call, just leave a message with the front desk."

"Perfect."

He started to follow Jennifer, then suddenly turned back. Pressing his well-worn gloves into my palms, he leaned down and whispered into my ear, "I'll feel better knowin' something of mine is keepin' you warm."

I stared wide-eyed at him as he winked.

On Christmas Eve, I entered our living room to find it overflowing with twinkle lights and garland. Andy Williams crooned from the hi-fi as the scent of cinnamon and cloves wafted through the air. The dining room table, weighted down with platters of skewered meatballs and fondue accompaniments, sat beside a makeshift bar tended by a server in a plaid vest and bow tie. Mother had begun the tradition of a Christmas Eve party while Daddy was still alive, but I knew she preferred the sophisticated Gstaad crowd to his eccentric artist friends. It was an annual event I usually dreaded, but tonight my insides fluttered with anticipation.

"*Principessa*, you look stunning!" Maria declared, coming out of the kitchen with another cheese platter. She set the food down and kissed me on the cheek. Mother sat perched on the sofa, sipping her wine and scrutinizing my attire.

"Is that Balenciaga?" An accusatory edge spiked her voice.

"Yes. I had a fitting this fall." Cristóbal was one of Mother's main rivals in the fashion world. I wore his sculptural ivory tunic, with delicate gold brocade accenting the hem and neckline, over matching pants. Green jade earrings dangled down to my shoulders, and I'd left my hair long and loose, center-parted. I would smile and charm her guests, but I would do it on my terms.

"It's quite beautiful," she grudgingly admitted. "Similar to one of my pieces a few years ago."

Turning to the bar, I poured a glass of white wine, likely the first of many tonight. "I forgot to tell you, Mother," I called over my shoulder, "though I mentioned it to Maria: I invited a friend to join us tonight. He's a photographer for *Vogue*."

"Yes, she told me, and I must say I'm surprised. I tried to get you to pose for Dick Avedon, but you had no interest. This boy must be quite the wunderkind if you're finally deigning to set foot in front of a camera."

"No, it's not like that. He's just a friend. He isn't photographing me for the magazine." No sense going into what our true relationship was, especially since I didn't know for sure myself. Did the mere fact that my pulse sped up and my muscles tensed every time we saw one another make him more than "just a friend"?

"Regardless," she continued, "after Maria told me he was coming, I spoke with Diana, and we agreed he should shoot the festivities. It will be fabulous advertising for the company. I do wish you were wearing one of my pieces, but you're already dressed, so no point in changing now."

I turned to her, angry. "Mother, you had no right to do that. Tex was to be here as my guest. Now he's going to think he's supposed to be working the whole time."

"Nonsense." She waved me off, leaning over to fluff a throw pillow. "He takes a few pictures, easy, then done. *Vogue* wanted us in the story, anyway; why not handle it tonight?"

I shook my head. "You don't understand. He has to take dozens of photos to get just one or two that will work for the article. The lighting has to be right, and the composition just so. He won't have a single moment to relax."

"Lighting? Composition? I didn't know my daughter was now an expert in the art of photography."

"*Principessa*, it will be fine," Maria said, approaching with a cold tray of caviar. "I promise we won't keep him working all night. Besides, you will also be busy, talking to other guests. Is Christmas, no? Time for cheer?"

I shrugged, resigned. At least I'd get to see him—that would have to be enough. "Fine. But if Roger Moore corners me again with a story about his crazy ex-wife, you're in charge of the rescue mission."

"*Lo prometto*," she agreed, giving my shoulder a knowing squeeze.

※

Two hours later, the party was in full swing. Tex had arrived with Jennifer Beardsley, and after briefly waving to me, began unpacking his camera and accessories from a leather bag. As usual, his height made it easy for me to spy on him from a safe distance. Behind the camera, he appeared confident and professional. It made me wish I had such self-assurance when it came to my music.

As guests chatted and nibbled on hors d'oeuvres, I made conversation with a French ambassador and his mistress, a B-movie actress Daphne had gone up against for parts. However, we were soon interrupted by Mother asking where I'd put the holiday records; it seemed we'd run through all the Andy and Bing.

"You know, I have my ukulele upstairs. Maybe I could bring it out, and we could all sing a few carols?" I suggested. Whether it was the wine or the mere presence of Tex that had emboldened me, I couldn't say. But in that moment, performing in front of a room full of people didn't feel so terrifying.

Her face twisted in scorn. "Caroline, this is not a Texas campfire. We do not have sing-alongs at a Leoni party. Besides, don't you think you would look a bit foolish with a tiny guitar and your Balenciaga pantsuit? Honestly. Cristóbal would never let me hear the end of it." She shook her head, bewildered.

My cheeks heated in embarrassment as the ambassador and his date looked away, having witnessed the public scolding. My heart sinking, I walked quickly to the stereo cabinet, bending down in search of more records. I felt the threatening pull of tears, but wouldn't give Mother the satisfaction. I wouldn't let her know that her put-downs and lack of faith in me were like a million tiny cuts breaching the armor of my couture. It was a pain I'd gotten used to; I didn't know why I'd expected anything different tonight.

As Mother huddled next to me, she whispered, "That photographer, Jack Fairchild—he really is quite striking, isn't he?"

"Yes, I suppose he is," I replied, concentrating on my task.

"It's no wonder you were drawn to him—you have my eye for attractive things. And that voice! It's like the ghost of your father."

"Because of the accent?"

"*Mio Dio*, that wretched twang—gah!" she grimaced. "If it weren't for Neiman Marcus, I'd say give the state back to Mexico."

Exasperated, I placed a Mancini album on the turntable. "Mother, where are you going with this?"

She held up her hands in surrender. "Relax, my darling, I'm just making conversation. You invited him; I assumed you might like to discuss him."

"Well, I wouldn't. And thanks to you, I haven't been able to say one word to him all night."

She sighed. "Again with this. All right, we will go right now and tell him to put the camera down and enjoy himself. It is a party, after all."

She linked her fingers with mine and marched us over to where Tex and Jennifer stood. He was fiddling with a lens when Mother reached up and tapped him on the shoulder.

"Mr. Fairchild, my daughter informs me that I am being cruel, making you work on Christmas Eve. Therefore, I am requesting that you put your equipment away, relax, and have a drink. I'm sure you've gotten what you needed by now."

"Ah, you must be Miss Emanuela. Al's told me a lot about you. Feel free to call me Tex—she does." He extended his hand, smiling.

"Al? Who is Al?"

"Sorry, just my little nickname for Caroline. She prefers it to 'ma'am,'" he explained.

"To be fair, it's no worse than her actual name. I begged her to change it when I did mine." I prepared myself for the well-worn sentence she was about to deliver. "*Carolina Leoni*—now *that* is a name." She emphasized her Italian pronunciation—Car-o-LEE-na. "Even her first name was not my choice. I wanted something like Isabella or Marianna, but my late husband insisted on naming her after his departed grandmother. Caroline. It sits there like a stone, does it not?"

"I think it's nice. What's the word I'm lookin' for . . . classic, maybe? But then again, I'm from West Texas and not as sophisticated as y'all," Tex said. He seemed amused rather than insulted by Mother's verbal ice picks, and I was relieved he could hold his own with her.

"Yes, well, nobody's perfect," she declared with a wave of her hand. "Miss Beardsley, you must come with me and meet Maria. She can tell you all about the House of Leoni and our preparations for the evening." Before leaving, she turned back to me and whispered, "Don't disappear, darling. I have a special surprise for you later." Then she was off across the room, with Jennifer trailing after her like a startled deer in headlights.

"Sorry about that," I apologized to Tex. "She can be a bit much. Sometimes she pretends it's the language barrier, but as you can see, her English is perfect."

"Not a problem. That went pretty much as I expected it to. So how's about that drink?"

I led him to the bar, where he ordered a whiskey on the rocks. The bartender refreshed my wine, and we made our way to a quiet window seat on the edge of the room. Outside, the stars twinkled through the trees, the moon illuminating snow-capped mountains beyond.

"You look beautiful tonight," he said quietly, staring through the glass.

"Mother was disappointed I'm not wearing one of her designs."

"Understandable. You're probably her best model; women would kill to look like you. Thing is, they don't realize your looks aren't even the most attractive thing about you."

"And what is?" I asked.

"Your talent. Drives me batty sometimes, wondering why it's not your voice I'm hearin' on the radio. Judy Collins can't hold a candle to you."

I shook my head, Mother's words still echoing. *Foolish.* "I'm sorry about the work assignment tonight. I had no idea she'd call the magazine."

"It's okay. And it hasn't been all bad. I may have snuck in a couple shots of you when you weren't lookin'," he admitted with a sheepish grin.

"That reminds me, I was a little surprised I didn't make the cut for the Acapulco spread."

"So you saw it? What'd you think?"

"Those pictures from the cliffs were amazing. You really are talented, you know."

"Nah." He shrugged. "It's easy to get it right when you've got such incredible subject matter. It's photographing the ordinary in an extraordinary way that takes real talent. I'm still working on that."

"I think you're already there. Those photos—they really brought me back to Mexico. They made me remember what it was like to be happy. Something I hadn't been for a long time." Not since that day Maria called with news that would change my life forever. The day everything stopped.

"And what about after Mexico?"

Memories of those desperate, empty weeks in Paris flooded back. I looked away, shaking my head. "I was even more miserable than before. Something I didn't think was possible."

He lifted his hand to tilt my chin back toward him. "You wanna know a secret, Al? Me too."

I exhaled, relieved I wasn't alone in my feelings. I wasn't crazy to think there was something between us.

"Fact is, I had another job all lined up, but when I got the call from *Vogue,* I dropped everything on the chance you'd be here," he confessed. "I know it sounds crazy, because we only had two days together, but I haven't been able to stop thinking about you. And that last night . . ." He trailed off. "It's like I turned a light switch off when I walked out of your hotel room, and now I can't find it again in the dark. I'm just fumblin' around, smackin' the wall."

"Oh, Tex, it's been awful! And then having you in Gstaad, knowing you were close, but I couldn't do anything about it— torture."

"I saw you in that damn pool the other day, and all I wanted to do was pull you out and put my arms around you. But there's this crazy game going on where nobody can do or say anything they really want to. It's all so polite, so hidden." He shook his head, exasperated. His face dipped closer to mine as my body pulled toward him like a magnet. "What would you say if I told you—"

His words were cut off by a sharp blast of cold air and the tinkling of bells strung on the front door. "Look who's here!" someone called out.

I turned, and there he was, brushing the snow from his thick, chestnut hair.

Henry Halliday.

EIGHT

HE SPOTTED ME across the room and headed toward our alcove. Dropping Tex's hand, I stood up to greet him. My face was probably as white as the snow outside.

"There's my girl!" Henry stepped forward with a hearty embrace, planting a quick kiss against my lips. "Merry Christmas, Caroline." He looked flushed and out of breath, the color in his cheeks high, as though he'd run all the way to Switzerland.

"Merry Christmas!" I said through a frozen smile. "What are you doing here? I thought you were with your family in Newport."

"A surprise change of plans. Your mother called last week and said you seemed blue. She insisted I come, so I caught a ride with Philip Smyth-Bates on his new jet." Henry encircled my waist with his hands, his bright smile beaming down at me. Not for the first time, I wished I could match even a fraction of his enthusiasm.

"It *is* a surprise. But I feel terrible—you've come all this way and I'm really fine. You know how Mother exaggerates. We could have cleared it all up on the phone." I shook my head, exasperated at the sudden turn of events.

"I admit, I had a more selfish reason for coming in person. Peter Notz has a car he's trying to sell, and I came for a test-drive. Figured I'd see how it handles the mountain curves. Being with you was a bonus. Though a great one!" he added somewhat belatedly.

That explained it. Henry's ferocious love of cars vied with his passion for art, so a possible new auto acquisition would have been too tempting to pass up. Although he didn't do much high-end racing, like some of the men in our crowd, he dreamed of building a pristine garage full of beautiful showpieces that would never see a speck of dirt on their tires.

"Henry!" my mother shouted. "You're here!"

He waved to her and kissed both her cheeks when she reached us. "Special holiday delivery! Sorry I'm arriving so late; we ran into a bit of rough weather."

"Nonsense, you're right on time. Caroline, are you happy about your surprise?" Her gaze ping-ponged between me and Tex. If she suspected anything, she didn't show it.

"Yes, of course, Mother, you know Henry's always welcome. But you made him worry for nothing. I didn't need cheering up; I've been perfectly happy here."

"Happy?" she scoffed. "Do happy people turn down an evening with Liz and Dick to lie in a bathtub and read an old issue of *Life*? I think not!"

My cheeks flamed, and next to me, Tex stood up.

"Henry, let me introduce you to Jack Fairchild," Mother continued. "Mr. Fairchild is here to photograph us for *Vogue*."

Henry held out his hand. "Nice to meet you, Jack. Henry Halliday of Halliday's Fine Art: New York, London, and Rome."

Tex shook it, a tense smile replacing his natural, easygoing grin. "Pleasure."

Mother looped her arm through Tex's. "Come now, Mr. Fairchild. Let's let these two lovebirds get reacquainted."

His inscrutable expression leveled me as Mother led him away. What had he been about to say before the interruption? Now I'd probably never know.

As I watched them go, Henry's voice buzzed like a wasp in my ear.

"... and you wouldn't believe the room they've put me in. The Palace is really going downhill these days. You're fortunate Gunter found you this property. Of course, you don't have room service, but with Maria cooking, you probably don't miss it." Henry stopped, his eyebrows pinching together. "Caroline, darling? Is something the matter?"

I took a breath and composed myself. "No, sorry, I'm listening. You're unhappy with your room."

"Yes, well, I understand it's all they could offer on short notice, but you'd think it was some other gallery's art lining their walls. As if my father didn't cut them an outrageous deal. Loyalty is obviously a thing of the past. God, it's hot in here." He removed his cashmere coat, flinging it onto the bench where Tex and I had sat only minutes before. "So, I plan on having a late breakfast tomorrow at the hotel, then we'll hit the slopes in the afternoon. I assume your mother will want to soak up what could be your last Christmas morning together. You never know what the situation might be next year." He smiled like he had a secret, and my stomach somersaulted at the implication.

"I don't know, Henry, you know I'm not much of a skier. Wouldn't you rather relax with us here?"

"Nonsense, you just haven't had the right teacher. When I'm through with you, you'll be zipping down the mountain," he promised, placing his arm around my shoulders. "Tomorrow night Peter's having a bunch of people round, and I said we'd come. It might make this car sale go a bit smoother. Wear something red; it's your best color."

"I can't just drop everything because you're suddenly here," I said, trying to get out of it. "I'd planned to see Billy and Daphne tomorrow night."

"Christ, I don't even want to know what kind of trouble those two could find here." Henry grimaced as he peered over my head and around the room. Probably looking for his next sales target among the guests. "Or worse, what they'd end up dragging you into. Caroline, don't you think it's time to start growing up, spending time with the right people?"

"And just who are the right people?" My spine stiffened.

"You know, people with the right connections. Maybe those who don't spend their lives on the pages of a gossip rag. If I'm to take over Halliday's someday, I need to consider all this. Of course, anybody I'm with needs to care about it too."

I shook my head, suddenly weary. "Henry, it's a party, and it's Christmas Eve. You don't need to talk about work all the time. Let's get you a drink, okay?" I gave him a small smile, mindful that he'd traveled all day to see me. That had to be worth something, I told myself.

From the corner of my eye, I spotted Tex and Jennifer Beardsley slipping into their coats near the front door. I shrugged out from under Henry's arm and pointed toward the other room.

"You go ahead to the bar. I'll meet you there. I have to say goodbye to some guests."

"That's my Caroline—always the perfect hostess." He smiled and headed off in search of a gin and tonic.

I caught up to Tex and Jennifer just as they'd finished packing up his camera equipment.

"Heading out already?" I asked. "The party's just getting going." I wished I could pull Tex back to our now-deserted corner.

He looked down at me, stone-faced.

"We've got everything we need," Jennifer explained. "Please thank your mother and Maria again for giving us access. I'll be sure to mention them in the story."

"Of course. So will you two be staying in town much longer?" I still spoke to Tex, even though he hadn't said a word.

"Probably until New Year's," Jennifer replied, tugging on a hat.

"Listen, Tex, I . . ." Words failed me. How to tell him I wished tonight had gone so much differently? "Merry Christmas," I finished, defeated.

He shook his head, like he was as disappointed with me as I was with myself. "Merry Christmas, Caroline. I hope you get everything you want." Then he turned and walked out the door.

A second later, Maria approached me. "A very charming man," she observed. "He seems to have a bit of a crush on you. I saw him sneaking looks at you all evening."

I frowned, staring at the doorknob. "It's nothing. And Henry's here now, so . . ." I turned to her and smiled. "The party really is lovely, Maria."

She cupped my face in her tiny hands and kissed my forehead. "Not half as lovely as you, *principessa*."

❋

I awoke on Christmas morning to the smell of strong coffee brewing. My head throbbed—the aftereffects of three martinis consumed after Tex left, during Henry's lengthy discourse on the merits of owning one's jet versus flying commercial. We'd said goodbye with a kiss, while I tried to hide my disappointment over how the evening had ended up.

Throwing a robe on over my nightgown, I went downstairs to face Mother and Maria. I found them sitting close together on the sofa, whispering and laughing.

"Ah, *principessa*, Merry Christmas!" Maria stood up to hug me. "Let me get you some coffee. It was a late night."

"Merry Christmas. Coffee would be great." I turned back to Mother. "Merry Christmas, Mother."

"*Buon Natale*." Her face was flushed and happy. "Another year, another holiday with my girls."

"I may have aged out of that title." I sat in an overstuffed armchair nearby.

She shook her head. "To me, you'll always be that little girl with the black hair who nearly wept with joy over the silly doll that wet itself. It was all you wanted to play with when you were six. Your father had filled the room with toys, but the doll was your favorite." She had a faraway look in her eyes, like she missed the child I once was. But that was impossible—she'd let nannies, Maria, and Daddy handle most of my upbringing, always too busy for things like make-believe and story time.

Maria came back with a tray of coffee and cinnamon cake. "Time for presents!" she exclaimed.

I smiled and got up to distribute the gifts. As we sipped our coffees, we oohed and aahed over perfume bottles, exotic jewelry, silk scarves, and in my case a new Leoni gown.

"I made this one myself," Mother admitted. "Your old *mamma* still has some tricks up her sleeve."

"You'll never be old. You'll go into the ground still looking thirty-five, and you know it."

Pulling the dress out of its box, I examined her craftsmanship, running my hand across the delicate stitching and silver palettes. It shimmered, the reflections of hundreds of tiny mirrored sequins casting rays of light on the walls. Modern and exquisite, it was almost alive.

"Oh, Mother, I can't wait to wear it on New Year's Eve!"

She patted my arm, visibly pleased. Stupidly, I basked in her glow. I knew it was silly to constantly seek the approval of a person who had let me down in so many ways, but I did. I couldn't help it. She was the parent who had stayed, and a part of me would always want to be the perfect daughter in the perfect dress.

"Henry won't be able to take his eyes off you. Not that he ever can," she said with a knowing smile.

I winced, wishing another man's gaze wasn't quite so paramount in my mind.

"Yes, and I love my new scarf!" Maria said, curling it like a meringue over her hair. She topped it with the canary-yellow beads I'd picked up for her in Rio last summer. "What do you think—too much?"

The three of us burst out laughing, succumbing to her silliness. I glanced back at the tree and noticed a scrap of red paper peeking out near the edge of the skirt.

"Oh, I think we missed one!" I walked over to retrieve the slim package. Checking the tag, I saw that it read: *For Al.* My pulse skipped a beat. Tex must have left it there last night when I wasn't looking.

"Caroline? What is it?" Maria asked.

"A gift for me. From Jack Fairchild."

Mother frowned, but Maria couldn't hide a small grin. I untied the gold ribbon and tore it open.

A simple silver frame surrounded a photo of me beside the pool at La Concha. My wet hair was slicked back, and my tanned skin practically burst to life. Behind me, the water shimmered in the sunlight. My expression was happy and mischievous, like I had a secret. It was the most beautiful picture I'd ever seen of myself.

"It's . . . it's a photo. From the day we met in Acapulco." I passed it over to them.

"Ooh, *principessa, sei così bella!*" Maria enthused.

"The boy is talented, I'll give him that," Mother acknowledged, handing the frame back to me. "Helps to have an attractive subject."

I finally had an answer to the question I'd asked myself a thousand times since Mexico. He had indeed saved my image, taking time to develop it, forcing my face to appear like a ghost through the watery chemicals. Perhaps he even had his own print— a reminder of me; of us.

"What's that on the back?" Maria asked.

I flipped it over to find a taped guitar pick, and a little note scrawled beside it: *You still owe me a song. One of your own.*—*Tex*

A hot wave of guilt washed over me as I thought back to the night before. He'd left this, knowing I'd find it today, even after I'd stood there numb, next to Henry, afraid to speak up. Afraid to say that Tex was someone who mattered; someone I'd already begun to care about. And now it was probably too late. No amount of retouching could fix the ugly mess I'd made of things.

NINE

THE BLACK FERRARI 330 zipped along the twisting road, gaining speed as Henry shifted into the next gear. We were already half a mile above Gstaad, climbing higher in altitude with each passing second. He'd invited me along on his test-drive, and desperate for some time away from the social fishbowl of the slopes, I'd accepted. Even though I knew almost nothing about cars, there was something thrilling about riding in this beautiful piece of machinery. Like a panther racing through the woods, the car was fast, precise, and dangerous. I loved it instantly.

"What's the verdict?" Henry raised his voice over the loud purr of the engine.

"Amazing! It's like we're flying!"

He smiled at me, flashing perfect teeth and a dimple on his cheek—the dimple that had half the girls I knew wishing I'd never met Henry.

"Then it's worth every penny Peter's demanding." He moved us into another gear, and my body slid toward the door as we went around another hairpin turn. By no means a professional,

Henry was still a competent driver. I felt safe with him, which went far in my book.

"Last night's party was crazy," I commented. "And gosh, marriage sure hasn't made Gunter any less of a cad. I couldn't tell if he and Brigitte were going to kill each other or make love when they got home."

Henry shook his head in bewilderment. "Probably both. I've never seen a more doomed pair in my life. By the way, I could tell Peter was charmed by you. As usual, he has excellent taste." Briefly letting go of the gear shift, Henry brought my fingers to his lips for a quick kiss.

"I think there's an overlook up ahead. Want to stretch your legs?" he asked.

"Yeah, that'd be nice. I bet the town is beautiful from up here."

A few minutes down the road, we came to a clearing with a little wooden fence. Henry pulled off, putting the car into park with a heavy jerk. I took a moment to catch my breath as he hopped out and jogged to the passenger side to help me out of the buttery leather seat. The crisp, clean air swirled into my lungs, already desperate for oxygen at such high altitude. Reacting to the cooler temperature, I reached into my pockets for a pair of gloves. Tex's gloves, I realized with a frown.

"This view is incredible!" Henry exclaimed as he leaned against the railing. Below us, Gstaad looked tiny and picturesque, like a fairy-tale village in a snow globe. Even though I'd experienced it from the helicopter, the town seemed even more special from this vantage point. Henry placed his arm around me, snuggling closer. "Cold?"

"A little," I admitted. "I'll be fine, though. I'm glad you stopped; I would have hated to miss this."

With his other hand, he clasped one of mine, his face registering surprise when he touched the rough suede of Tex's oversized glove.

"Whose are these? Surely not yours . . ."

Thinking fast, I answered, "They're Billy's. I forgot mine at the skating rink when I took them off to untie my laces." In truth, I hadn't been ice skating once this week.

"I wish I'd known; I could have bought you another pair. I guess you'll just have to settle for my other gift." He grinned, pulling a small velvet box out of his coat. I sucked in a breath, relieved it was too large to be a ring box, but scared that it easily could have been.

"Henry, we said no gifts, remember? I don't have anything for you."

He shook his head, his smile mischievous. "I know what we said, but I like to spoil you. Come on, open it."

I removed Tex's gloves and, with trembling fingers, lifted the lid. Inside was a pair of the most beautiful diamond and emerald drop earrings I'd ever encountered. They looked old, perhaps Art Deco. Also extremely expensive.

"Do you like them?" he asked, excited. "I know it's a little extravagant, but I saw them at the Helena Rubinstein auction and couldn't resist."

"Henry, I don't know what to say. They're exquisite!" His grand gesture had knocked me off-balance. Dazed, I kissed his cheek.

Henry opened his mouth as if to speak, then hesitated.

"What is it?" I asked.

Biting his lip, he looked into my eyes. "Do you remember that party in the Hamptons, when you were ten and I was twelve? The one at Jackson's, that summer he went off the deep end?"

I unspooled my memories, already blurred by the passage of time. "When he smashed the coffee table?"

He nodded. "There were so many people there. All the adults were drinking too much, arguing over reviews and about who'd slept with whom. My father and yours were arm wrestling in the corner, and your mother was chain-smoking, rolling her eyes at something Clem was saying. The air smelled like cigarettes and sweat and turpentine, and I just wanted to get out, go anywhere but there. So I slipped out the back door and saw you lying on a picnic table, staring up at the stars. Remember what you said to me?"

I smiled, recalling the skinny, dark-haired boy who'd looked as lost and forgotten as I was. *"What took you so long?"*

He nodded. "I think about that all the time. Finding you there, like this shelter from our parents' drama. You've always been a safe place for me, and from the moment I met you, it felt like we were meant to be with each other because we're the only ones who truly get what this life is like. How it can be ridiculous at times, but also exhilarating. But when I stood in front of that jewelry case, I hesitated. Should I have chosen a ring instead of the earrings? Because damn it, Caroline, what's taking us so long?"

My stomach twisted. I didn't have an answer for him. Inertia had gotten us this far, but I didn't know how to force my body, and my heart, to propel us further. "You know me too well," I answered. "Better than I know myself, maybe. And that's the problem, isn't it? *I* don't know what I want. In a partner, in life, all of it. I guess I'm still figuring things out."

"And you don't think we could figure it out together?"

"No." I shook my head, wrapping my arms around myself. "It would be too tempting to get lost in you. To become your shadow, like all the other wives who follow their husbands around, planning their dinner parties and trips, taking care of the children, until eventually they become invisible. And that's not what I want, for either of us."

He nodded, looking down at the valley instead of me. "It sounds like earrings were the right choice, then, after all."

It was horrible, seeing his disappointment in me. In us. He'd been so kind, and I . . . I had to try. Taking a step toward him, I grasped the lapels of his jacket, moving my face closer. He turned, searching my eyes, gradually bringing his lips to mine. The kiss was tentative at first, gentle, before instinct took over and passion unfurled. He stroked my neck, putting pressure on sensitive spots.

Despite the mild stirring his enthusiasm aroused in me, a tiny voice told me I was simply going through the motions. *A touch here, a whimper there, now move an inch to the left* . . . I wanted to tangle his hair between my fingers, wreck his perfect facade for just a moment to see how he'd react, but something inside held me back. Somehow, my body understood that Henry wasn't built for ruin.

Sensing something was off, his mouth stilled against me.

"What's wrong—why'd you stop?" My breath puffed in the wind.

"You're here, but you're not," he replied, frustrated. "For a long time, I thought it was because of me, something I was doing wrong. But now I'm starting to wonder if there's more to it than that."

Tears formed as I realized my fear and uncertainty had been hurting more than just me. Henry was my friend, before anything else, and he didn't deserve this. "You're right. I'm the problem. I'm the one who's incapable of being happy. I can see it in front of me, I reach for it, and there's just nothing there. Like I'm grasping at smoke."

He frowned, staring back out over the mountain. "I'm not smoke, Caroline. I'm right here, flesh and blood."

"I know." I clutched the velvet box tighter in my hand.

"Just tell me, should I be worried about that guy you were with on Christmas Eve? The one who was taking pictures? I saw the way you looked at him as he was leaving. Like he was something you craved. You've never looked at me like that."

I shook my head, unable to explain the constant push and pull I felt around Tex. "It's not just about him, but I won't lie and tell you there's nothing there. We'd met before, in Mexico, and he came here because of me. It's just—he sees me, you know? And not only through the viewfinder in his camera. He heard me singing and didn't laugh or make me feel like an oddity or a charming bit of entertainment for a cocktail party. He didn't meet me and ask why I'm not married yet; he asked why I'm not on the radio yet."

"I don't think you're odd, and I would *never* laugh at you, but I'm also not going to pretend that I think you're the next Dusty Springfield," Henry argued. "I don't want to stifle your hobbies, but there comes a point where people just have to grow up and be realistic about things."

"Right there." I pointed at him. "You say hobby, and he says destiny. And I'm just asking for more time to understand which one it is."

"I can give you time. A lot of it, in fact. Maybe this thing between us—maybe it needs to be done," he said woodenly.

"You're right," I agreed. "We should go back to being just friends and let go of all the complications."

He frowned. "No, that's not what I meant. I don't think we should see each other at all anymore, even platonically. I can't erase my feelings and pretend I never had them. We can't go back; not now."

"So that's it?" I asked incredulously. "Twelve years of friendship down the drain? I'm supposed to forget about the only other person on the planet who knows my father once snuck us into the Met after hours and let us run wild through the galleries? The person who called me at three a.m. every night for weeks after the funeral because he knew I'd be awake? I'm supposed to just lose him forever? Henry, that's not what I want."

"We don't always get what we want." His voice was tight with anger. "And it pains me to realize we were probably viewing the last twelve years through very different lenses. I thought I did see you, the real you, but now you tell me this photographer sees even more. I can't trust you, and now I can't trust the memories. So please—just stop."

I swallowed the lump in my throat, along with the guilt that came with knowing how much I'd disappointed him. With the wind turning the surrounding air even colder, I nodded and got back in the car, Henry following seconds later with an abrupt door slam. Deep down, I think I'd always known this reaction was a possibility, but I'd never imagined how much it would hurt to finally express what my heart had been screaming for months.

※

The drive back to town was one of tense silence, neither of us bothering to turn on the radio. I relaxed as soon as our chalet came back into view, Maria's car gone from the driveway. Cutting the engine, Henry slumped in his seat and stared straight ahead.

I tried to hand him the earring box, but he shook his head. "No, those are yours. I bought them for you."

"But I don't feel right about taking them now that . . . well, you know."

"Wear them on New Year's at that damn party they throw at the Palace. Consider it a parting gift."

"You won't be there?" I asked, surprised.

He shook his head. "No, Father needs me in Rome. There's a big gala. Important contacts for the new gallery, et cetera, et cetera."

"Oh." I'd pushed him away, yet this hasty retreat made it feel real, and terribly final. "I guess this is goodbye, then."

He exhaled, then reluctantly leaned over to kiss me on the cheek. "Take care of yourself, Caroline. Be safe," he said against my ear. "For what it's worth, I still think '67 will be a big year. For both of us."

I nodded, wrenching my body away. Not wanting to prolong the uncomfortable moment, I got out and started walking up the path to the house, before remembering something I wanted to tell him. Turning back, I knocked on the passenger-side window. Henry leaned over and rolled it down, his eyes cautious.

"Promise me if you buy this car you'll actually drive it," I implored. "Beautiful things aren't meant to be caged."

TEN

THE SILVER PALETTES of my dress sparkled under the lights of the Gstaad Palace ballroom, while tiny bubbles in my champagne coupe rose steadily to the top. There'd been rumors of renovations for the grand hotel, including a new disco and indoor swimming pool, but tonight it looked the same as it always had—dark wood, gold fixtures, jewel-toned upholstery, and the air of old money. Dionne Warwick sang from the stage, her flawless skin luminescent as she covered us in a blanket of melodies.

At our table, Billy regaled us with the tale of a ruined wig meeting its final destiny in a snowbank, while Daphne had us in stitches over her date with a Le Rosey student. She'd assumed he was in his final year, but it turned out he had quite a few left to go. Having deposited him drunk and disappointed at the train station, she could finally admit that it might be time to find a new Gstaad tradition.

"Caroline, darling, I must know who designed your dress," Penelope "Pidgy" Worthington said between puffs from her cigarette holder. "It's absolutely divine."

"It was a gift from Mother. She made it herself."

"Really? I didn't know Emanuela still sewed. I assumed she had dozens of cutters and seamstresses working for her."

"She does, but she wanted this to be a special gift for me. And I doubt she trusted anyone else to get the palettes right. You know what a perfectionist she can be." I smiled ruefully.

"If she decides to put that design in her spring line, ring me and let me know. It would be marvelous in Portofino."

"Oh, aren't we all just bored to death of Italy?" the Viscount de Belange lamented.

"I've heard good things about Beirut," Billy replied. "The Paris of the Middle East, they say."

As my tablemates debated the appeal of various destinations, my attention drifted to Mother and Maria at David Niven's table. They smiled at one another, clearly relaxed and enjoying themselves. I wished I was able to do the same.

"Don't look now, darling, but you-know-who just walked in," Daphne whispered into my ear. I looked over her elaborate column of hair to the doorway of the ballroom. Tex stood on the threshold, appearing confident in a tailored tuxedo and slicked hair, his hands resting on his Leica. As usual, the sight of him stole the breath from my lungs.

"Should I go say something?" By this point, Daphne knew the full story of what had happened at Mother's Christmas Eve party.

"Definitely. Thank him for the photo he left for you. That's your in."

"You're a genius!" I squeezed her forearm.

"I know, darling, but it's always nice to be reminded. Now go!"

She waved me off, her thick-lashed eyes bright with encouragement. I blew her a kiss, and she pretended to slip it into her pocket with a wink.

Smoothing my dress down, I felt Henry's earrings bobbing against my shoulders as I walked. I'd kept my promise, even though it only amplified my feelings of guilt. Approaching Tex from behind, I waited until the shutter clicked and his body relaxed before tapping him on the shoulder.

He jolted in surprise, turning to face me. "Caroline! Where did you come from?"

"Daphne and Billy and I have a table over there with a few others." I pointed in their general direction. "I hardly recognized you when you arrived."

"You mean in this monkey suit? 'Required dress code,' according to the *Vogue* higher-ups. Believe me, I feel mighty ridiculous."

"Still, I'm glad you're here, because I wanted to thank you for the Christmas present you left."

He paused to choose his words. "Don't worry about it. I came across that image when I was processing negatives and thought you might like it. I packed it in my suitcase, hoping I might see you. Seemed a shame not to give it to you after all that."

"I'm happy you did." I wanted to say so much more, about how my heart beat wildly at the idea of him staring at my face in the darkroom, and that while he'd been thinking of me, I'd been thinking of him too. More than was probably healthy, in fact. I just couldn't get the words out.

"So where's Henry?" Tex asked, looking around. "He your date tonight?"

"No, he had to go to Rome. And about Henry, you should know—we're not seeing each other anymore. All of that, whatever it was, is over."

Surprise flashed across his face. "Oh yeah? Since when?"

"Since he saw the way I looked at you the night of Mother's party." If I'd just revealed too much, I didn't care. It was time to lay my cards on the table.

Tex sighed. "This world of yours—relationships starting and ending like they're nothin'. It's not my scene, and it probably never will be."

"I'm not sure it's mine either," I argued.

"But you're here, you're in it, and it's becoming harder and harder to do this with you. Every time we see each other, I walk away feeling like I just got punched in the gut. I keep waitin' for you to come up to me and say, 'Hey, mister, it's been fun, but didn't you know I was just kidding?'" He shook his head. "I don't want to play the game when I don't know the rules."

"But don't you see? I want more for us too. That's why I finally gave up on the idea of a future with Henry. My heart is yours, if you want it." That desperate organ pounded in my chest, on full display through my shimmering dress.

Tex frowned. "But did you really give him up, though? Sounds to me like *he* gave *you* up. Tell me—if he hadn't seen us together that night, would you still be with him?"

My mouth opened and closed as I tried to think of a response. "I don't know," I said finally. I thought I'd been the one to put an end to things on that mountain by at long last being honest about what I did and didn't want, but Tex's words had me twisting it all around now. Would Henry have been able to live with my uncertainty about the future if I hadn't admitted to having feelings for another man? And would I have let him?

"I need more than that, Caroline. I need to know you're brave enough to come to me, and not as a consolation prize. As a choice. And I don't think you're capable of that yet. Not from what I've seen."

I felt the flush of embarrassment on my cheeks. "I—I'm sorry. To have wasted your time," I apologized, my voice cracking. "You have a happy New Year, Jack. And just so you know, it was never a game. Not to me."

Walking away quickly, I was desperate to find a private space before losing control. I thought I heard him call, "Al, wait!" but I couldn't turn around. There was no denying it—I was a silly girl in a silly world. I had nothing to offer him; nothing that mattered.

I rushed into the empty ladies' room, startled by the sight in the mirror: my eyeliner and mascara muddled by tears, the black streaks turning my face into a macabre watercolor. I gripped the back of a chair for support.

The door opened, and I turned, relieved to see it was only Daphne. Billy followed a second later, locking the door behind him.

"You're not allowed in here," I pointed out.

"Don't care." He shrugged. "You need us."

"We saw you run away from Tex." Daphne took a tissue from the nearby box and handed it to me. "What did that wanker say to you?"

"Nothing I hadn't already thought myself a dozen times. We're too different. Starting a relationship with him was just a ridiculous fantasy."

"I realize I'm not the authority on mature behavior here, but even I know you don't make a girl cry," Billy fumed. It was touching, if misguided. "Maybe I should go talk to him."

"No, please don't. I'm okay. I just want to get out of here."

"Well, darling, it just so happens that there's a fabulous party in one of the tower suites. I've been promised a New Year's Eve we'll never forget. You up for it?" Daphne asked, a gleam in her eye.

"God, yes." I needed an escape. "I don't want to think for the rest of the night."

Daphne and Billy flanking me, we left the bathroom in search of distraction, debauchery, and a fête fit for a March hare. It was painfully obvious now—I belonged with the mad ones.

Reaching the end of a long hallway, I heard the faint notes of music through a door. "Whose room is this, anyway?" I asked Daphne as she removed her satin glove to knock.

"A Rothschild, I think."

"Which one?"

"Does it matter?"

When the door opened, we were immediately confronted by a gyrating amoeba of psychedelia. Someone had draped colored scarves over the lampshades, while another light spun in the corner, emitting tiny moving dots along the walls. Antique furnishings surrounded the partygoers, some in eveningwear from the ball downstairs, others in casual fashions. A cloud of marijuana smoke filled the dark room, making it difficult to see more than three feet in front of us. Tapestries hung limply on the walls as writhing bodies swayed to the high pitch of a sitar's wail.

"Far out," Billy murmured, awestruck.

"Welcome, my friends," a short man with shaggy hair and a thick French accent greeted us, drawing us in. He wore tuxedo pants and a white shirt, unbuttoned at the collar. He was also barefoot. "Daphne, wonderful to see you again. You always arrive with the most beautiful guests."

She kissed his cheeks in rapid succession before introducing us. "This is Caroline Kimball and Billy Lloyd."

I noticed she didn't tell us our host's name, a sure sign she'd forgotten it.

"Billy Lloyd—I know you by reputation, of course. Come, there are some gentlemen I'd like you to meet. This way." He ushered Billy toward the back parlor of the suite, where the lighting got even dimmer. "Punch is on the sideboard, ladies. Help yourselves," he called over his shoulder, winking.

Billy glanced back at us and shrugged. Where he was headed, I knew we couldn't follow.

Daphne and I walked over to the makeshift bar. There was a large bowl of red liquid, with glass cups on a tray nearby.

"Punch?" I asked, tilting my head. "Has the European aristocracy started reading _Ladies' Home Journal_?"

"Hmm . . . I don't see any spare bottles of vodka lying around, so it looks like we'll have to make do." Daphne eyed the bowl with a grimace. She took two glasses from the tray and ladled in the mystery concoction. Handing me one, she toasted, "Bottoms up."

We drank in unison, the warm, sweet liquid filling my mouth. I couldn't taste any alcohol. Daphne's eyebrows pulled together in confusion.

"Am I missing something?" I held my now-empty glass upside down.

"Yes, the booze." Turning, she tapped a girl behind her on the shoulder. "Excuse me, is there another bar set up somewhere?"

"I think there's some champagne in one of the bathrooms." She pointed toward a doorway on the side of the room.

"Are you sure this is a Rothschild's party?" I whispered to Daphne as we headed that way. "Why would they hide the alcohol like this?"

"You've got me. Maybe Philippe had a bad year." We reached the bathroom, filled to the brim with people. I recognized several faces, including two men who'd flirted with Daphne at the Eagle Ski Club a couple days before. As we claimed a bottle from the ice-filled tub, they shuffled through the crowd toward us.

"Finally, some class in this place!" one of them exclaimed. "Roger was just saying we're surrounded by French hippies."

"Dickie!" Daphne turned around to greet them. "Caroline, this is Dickie Waddlestone and Roger Northridge. We met at the Eagle."

"Yes, I remember. Caroline Kimball." I extended my hand.

Roger clasped it in his sweaty one, flashing a grin. "Pleasure."

"Say, let's get out of this mixing bowl and grab a seat somewhere," Dickie suggested, pointing toward the door.

"Good idea." I tucked a bottle under my arm and followed him back out to the living room. Managing to find some empty cushions on the floor, Daphne and I lowered ourselves down as gracefully as we could in our dresses.

For the next half hour, the four of us passed the champagne back and forth and chatted about our winter plans, Dickie's new boat, and Daphne's upcoming film premiere. Roger continued to edge closer to me, at one point touching my knee in a way that made me uncomfortable. The room continued to fill as inebriated guests began giggling and flopping to the floor all around us. The Beatles album *Revolver* played on the hi-fi, the entire party swaying in time to "Tomorrow Never Knows."

I tried to keep up with the boys' conversation, but by that point, I'd begun to feel slightly off. The room's atmosphere, once so dim, was suddenly bursting with color. My dress created patterns on the ceiling as light reflected off it, like dancing constellations. I lay back to watch them, mesmerized.

"Oh man, she is gone!" Roger laughed.

"What's wrong with her? Is she blotto?" Dickie asked from far away.

"Didn't you know? There's LSD in the punch over there. They must have drunk it. Look at that one's pupils."

I glanced sideways at Daphne, who was now staring at the wall like it was saying something terribly important.

I didn't know how long I lay there, staring at the sparkling rays above me—it could have been hours or minutes. Eventually, a voice slithered into my ear. "Time to go, sweetheart."

"Tex?" I mumbled weakly. Turning my head, I saw Roger pulling me to my feet. This was all wrong. I wanted to stay in this cocoon of beautiful people and colors and music that mirrored my soul. It was Wonderland, come to life. I wanted Tex's fingers to be the ones skating across my body, making my blood run hot and cold. Instead, the hands on me were clammy and thick, bruising in their lack of finesse.

"Just one more song," I begged.

"You can listen to music in my room," he promised.

I looked back at Daphne, but she was awash in a pool of blue light, stroking Dickie's face and smiling. Roger urged me to the door, and we floated through a tunnel of mannequin bodies. I smiled at them, still in a daze.

Out in the hallway, the light was too bright, forcing me to shield my eyes.

"This way to the elevators." Roger's voice sounded far away yet inside my ear at the same time, like a seashell.

I looked to where he pointed, then back at him, but in place of Roger's handsome face was a sharp-toothed wolf's head. My back hit the wall, my body quaking with fear.

"Caroline?" the wolf asked in a disturbingly human voice. "What's the matter?"

"Get away from me!" I cried, swatting at him.

He moved closer, placing one hand around my neck and the other on my thigh, his body pinning me to the wall. His breath came out in hot bursts, and the fur of his muzzle scraped against my chin. His pupils glowed red as fingers traveled under the hem of my dress.

"Come on, baby, I thought you liked me. You've been flirting with me all night."

I tried to struggle free, but his claws dug into my skin. "No, no, no!" I started to scream, tears spilling down onto my neck. "Please let me go, please!" My whole body shook as I beat against his chest.

"You there, young man! What's going on?"

Turning my head, I saw a man and a woman dressed in their finest evening clothes. He had the head of a pigeon; she, the head of a fish.

"Take your hands off that girl!" the pigeon exclaimed.

The second the wolf's grip loosened in surprise, I ducked under his arm and made a mad dash down the hall.

"Dear, are you all right?" the fish asked as I bolted past.

I was unable to stop and thank my saviors; I just had to get away. When I reached the elevator bank, I pushed the buttons in rapid succession. Shivering and clutching my middle, I squinted against the blinding overhead lights, which were like fire on my retinas. A ping sounded, then another, as two doors opened simultaneously, side by side.

On the left, a couple was clutched in a tight embrace, their kiss passionate and intense. My eyes were still playing tricks: it looked like Maria and a woman with a lion's head. The creature wore one of my mother's designs, a black crepe dress ringed with fur trim around the collar. I stood dumbstruck for a second, then dashed between the closing doors of the other car. Slamming my hand against the button for the lobby, I exhaled in relief.

As the elevator descended, my stomach lifted and pitched. I floated through the air of the tiny box, the sequins of my dress tinkling, their pattern and movement like reptilian scales. *Goodbye, feet.* But with a startling jolt, I came plummeting back to Earth as the door opened with a swoosh. Staring back at me was a pack of wolves in tuxedoes, lying in wait. I screamed and ran toward the lobby, praying they wouldn't follow. My shoes flew off as I strained for traction on the slippery floor, the ceiling mural dancing and swirling above me, a tsunami wave crashing against the walls. A countdown of numbers and an explosion of "Happy New Year!" shouts rang out from the bar, but I didn't stop. Pressing myself through the revolving glass door and into the cold night, I gulped in air like the drowning victim of a shipwreck.

The snow-covered lawn bordering the hotel appeared before me as a dark ocean, eerie in its stillness. Trees swayed and tilted, reaching their branches out to claim me. I dashed into the field, searching for refuge. Icy needles lashed at the soles of my feet, the shock too much to bear. Trapped in this arctic quicksand, I knew I had to keep moving, but my legs wouldn't cooperate.

"Caroline!"

I turned to see Tex running out of the hotel, his camera still around his neck.

"Jesus Christ, it's freezing out here!" he yelled, finally reaching me. "Where's your coat? And your shoes?"

"I—I . . ." I couldn't find the words to tell him what had happened, or what I'd seen. My chattering teeth opened and closed helplessly.

"You're comin' with me," he ordered, bending down to reach behind my knees with one arm while he placed his other behind my shoulders. I felt myself being lifted as his small Leica dropped into my lap. "Hold that, will ya?"

I rested my head against the chest of this white knight and closed my eyes.

ELEVEN

A DULL ACHE pounded in my forehead, welcoming me to 1967. As my vision focused, sparse furnishings began to appear, along with a variety of men's clothing items strewn about haphazardly. Across the room, a silver dress hung limp over the desk chair. My muscles tensed with panic before I patted myself under the bedsheets, relieved to find my underwear and bra still on. I spotted a piece of stationery on the nightstand and reached across the mattress to grab it. *Hotel Olden* was stamped in cursive across the top.

Peering over the edge of the bed, I saw a long figure rolled up in a blanket on the floor. There was no mistaking the golden hair resting on a pillow: Tex. Last night's events came flooding back like spliced frames in a filmstrip: the party in the tower; the punch; Roger; running outside the hotel; falling asleep in Tex's arms. He'd saved me—a girl he'd already rejected, yet still he came to my rescue.

Embarrassed and disheveled, I slipped out of bed to retrieve my dress. Not finding my shoes anywhere, I took a pair of hotel slippers from the floor in the corner. There were things that needed to be said, but I was in no shape to say them at the moment.

Grabbing a pencil, I jotted down a quick note:

> *Tex—*
>
>   *I'm sorry to leave like this, but I need to go home and put my head back together. Will you meet me here at the bar, two o'clock? Please?*
>
>   *—Al*

I didn't have a watch, but I knew from the weak light peeking through the curtains that it must be early. Spotting Tex's wallet on a nightstand, I took out a few bills for taxi fare to the chalet. Surely the Olden's concierge had seen worse than a girl in cocktail attire, slippers, and no coat sneaking out of a man's hotel room at dawn. It was Gstaad, after all.

Leaving my note on the bed pillow for Tex to find, I crept past him and silently stepped into the hallway. There would be time for explanations and apologies later.

※

After the taxi deposited me in our driveway, I paid the fare, walked up the cleared path, and let myself in through the side door. It was warm inside the chalet, and I couldn't wait to take a hot bath and lie down. Although I had slept a few hours the night before, my dreams had left me exhausted.

In the dining room, I discovered my evening bag, coat, and shoes piled neatly on the table. I stopped to examine them, wondering how they'd managed to turn up here. Tiptoeing next into the living room, I came upon two figures slumped together on the couch. The light was dim, but I could just make out the fur trim on Mother's dress, along with Maria's beehive hairstyle. They were asleep, Maria's hand on Mother's thigh, their heads pressed together on the back cushion. A glass of amber liquid rested on the end table, with a pack of cigarettes next to it.

As I stood staring, my attention returned once more to Mother's dress. A blurry image began to form through the fog clouding my brain, of an elevator and a lion. A kiss, and that same fur trim. Blood pounded in my ears, and in that second, I knew. As sure as I knew C came after B, and two and two would always make four. Hushed words, surreptitious touches, a million little things I'd always ignored because I didn't want to see the full picture. But now it was here, clear as day, lying peacefully on the sofa.

I backed away slowly, retreating to the kitchen. Filling a glass with water from the tap, I gulped it down, trying desperately to lock the truth back in its box, that corner of my brain where all the confusing things could be set aside. Things like a smudge of lipstick on the collar of a dress, or a curious noise coming from Maria's room, or the way Mother's eyes got soft when she looked at her longtime companion—softer than they'd ever gotten for my father, or for me.

"Did you enjoy yourself?" a voice behind me asked.

Turning, I came face-to-face with Mother.

"I honestly can't remember," I said, my voice shaking. "Was it you who collected my things?"

"You can thank Maria. She heard about your episode in the lobby and stopped at the front desk before we left. Your coat had been left unclaimed, your evening bag was turned in by someone named Dickie Waddlestone, and your shoes were found on the floor outside the ballroom. Dare I ask what happened?"

"I'd rather not talk about it right now."

"It's not such a secret, Caroline. Half the hotel saw you shrieking like a *strega*, high as a kite. I had hoped my daughter would be more discreet if she made the stupid decision to experiment, but I see that was giving you too much credit."

Reacting to her condescending tone, I leveled my stare at her. "It seems we both have open secrets. Would you like to talk about yours? Or maybe I should ask Maria? Should I ask her what happened in the elevator last night? And who kissed you at midnight?"

Her face paled, and she looked vulnerable to me for the first time in twenty-two years. "You must be tired after staying out all night. Perhaps a nap would be best."

Dismissed, I grabbed my things from the dining room and retreated quickly up the stairs. Reaching my room, I slammed the door and rushed into the adjacent bathroom. Arms over my abdomen, I retched over the toilet, forcing the bile in my throat to expel itself. Nausea, and the realization that my life had spun out of control, made it clear I couldn't stay here any longer, in this house of lies and half-truths. I needed to be with the one person who didn't live his life as a slave to image; the one person who made me feel like I could do the same.

I pulled up at the Hotel Olden just before two in Maria's rented wagon. Turning the engine off, I sat for several moments, listening to the engine tick. I could do this, I told myself. I *had* to do this.

Gathering my courage, I got out and headed to the entrance. Inside, the fireplace crackled, imbuing the room with velvety warmth. Tex rested against the bar, a drink in front of him.

I took the stool next to his and greeted him with a quick brush against his arm. "Hi, cowboy."

He looked up from his mug of beer in surprise. "You made it. I wasn't sure if you'd be feeling well enough."

"I've been better," I admitted. "So you got my note, then?"

"Yeah. I was worried when I woke up and you were gone."

"A drink, miss?" Hedi asked from behind the bar. She and her husband owned the hotel, and had been serving the rich and famous their schnapps and lager for years.

"Just coffee, please," I requested, knowing that alcohol was the last thing my body needed right now.

"And another round down here, Hedi. When you've got a moment," a deep English voice said to my right. I glanced over and spotted Richard Burton, perched on his usual stool, trying to bankroll the Olden's bar all by himself.

I turned back to Tex. "Thank you for meeting me. And thank you for last night. I know I didn't deserve your kindness after what I've put you through."

"What happened to you before I found you? You acted like you'd lost your mind."

"I had, a little bit. Daphne took me to a party, and someone spiked the punch with acid. We didn't know and drank it by accident."

"Ah." He nodded as though I'd just provided the missing clue. "That makes sense now. I knew it couldn't be just alcohol. Or even grass. But why the hell'd you run outside without your coat? Or shoes?"

I shook my head, massaging my still-aching forehead. "I've no idea. I think I was running away from someone. A wolf, or a man— it's all a bit hazy . . ." Hedi set my coffee down in front of me, with cream and sugar. "I'm just glad you were there to find me."

"I didn't know if I should take you to a hospital, but you were still breathing and basically alert, so I just put you in the back seat of Jennifer's car and brought you here. I hope you don't mind that I took your dress off; those sparkly silver things all over it looked uncomfortable to sleep in. I swear I didn't peek. Much." He grinned sheepishly.

"I wondered about that. The last thing I remember is you picking me up."

He looked down at his beer, and an awkward silence stretched between us. I didn't want to rehash what we'd said in the ballroom, and maybe he didn't either. But I couldn't let him walk out of my life without telling him how I really felt.

"After I got home this morning, I thought a lot about what you said to me—about not being brave enough. I haven't been fair to you."

He turned to me, taking my hand. "Oh Christ, don't you see? It's not just about me; it's about bein' fair to yourself. I can't sit here next to you and pretend that night in Acapulco didn't happen. It meant something to me, and I know it did to you too."

I closed my eyes for a second, allowing that moment in the water with him to replay in my head, like a movie I'd watched a thousand times. "You're right. It meant *everything*."

Knowing there was no turning back now, I closed the distance between us. All the heat from the pool in Mexico came rushing back as my mouth met his, glimmering like the first ray of sunshine on a dark, frozen pond. Wonderful and shattering all at the same time.

He returned the kiss, bringing his hand around to cup my head. I didn't care who saw us; to hell with Richard Burton and all the other refined drunks in this place. The only thing that mattered was the way Tex made me feel: dizzy and delirious with every sweep of his tongue, every press of his lips.

Gradually coming down from the clouds, I pulled back and breathed the sentence flowing through my head like a prayer: "Run away with me."

A line formed between his brows as he processed the words. "What do you mean?"

"Just what I said. I can take us someplace where nobody will bother us. Where we can say all the things we've kept hidden, and neither of us will have to pretend to be something we're not. I don't care if it's reckless. I'm tired of being afraid." Now that I'd said the words out loud, I realized this was what I needed most. To stop living the life other people wanted for me and figure out what *I* wanted.

"And where is this magical spot?"

"Formentera. That little island in Spain I told you about once? Daddy had a house there; it belongs to me and Mother now. I haven't been back in years, so I don't even know what condition it's in, but I want to see it again. I *need* to see it. Please, Tex, come with me."

I watched him consider it. "Let's say I did follow you down the rabbit hole—how long would you want to stay?"

"A week? A month? Forever? I don't know!" I laughed, giddy with the rush of doing something so impulsive.

"Well . . . I don't have another assignment lined up yet. I guess I better call my roommates and tell them I won't be back for a while. Just so they don't panic and think I broke my neck on the slopes."

"Is that a yes?"

He smiled. "It's a yes, Al. When do you want to leave?"

"As soon as you're packed. I've got a bag waiting in the car."

He raised an eyebrow. "That's presumptuous."

"To tell you the truth, I would have left Gstaad with or without you. But I'm so glad it's with." I kissed him again, feeling his happiness against me.

"Okay," he said, once we'd finally pulled apart. "You wait here, and I'll get my stuff gathered up. Don't disappear this time."

I shook my head and smiled. "I'm afraid you're stuck with me."

"Not sure I'll believe it till we're on the plane."

"Oh, did I forget to mention? We're taking a train."

He tilted his head in confusion. "I thought your crowd preferred to fly."

I shrugged. "Jets are overrated."

FORMENTERA

January 2nd, 1967
Estació de França train station
Barcelona, Spain
(Formentera-bound)

Dear Daddy,

What a curious thing—the tiny gears of the surrounding clocks have all ground to a halt. People tap their watch faces in confusion, wondering if they're late or early. Time has stopped; there is no yesterday or tomorrow, only this stolen second.

I'm eager to introduce Tex to the things you left behind. The little lines near the doorjamb where you marked my height. The ugly mugs in the cupboard that were always chipped and cracked (you were the patron saint of struggling potters). And most of all, the smell of the sea that clung to your skin and clothes like paint on a canvas. I'll tell him the stories, and I'll sing him our songs, like I sing them to myself.

Hasta luego,
Caroline

TWELVE

REFLECTIONS OF SUNLIGHT on the sea shimmered like crystals as the fishing boat drew closer to Formentera. We sat facing the bow, Tex's arm around me, shielding my body from the strong winds. After almost two days of travel, from train to bus to ferry to our current vessel, fatigue was heavy in my bones. Nevertheless, I felt the thrill of a hasty escape, like jewel thieves running from the scene of a crime. Only it wasn't a crime; it was my life.

Tex watched the passing scenery through red eyes and tousled hair. I knew he couldn't have gotten much rest on the bus last night, not with me using his shoulder as a pillow. He said I twitched in my sleep, like a Mexican jumping bean.

"Is your family's cottage close to the port?"

"About a fifteen-minute drive," I answered through a yawn. "There's usually a taxi waiting around the docks. Once we've settled in a bit, we can ride bicycles around the island. There might still be a scooter in the garage too."

"What's the house like?"

"Small, but cozy. There's a little pool off the patio. Nothing fancy, but it feels good on a hot day. Daddy had the house outfitted with all the necessary conveniences when he bought it. Water pump, electric generator, septic system. It might not look like much from the outside, but it's a lot more modern than the rest of the island."

The boat hit a swell and our bodies came down hard on the seat, causing me to grip his leg in surprise.

"When's the last time you were here?" he asked, trying to distract me from the choppiness.

"Not since the funeral, five years ago. Daddy always said he wanted his ashes to be scattered into the sea, over the fields of Posidonia grass that grows underwater."

I thought back to that sad day. Little old Spanish women from the village draped in black, standing in contrast to the cosmopolitan art patrons and colleagues who had made the arduous trip to the island to say goodbye. It was strange and beautiful, like a scene from a Fellini film.

"How did he die?" Tex's gentle tone coaxed me to say more, but only if I was ready. "I know from the papers it was suicide, but I don't think I ever heard the details."

"He hanged himself from a beam in the shed beside the house. Mother found the body." I swallowed down the lump in my throat, picturing the horrific scene. "I was in my last year at school with Daphne when Maria called with the news."

"Jesus." His hand tightened around my shoulder.

"He didn't leave a proper note explaining why, and I never understood how he could abandon us like that. Mother was particularly angry about that part—not for herself, but more for me. About all the milestones I'd have to experience without him. I never saw her cry, but god, she had rage."

Tex kissed the top of my head. "We'll create better memories this time around, Al. And damn, would you look at that water. I don't think I've ever seen anything so blue."

As we pulled closer to the rocky shore, the Mediterranean shifted to a lighter, brilliant turquoise color. It was a painter's masterpiece, almost too beautiful to be real.

"I told you." I smiled, happy to share this long-buried part of myself with him.

He hugged me closer, reaching his lips down to mine. The soft brush caused my flesh to break out in goose bumps, heat rising up my neck. It had been like this since we got on the train together. Quick kisses, the stroke of a hand, the intertwining of fingers— constant sensual awareness becoming almost too much to bear. I ached for him in a way that made me feel weak and starved. It was something I'd never experienced before, especially not with Henry.

At last our boat bumped up against the dock, and the captain bellowed, "La Saviiina!"

As we collected our bags, the first mate called out, "*Buena suerte, bella.*"

Tex set the luggage ashore, then turned back to help me off the boat.

"What did he say?" he whispered as we walked toward a waiting taxi.

"Good luck."

But we didn't need luck; I had a feeling things were developing just as they were supposed to.

We pulled up to the cottage, a quaint stone house set at the end of a dirt road. After paying the driver, Tex and I stepped into the chilly air—the temperature hovered around sixty degrees at this time of year. He lifted our luggage from the trunk, and I reached in for my ukulele. My bags were filled with the few necessities I'd purchased from a shop near the train station in Barcelona, to supplement the sweaters and pants I'd brought from Gstaad. Tex had one for his clothes and a separate one for his film and camera equipment. I was sure his camera bag was just as precious to him as my ukulele case was to me.

"Well? Shall we?" I shuffled toward the house. There was no telling what awaited us inside, and I didn't know if Mother had hired anyone to maintain it after Daddy's death. She never talked about coming here, and I'd never asked. A chill crept up my spine at the entrance, and it finally hit me—I was returning to the place where my father had ended his life. The place where he'd decided Mother and I weren't enough of a reason to stay and fight the demons he held inside. It was just a house, but to me it was also his ghost.

"Hold up a sec." Tex dropped the bags on the rough fieldstones of the front patio. "Give me your hand."

When I offered it to him, he placed it around his shoulders, then brought my other one to his neck. He leaned down as if to kiss me, and I closed my eyes in anticipation. After all, there were worse ways to calm a person's anxiety. But suddenly, he lifted me from the ground.

"What are you doing?!" I shrieked.

"I know you're not a bride, and I'm sure as heck no groom, but I figured I'd carry you over the threshold just the same." He grinned as I held tight to him. "You got a key to this place, darlin'?"

"In my purse." I reached down with one hand to access the pocketbook in my lap. I dug through until I found the rusted key I'd kept with me all this time, perhaps as a sort of talisman. I handed it to him, my heartbeat kicking up again as he slipped it into the lock and moved us inside.

As my pupils adjusted to the darkness, I saw furniture covered in white sheets, paintings still lining the walls, and dust mites swirling through the air. In spite of the gloom created by the shuttered windows, nothing had changed. The weight of memories hit me like a wrecking ball.

"It's just like I remember it," I marveled, after being set gently on my feet. "Mother hasn't moved a thing." My attention snagged on the guitar case propped against the wall. I'd left it here because I wasn't ready to deal with the pressure of Daddy's last gift. I told people I played the ukulele because it was easier to travel with, but the truth was, I didn't feel grown enough for the guitar. Not yet.

"Maybe we should get some light in here." Tex walked to a window, clearing his throat. I wondered if it had just hit him, too, that we were finally alone. *Alone*, alone. The nervous flutters in my stomach resumed their dance.

He wrenched open the wooden shutters while I flung off the sheet covering the sofa. Coughing on dust, I asked, "So, is it still paradise?"

He took it all in, then responded, "With you here? Absolutely."

Then, after a pause, he asked, "What happens next in *Alice's Adventures?*"

Though my blood hummed with adrenaline and lust, my brain couldn't quite keep up. "I think . . . sleep." Involuntarily, my mouth stretched into a yawn.

He smiled and nodded, understanding flashing across his features. "I'll get the bags."

During my inspection of the house, I found a back room filled with easels of paintings in progress, rough drawings, and various art supplies—overflow from Daddy's studio. Old furniture and boxes cluttered another room, but luckily the largest bedroom was still usable. An iron bed took up most of the space, with wooden nightstands beside it. While Tex brought in luggage and logs for the fireplace, I located a cotton sheet set and quilt in the armoire. I started to make the bed alone, before he eventually stepped in to help. Placing down-filled pillows at the head, I dusted my hands off. "There, that's done."

Tex looked at the finished product, then at me. Tension flickered between us.

"You can stay in here with me," I blurted, just as he said in a rush, "I can clear out one of the other bedrooms."

I laughed, and he smiled, a telltale blush creeping up his neck. "Tex, it's okay. I want you in here. Besides, it's too cold to sleep alone." And though I didn't say the words aloud, having him beside me would keep the ghosts at bay.

If he could see through my flimsy excuse, he didn't let on. "All right, lady, but no funny business. I'm tired as all get-out."

"No funny business." I exhaled in relief. Though I wanted more eventually, right now I just wanted to fall asleep with his arms around me.

As he lit a match under the kindling, I grabbed a pair of gingham pajamas from my suitcase. Taking my nightwear and makeup case into the bathroom, I turned on the sink's faucet, glad to see the well hadn't run dry. Cleaning the day's travel off, I scrubbed my face with cold water as fatigue battled with apprehension over the prospect of my first night alone with Tex. Although I wasn't a virgin, I'd never actually spent all night with a boy before. As for Tex, had there been other girls before me, and if so, how many?

Back in the bedroom, a fire crackled in the hearth as Tex lay reclined on the bed, still fully dressed. He'd lit the oil lamps on the nightstands, thawing the room's gothic pallor. Outside the window, dusk had settled over the island.

"The bathroom's free if you need it." I peeled back the quilt as he jumped up, grabbing his shaving kit and stack of clothes. The bed, though a little lumpy, was heaven under my weary bones. I stared at the ceiling, still not quite believing that I'd made my way back to Formentera after all this time. *I'm home, Daddy.*

I must have dozed off, because the next thing I knew, the weight of Tex's knee depressing the mattress roused me awake. He wore pajama pants but no shirt. I tried not to ogle, but it was hard to tear my eyes away from the wall of taut skin as it pulled over sinewy muscles. He slipped under the covers, turning to face me, then lifted his hand to touch my nose.

"I never noticed your freckles before."

"I usually wear makeup to cover them," I explained sleepily.

"You shouldn't ever hide them," he whispered. "Not with me."

We studied each other for a moment, caught up in the spell of yearning.

"Tex? Do you think we did the right thing? Coming here, I mean?"

After considering the question, he said, "Bein' with you feels like the rightest thing I've ever done in my life." Then he yawned and turned us, gently bringing my back to his front. He curled his arm around my midsection, squeezing me tighter. "Close your eyes. We've got all the time in the world, Al."

I felt the press of his lips against the back of my neck, as my mind swirled with images of blue water, rocky cliffs, and the sweet nothingness of contentment.

THIRTEEN

COLD AIR LAPPED at my face as Tex's body warmed me from behind, the chirping birds outside signaling an approaching dawn. Across the room, gray ash filled the bottom of the hearth, the fire having gone out hours ago. Lingering smoke mixed with old turpentine fumes and an earthy mustiness from sheets kept too long in a closet. An olfactory jolt, the smell of the house was like a trip back in time. I half expected Daddy to be making lopsided pancakes in the kitchen.

As my legs shifted, Tex tensed behind me before groaning and pulling me closer. His hand found the skin of my stomach, and I felt the gentle caress of his thumb.

"Too early," he mumbled. "Go back to sleep."

I liked this rumpled, drowsy version of him. "We've been asleep for hours and hours," I whispered, smiling. "I've had enough rest."

Turning, I found myself within inches of his heavy-lidded eyes, as one side of his mouth ticked up. "Now that's a morning view I could get used to." He leaned in, pressing his lips to mine.

We kissed slowly, languidly, as my body began to respond. Against my thigh, I felt the rest of him waking up too. Our tongues tangled as I finally groped his bare chest, the skin warm and smooth. Muscles flexed and tightened as we moved together, hinting at a strength he kept tightly coiled.

Pulling away for a moment to catch his breath, he panted softly, "Damn, what you do to me." His palm dipped lower, stopping on the exposed skin of my stomach where my top had ridden up. Fingertips stroked underneath the gingham fabric, grazing the underside of my breast. I shivered, biting my lip, my body aching with need. I kissed him again, pressing myself into his hand, as a quiet rumble escaped the back of his throat.

"If you keep this up, I might not be able to stop," he murmured against my lips.

"Maybe I don't want you to stop."

His movement stilled, and he leaned back to look at me. "Are you sayin' what I think you're sayin'?"

"I want you, Tex. I do." I'd never wanted anything more.

"Have you . . . have you ever done that before?"

Reluctantly, I nodded. Would he think less of me, knowing he wasn't my first? The experiences had been disappointing and unremarkable, but still, they'd happened.

"Were you in love?"

I shook my head. "Hardly. The first time was with a boy I met at a party. It was six months after Daddy died, and I just wanted to feel something other than sad. He was timid and awkward, but that's better than the alternative, I guess. Another time was last year. It wasn't anyone special, just an actor who happened to be at the right place at the right time. The right time for him, at least. I regretted it almost instantly, but luckily nobody ever found out. Not even Daphne or Billy."

"So you've never been with Henry?"

"No. Henry wouldn't dream of being so reckless. Certainly not with me, anyway."

"You ever wonder if he's maybe a little . . . like Billy?"

I shook my head vehemently. "It's not that he doesn't like girls, it's just that he put me on some kind of pedestal, like a delicate flower behind glass." I hesitated before asking the question I'd been thinking about since last night. "What about you? Were there other girls?"

"A few," he admitted. "I had a girlfriend back in Texas, and we made it after a high school dance. Cliché, right?" I shrugged and laced my fingers through his, trying to reassure him that whatever he revealed wouldn't change my opinion of him. "And then, after I moved to New York, there were a couple more. Secretaries, waitresses, you know. Nobody serious. I guess I was just lonely. Hell, they probably were too. New York is full of people, but somehow it feels awful empty when you haven't found the one who really understands you."

I could relate, given my own tendency to feel alone in a crowded room.

"Listen, Al—I get that we're here together, sharin' a bed and all, but I want you to know I don't expect anything. It's enough for me just to be here with you. Even if all you want to do is sleep, that's okay with me."

I smiled, knowing sleep was the last thing on either of our minds this morning. "That's nice of you to say, but I can think of a much better way to pass the time."

We quickly picked up where we'd left off, discovering one another as his lean body moved against mine in a sensual ballet. My blood heating, I moaned as his kiss traveled over my shoulder, his hands gliding ever so smoothly over my—

KNOCK-KNOCK-KNOCK.

A sharp pounding on the front door jolted us apart.

"Does anyone know we're here?" Tex asked, staring wide-eyed at the bedroom doorway. His cheeks were flushed, and his hair stuck up in pieces. I stifled a giggle.

"I didn't think so." Quickly, I tiptoed across the cold room, rifling through my bag to find a pair of slippers. Realizing I'd neglected to pack a robe, I grabbed a large cardigan sweater and pulled my arms through it.

"Coming!" I shouted, scurrying toward the living room. Reaching the front door, I cracked it open just enough to see who was outside. On the stoop stood a small older woman holding a bucket and knapsack.

"*Buenos dias.*" Her voice was as salty and weathered as the sea.

Confused, I opened the door wider. In my limited Spanish, I asked, "Can I help you?"

"I am Valentina," she replied in heavily accented English. "Maria hire me to care for the house. There was word in village of two people arrive here last night."

"OH! Yes, please come in!" I shuffled aside. "I'm Caroline, David Kimball's daughter."

The old woman gave the sign of the cross at that.

Tex strolled out from the bedroom, trying to flatten his hair down.

"This is my . . . husband. Jack Fairchild," I explained by way of introduction.

He stopped in his tracks, eyes widening in surprise.

"¿*Esposo?*" Her mouth twisted into a skeptical frown. "¿*O tu amante?*"

I pretended I didn't understand, though I could easily translate her suspicion that he was my lover and not my spouse. Spain was still largely conservative, and I didn't know if Franco's reach extended all the way to the islands. A fake marriage was our safest option.

"I didn't know Maria had asked anyone to look in on the house."

"She pay the bills, me, and the gardener, Jaime. He take care of the pool. Is too cold for swimming now," she explained. "Maria know you are here? With him?"

"No, I didn't tell her. It was all very last-minute."

She trained her eye on Tex as she spoke, like he was a dangerous predator. "Washing is beside the house; you dry outside on line. Jaime come every two weeks. How long you stay?"

I shrugged. "I don't know yet. A month? Two?" I glanced at Tex, but his expression was as clueless as mine. We'd only just gotten here; it was too soon to think about an end date.

"I come back next week to clean. You ask for Valentina in village if you need anything. My house no has phone."

Thank heavens for that. There was no easy way for her to call Maria to tell her the house had unexpected guests.

"*Gracias, Valentina. Encantado.*" I extended my hand to her.

With a curt shake, she sniffed and turned to leave, muttering to herself in Spanish. I caught the word *pecadora*: sinner.

"Wasn't she just a barrel of fun," Tex said once we were alone again. He came deeper into the living room and plopped onto the couch, fiddling with his camera. "I hope it was a nice wedding— wish I could remember it."

"Sorry about that. It's just that Mother's always warned me about Franco and his disciples. I don't think they'd look too kindly on our arrangement."

"And what arrangement is that?" he asked, raising the view-finder to his face.

"The kind where we sleep in the same bed without rings on our fingers, and you come out of the bedroom with messy hair." I made a silly expression just before he snapped a photo of me.

He chuckled. "Nice try. You're still gorgeous."

I sat down on the opposite end and curled my legs under me. "We should head into the village later to get some groceries. Just to warn you, I'm not exactly the best chef. Finishing school taught me to hire them, not to be one."

"I cook for myself most nights in New York. If you don't mind baked beans and frankfurters, we won't starve."

I grimaced.

"I'll need to find the post office too," he continued. "I've got to send the negatives from Switzerland to *Vogue*."

"You didn't do that before we left?"

"There wasn't time. Will it be a problem to send them from here?"

"No, it's just a little slower. We'll get a post office box, and I'll send Daphne the address. We like to write to one another when we're not in the same place."

He fiddled with his lens, clicking a few buttons on the side of the camera. "She's a really good friend to you, huh?"

"Yes." I nodded. "Most people don't understand our connection, but I've honestly never met a more loyal person than her. Once she lets you in, you're in for life. I know she'll always be there for me if I need her, and she expects the same from me. It's just how we are."

"I think she's a hoot," Tex said with a smile. "You know, after I first saw you again in Gstaad, she took me aside and said, 'Now, don't you bloody well give up on that girl. She'll figure it out; just you wait.'"

"Figure what out?"

"This." He gestured between the two of us. Raising the camera, he snapped a picture of my head resting on the back of the sofa, lazy grin on my face.

Click.

✳

After I showered and put on jeans and a striped sweater, we went outside to find the bikes Daddy and I had used for trips into town. I made Tex go into the shed without me; I wasn't ready to see it yet. After a few minutes, he emerged victorious. Though the bikes were slightly rusted, a wicker basket still adorned the smaller of the two, and we quickly refilled the tires with a hand pump he'd located. The road to Sant Ferran was flat and easily traveled in about half an hour, making for a pleasant ride on a sunny day like today.

Tex and I pedaled mostly in silence, taking in the beautiful scenery. Wild, gnarled trees dotted the countryside, and occasionally

I'd point out something remembered from previous visits. Reaching the small village, we parked the bicycles outside a general store and went in with canvas bags I'd found in the kitchen. Tex and I browsed the tiny shop, picking out grocery staples along with sharp cheeses and cured meats that would keep. He even surprised me with a bouquet of flowers, smiling as he handed them to the cashier. Maybe we were playing at being married, but it didn't feel like make-believe to me.

Using my language skills, we obtained a box at the nearby post office, c/o Caroline and Jack Fairchild. My heart fluttered, seeing our names like that on the form. While Tex filled out the additional paperwork to send his film to the *Vogue* offices, I sat at a small wooden table and composed a quick letter to Daphne:

Dear Daphne,

Tex and I decided to run away to Formentera. I promise, I'm okay. We're staying at my family's old cottage, but you can reach me at the return address on this letter. Hopefully Mother and Maria didn't give you any grief after I disappeared from Gstaad. I'm sorry there wasn't time to say goodbye in person, but I hope you survived that awful punch. Safe travels to wherever you're headed next, and please write as soon as you can. And if you wouldn't mind, could you send one of your famous care packages? I'll owe you forever. Say hi to Billy for me and tell him not to worry. I'm right where I need to be.

Love always,
Caroline

I sealed the envelope and wrote Daphne's mother's Paris address on the outside, giving it to the postmaster with some coins for postage.

"All set?" Tex asked from behind me.

"Yes. I hope this gets to her before she leaves again."

"You don't want to call? I saw a pay phone in the corner over there," he offered, pointing.

"No, a letter is better for now. If we talk on the phone, she might point out how crazy it was to run off like we did, and I'm not ready to have anyone spoil it."

"You don't think she'd be happy for us?"

I shrugged. "Oh, probably. But that doesn't mean she wouldn't question my sanity." I took his hand and squeezed it. "For now, let's just enjoy being on our own."

Tex nodded, bringing my knuckles to his lips for a quick kiss. We walked back to our bicycles, and as he swung his leg over the seat, he called out, "Last one back to the house has to make lunch!" Pulling away, he flashed a devilish grin over his shoulder. I laughed and hurried to catch up.

※

As day turned to night, we relaxed into an easy rhythm with one another, working in tandem to make the house a home. Once our things were finally organized, I enjoyed a glass of Tempranillo, humming a song, while Tex tended the outdoor grill. Sitting at the battered kitchen table later, we ate our feast of beef and seasonal vegetables under the dim light of the flickering candles I'd set in Mother's candelabras, while Daddy's Billie Holiday album spun on the old player. It was a perfect meal, made even better by the fact that we could finally talk without a roomful of prying eyes and ears listening in. He told me about his time in Gstaad, and I told him the truth about what had happened on New Year's Eve—as much as I could remember. When I got to the part about Roger and the hallway, his face turned to granite.

"That asshole was ready to take advantage of a girl out of her mind on drugs. I don't even wanna think what might have happened if he wasn't interrupted."

I didn't have the heart to tell him my tale was an all too common one; I knew plenty of girls whose story hadn't concluded in the hallway. "Well, he was. And I'm okay. The right guy found me in the end. My knight in shining armor."

"Nah. You were the one in shining armor. That silver dress was somethin' else. I was almost scared to touch it when I got you back to my room. Like it might sear my hand when I took it off."

My face flushed from the wine and the image of him removing my clothes. Getting up, I busied myself taking our dishes to the sink.

"Do you want to light a fire?" I called back to him. "It's getting a little chilly now that the sun's gone down."

"Sure. In the living room?"

"No . . . I think the bedroom." I let those words hang between us, the moment charged with a current of possibility. Maybe even inevitability. Silently, I started to scrub, glad to have something to occupy my hands.

Seconds passed before he approached from behind. Wrapping his arms around my waist, he rested his chin on my head. "Nothin' to be nervous about, Al. Like I told you this morning, I don't expect anything. You can trust me."

I set a plate on the drying rack and covered his forearms with mine. "I know. We wouldn't be here if I didn't."

Appeased, he brushed his lips against my ear. "I'll get going on that fire." Then his body was gone, its absence haunting me like a phantom limb.

I stared out the window to the darkened swimming pool beyond. Tex had uncovered it earlier because I'd said it made me happy to be near water, and it shined like black obsidian under the moonlight. Seeing it gave me an idea, and before I could talk myself out of it, I took another big sip of wine and walked to the patio doors. I turned on the light to the pool, illuminating the green water from below. Knowing it would be cold, but craving the rush, I stepped onto the patio, slipped off my canvas shoes and sweater, and unbuttoned my dress. I removed my bra and panties and, mustering every ounce of courage, dove headfirst into the deep end.

The water was like a bucket of ice, causing my limbs to kick violently in retaliation. As thoughts of hypothermia flashed through my mind, I surfaced and drew great gulps of air across my chattering teeth. Although the cold was nearly heart-stopping, it was the one thing that always kept me from crawling out of my skin. The one thing that grounded me.

"Caroline?" Tex called from inside the house.

I swam to the edge of the pool and waited for him. Finally, his tall form stepped through the doorway, holding a camera. He looked at me, and I could almost hear the small intake of breath when he realized my clothes were scattered on the ground.

At last, he spoke. "That pool has to be mighty cold, Al." He raised the box to his face, and the shutter clicked. Lowering the camera, he moved closer. I saw the hunger in his gaze as his thumb advanced the film.

"It's not so bad," I lied, my voice trembling. I looked boldly at his lens, and the shutter released again. "Want to join me?"

"Maybe another time." *Click.*

Tex and the camera worked in tandem, devouring my form beneath the surface. I swam to the ladder and pulled myself up. Icy droplets rolled down my naked body as the shutter released once more. *Click.* Adrenaline tangled with the cold night air, and I resisted the urge to race him inside. Instead, I walked carefully to where he stood, letting the island breeze tease my skin, stimulating every pore. Once I finally got to within inches of his body, he lowered his hands.

"Pictures are never good enough. Not when it's you," he said thickly.

I took the camera and set it on a nearby table. My hardened nipples brushed his T-shirt as the labored rise and fall of his chest heightened the sensation. I twined my fingers together behind his neck and leaned in. As our lips made contact, his warmth soothed my trembling body.

"Take me to bed," I pleaded against his mouth.

With ravenous eyes that had turned as black as the night surrounding us, he took my hand and led me inside.

Acutely aware of my nudity as soon as we stepped across the threshold, I wrapped an arm across my breasts while he locked up behind me. Before I could turn away, he tugged my wrist.

"Please don't hide," Tex begged. "I've seen some of the most beautiful things on this planet, but they're nothing compared to you, right in this second. Let me savor it."

Raising my eyes to meet his again, I nodded softly. My hips swayed as I walked to the bedroom, arms loose at my sides. Water from my hair dripped down my backside, making tiny dots on the stone floor. I could feel his eyes on me, but I didn't look back. We were not Orpheus and Eurydice—I trusted him to make it into the light.

In the bedroom, a fire danced in the hearth, casting shadows across the wall. The room glowed with a sultry warmth, loosening my inhibitions with every breath I took.

"You're overdressed," I said, turning back to Tex. He reached for the hem of his shirt before I placed a hand over his. "Let me."

I pulled the cotton T-shirt over his torso as he raised his arms, bending down so I could lift it over his head. Flinging it across the room, I let my hands wander to his chest, noticing how the skin pebbled beneath my touch. *Oh, he liked that.*

My attention then traveled to his belt and the hardness pressing against his jeans. Hesitating just a fraction of a second, I moved to pull the leather through the buckle before he stopped me.

"Are you sure? You don't have to, you know."

"I'm sure," I promised him. And I was—I wanted his body more than anything I'd ever wanted in my whole life. "I'm just a little nervous because it feels different than those other times. I've never done this with someone who matters. Someone who's watching every move I make and looking at me like I hung the stars."

He shook his head. "I don't think you hung the stars; I think you *are* a star."

"If I'm a star, then you are too. We're equals tonight—that's how it has to be."

Understanding washed across his face as he pulled me to him. Tex hugged me for a moment before walking me backward. Feeling the bed against my legs, I sat down slowly, reaching for him once more. I looked into his eyes, letting him know I was exactly where I wanted to be. Where I needed to be. He might have been more experienced, but none of that mattered now. Stripped of our pasts, we were one and the same.

With our clothing finally shed, we collided on top of the old quilt, neither of us moving to pull it back. Though I couldn't read his mind, I knew he felt as I did—that to cover any inch of ourselves would have been a travesty. I wanted to look my fill, as he had done of me. I wanted to see his muscles contract and release as I slid slowly on top of him, the red flush of his skin as he moved beneath me, the joining of our hands as we inched ever closer to ecstasy. And when it finally happened, and my voice cried out in release, I wanted to see my own trust and adoration reflected back. Wanted to see what it looked like when, with ragged breaths and shaking limbs, two stars became supernovas.

FOURTEEN

A FEATHERY TOUCH against my hip woke me from a dreamless sleep. Gradually remembering where I was, I lengthened and stretched through the soreness in my legs and thighs.

"Mmm, good morning." I yawned, tightening my hold on Tex. He lay on his back, my cheek resting against his chest. Violet light seeped in through the windows, and I knew it must be early. "One of these days we're going to have to learn how to sleep in."

"Wasn't it just yesterday you said there were more interestin' things you wanted to do?" he teased, the Southern accent heavy in his voice.

"Didn't we do them already?" I asked, raising an eyebrow.

"I can think of a few variations worth tryin' out."

I leaned up for a kiss as he pulled me on top of him.

"So, no regrets? About being here with me, or what we did?" He ran his fingers up and down my spine, gently playing with my hair.

"No regrets." I shook my head.

He squeezed his arms tighter around me in silent agreement.

"And you don't have to worry about getting me in trouble," I continued. "I'm on the pill." Fortunately for us, contraception had never been more accessible. Daphne had taken me to her doctor as soon as it'd come on the market.

Tex scrubbed a hand over his face, looking embarrassed. "Oh shit, I didn't even ask. You must think I'm such a dolt. I bought some rubbers at a pharmacy in Switzerland, but I got so distracted last night that I forgot all about 'em."

I squeezed his thigh in reassurance. "No, it's okay. If it were a big deal, I would have told you. But I knew I had it taken care of, and I didn't want to break the moment. It was a pretty great moment."

"Yeah, it was," he agreed, a gleam in his eye. "Now you're here, naked, looking more beautiful than anyone has a right to look first thing in the mornin', and I really want to have another one of those moments. Only I think there's somethin' else I want even more."

"Oh yeah? What's that?"

"A song. One of your own. And don't go sayin' you don't have one, because that pile of words over there proves you do." He pointed to the notebook I'd left on the nightstand.

Biting my lip, I hesitated for a second, then jumped up. I'd said I wanted to be brave with him, and here was my chance. I picked up his shirt from the floor and slipped it over my head before retrieving my ukulele case.

"I saw a guitar in the living room, Al. You want to play it on that instead?"

I shook my head. "Not yet. I know Daddy left it for me, but I don't think I'm ready for that yet. At least, not today. Today you get four strings, not six."

I brought the ukulele up to my chest, taking it out of standard tuning. Most of the songs I'd come up with sounded wrong that way; they needed to take their own path. Once I had it adjusted to my satisfaction, I sat down and took a breath. Tex smiled at me, relaxed and shirtless against the pillows. God, he was handsome. And wonderfully distracting.

"This is just a little something I wrote in Acapulco. I was reading Rimbaud at the time, and one of his poems stuck with me. It's called 'Sun Meets Sea.'"

I strummed the first notes as my lips parted to sing. Leaning my head back, I let the music emanate from someplace deep inside.

Early one morning,
such a bright, brilliant day
Open the window
Time to go out and play

The water, it shimmered
Like cellophane flags
And the beachgoers beside
Lay limply like rags

Where the sun meets the sea
There you'll find me
Wishing, watching, waiting, hoping,
Eternity
Eternity

When the light got too bright
You pointed to my lids
Close them, you said
Don't regret what we did

But oh, in my dreams
We stood even higher
You were my altar
And I, the brave diver

Where the sun meets the sea
There you'll find me
Wishing, watching, waiting, hoping,
Eternity
Eternity

Finishing the second refrain, my fingers slowed on the strings. I opened my eyes, finding his transfixed on me. The silence sat between us, heavy and uncertain.

"Well?" I asked nervously. "Was that okay? Was it trite?"

"Come here," he said thickly, plucking the ukulele off my lap and setting it on the floor. Then he pulled me under him and kissed me with surprising intensity, stopping only to say, "Don't ever let anyone tell you that you weren't meant to make music. Your daddy was right—you soar above 'em all."

※

Finally extracting ourselves from the bed later that afternoon, Tex and I took the scooter into town. I clutched him tight around his midsection, smiling against the back of his shoulder. The sun dappled through the trees as the wind whipped and swirled my hair out behind me. We were flying, or maybe that was just my heart.

After ordering two coffees at the Café Sirena, Tex sat back and looked at the stucco walls and wooden tables surrounding us.

"This place reminds me of West Texas. Sparse and Catholic." He pointed at the small crucifix on the opposite wall.

"I guess there's some crossover. Did you have many Mexicans in your hometown?"

"Oh, sure. Mostly ranch hands and their families. That girlfriend I told you about? Consuela was her name. Her dad worked our land, with the horses. I took quite the beating when my folks found out we'd been sneakin' around."

"Ah, now I see. You have a taste for raven-haired women," I teased.

He laughed, shaking his head. "Maybe so. Anybody ever confuse you for Mexican down in Texas?"

"Ha! No way. Mother made sure to let all of Daddy's snooty Houston relatives know she came from European nobility." I rolled my eyes. "It didn't matter so much in New York. Maria made sure I learned about other cultures; she thought it might be useful to me someday." It was strange to talk about Maria as though I didn't know what she really was to my mother. What she probably always had been.

"I've heard you speak Spanish, but what other languages do you know?" he asked.

"My French and Italian are pretty good, and I know enough German to get by. I'm hopeless in Asia and Greece, but there's usually someone around to translate. What about you?"

"A little Spanish, that's about it. Though it sounds mighty different here than in Texas."

The waitress arrived with our coffees and a slice of almond cake dusted with powdered sugar. As I splashed a bit of cream from the earthenware pitcher on the table into my cup, the door behind Tex creaked open, and an old man shuffled into the café.

"Oh my goodness, it's Gerhard!" I exclaimed. The sight of him was like discovering my favorite sweater in the back of the closet.

"Who?" Tex asked, glancing over his shoulder.

"Gerhard Nussbaum. He owns the farm next to our property. It's in the opposite direction from town, so we haven't passed it yet."

Tex looked back at me, stunned. "Wait, *the* Gerhard Nussbaum? The writer?"

"Yes, have you read his book?" It had taken me several months to get through it myself, the pain on the pages almost unbearable.

"Of course, hasn't everybody? That poor guy . . ." He shook his head, his voice heavy with sympathy.

Gerhard Nussbaum's famous memoir, *Notes from the Inferno*, described his experiences as a German Jew under the Nazi regime. In horrifying detail, he'd chronicled years of starvation, torture, and the eventual loss of his family to the gas chambers. Gerhard had clung to life in a work camp, only to be left with nothing when Hitler was finally defeated. He'd written his memoir with journalistic detachment, yet there was no escaping the harsh truths about man's capability for prejudice and cruelty.

Most people didn't know Gerhard had been living on Formentera for more than a decade.

As he shuffled closer, leaning on his cane, I stood to greet him.

"Oh my. Caroline. *Das kleine Mädchen*. Is it you?" he asked in his soft German accent.

I moved closer to grasp his shoulders and kiss his cheeks. "Gerhard! I can't believe it! It's been so long."

His shining eyes took in my long dark hair, scuffed sandals, and belted white dress. I had probably changed quite a bit since he'd last seen me.

"Please—join us," I invited, gesturing to our table. "This is my friend Jack Fairchild. I call him Tex."

Tex stood to greet him. "It's an honor to meet you, sir."

Gerhard waved him off, plopping himself into a chair next to our table. "Sit, sit. So much fuss."

Tex signaled the waitress back over.

"Caroline, dear, have you the time?"

I glanced at my wristwatch. "Two thirty in the afternoon."

"Too early for brandy, then. *Café cortado*," Gerhard requested. Turning back to us, he explained, "Before five o'clock, coffee. After five, brandy. The one rule I still follow."

"A good one." I smiled. "I'm so pleased to see you again. And happy you remembered me."

Gerhard shook his head. "How could I forget the charming girl who used to run through my olive trees? I still remember the face you made when you tasted the bitter fruit of my 1957 crop." He and I both laughed at the memory. "Tell me, Caroline, are you still writing poetry?"

My face turned beet red at the prospect of discussing my song-writing in the company of an actual, world-renowned author.

Tex grinned, nodding his head enthusiastically. "She sure is. But she turns those poems into songs now, and what a talent! I was lucky enough to hear her sing earlier."

"It's nothing," I said, shaking my head. "Just something I like to do for fun. Daddy taught me to play the ukulele, and I've tried to keep it up."

"A singer!" Gerhard exclaimed. "Your father predicted it. He told me his girl had more talent in her little pinkie than most of the artists in his stack of records. That she saw things in a way nobody else did." He pointed at me, looking at Tex. "This one—always with her journal, scribbling away. I still remember your pencil flying across the paper; you wrote so fast it was like your hand couldn't keep up with your mind."

"It still can't," I mused, taking a bite of cake. "But it's not like I'm an actual writer. Not like you."

"I used to say my photos were no big deal until people started payin' me," Tex cut in. "Maybe you should try to get a gig some-where."

The waitress arrived with Gerhard's coffee, and he scooped a tiny bit of sugar into it. Stirring, he regarded Tex. "Photos?"

"Yes, Tex is a photographer in New York," I said, ignoring his suggestion about a gig. There was no way I was ready to perform in front of strangers. "He just had a spread in *Life* magazine. We met when he was on assignment in Acapulco." I smiled at the memory of his tall frame looming over me at La Concha Beach Club.

"A very powerful thing, photos," Gerhard mused. "They tell a story better than words ever could."

"Not better than your words, sir. And I don't know that photos are ever enough on their own. Take, for example, the first one I shot of Caroline. In it, there's a beautiful girl with brilliant green eyes, perfect skin, in an exotic setting. But that image doesn't tell her whole story. Doesn't even come close."

"That's not true. It's the best picture ever taken of me," I argued.

Tex shook his head. "It only scratches the surface. I'll take a better one someday."

Gerhard smiled, glancing between the two of us. "I'm so happy you're back, my dear. The island just isn't the same without Herr Kimball and his stylish family. I saw your mother and that woman she's always with in town last spring, but they kept to themselves."

I stiffened at the mention of Mother and Maria. I didn't want to think of them here, together at the house that had become my sanctuary with Tex. "I can't keep track of their comings and goings," I deflected. "I'm just glad they're maintaining the cottage. Even during the winter months."

"It is quiet this time of year. You two must come for an early supper tomorrow night! You'll tell me everything you've been up to."

"Oh, we couldn't impose, sir." Tex still seemed a little intimidated by our famous neighbor.

"Nonsense!" Gerhard insisted. "Caroline knows the way. Five o'clock. We shall have brandy, then sample the fruits of my labor."

"We'd love to," I cut in, silencing the protest rising on the tip of Tex's tongue. "What can we bring?"

"Just one of your songs, and some of this one's photos." Gerhard pointed his thumb at Tex. "I want to see who you've gotten yourself mixed up with."

I laughed. "All right, then. We should probably get going and let you enjoy your coffee." Standing up, I leaned back down to kiss him again on his cheek. "*Auf wiedersehen.*"

"Charming girl . . ." He smiled, lightly tapping my chin.

"Good to meet you, sir," Tex said, extending his hand once more. "Really is a pleasure."

Gerhard shook it, then waved us off. "*Bis morgen.*"

Once outside the café, Tex turned to me. "Did that just happen? Did we actually have coffee with Gerhard Nussbaum?"

I shrugged, standing next to the scooter while Tex hopped on and started the motor. "What can I say—you just never know what'll happen when you're with me. Or who you'll meet."

The next evening, Tex and I began our short walk down the dirt path to Gerhard's property. The sky had turned amber as the sun sank behind the gnarled trees, and lights flickered through the small windows of his farmhouse. I wore a belted blue house-dress under my cardigan, and Tex was bundled up in a thick navy sweater. It was colder this time of year, but that just made me want to snuggle closer to him. I carried my ukulele in its case, butterflies in my stomach at the prospect of performing a song. I knew Gerhard was a friendly audience, but still, my nerves were stretched.

"Are you sure we shouldn't have brought something besides the wine?" Tex pointed to the bottle cradled in my other arm.

"Trust me, Gerhard was always envious of our cellar." I could still remember him sitting with Daddy on our patio, several bottles between them, talking well into the night.

"I still can't believe he invited us over like this."

I nodded, staring at the house in the distance. "He probably gets lonely. After he wrote the book, it became too hard for him to stay in a big city. People would come up to him, sympathizing but not totally understanding what he went through. Unless you'd lived through it yourself, you couldn't. In the end, it was just easier to walk away from all that."

"And he never thought about going to Israel? To be with other survivors?"

I shook my head. "No. You see, here he's not known for being Jewish, or a writer; he's just the nice old man with the olive oil. I'm sure Franco knows he's here, and maybe he's even being watched, but as Daddy always put it, 'Little Caudillo has an image problem that won't be solved by backhanding the one man the rest of the world wants to embrace.'"

The front door opened as we got closer to the house, and Gerhard appeared, backlit. With his stooped shoulders, wrinkled pants, and glasses resting on the bridge of his nose, he looked every bit the part of an aging writer.

"*Wilkommen!*" he called. "I spotted a young, handsome couple walking and knew it must be time for our little party. Come, you can help with the food."

I laughed, bending to greet him as we stepped into his tiny foyer. "I'd be happy to. But you know Maria is the cook in our family, not me."

"*Psht*, you will do fine. I am an excellent teacher." His eyes warmed as he clasped my cheeks. "And Tex! Come in, my boy," he directed, ushering him inside. "You shall entertain us with stories of the American West. With a name like that, you must have dozens."

"Aww now, maybe a few. Do you know anything about Texas already?"

"Just what I've seen in the movies. They showed the picture *Riders of Destiny* at a little theater in Berlin before the war. Singing cowboys, John Wayne—it was enchanting!"

Tex laughed in surprise. "Well, I can tell you that life on a ranch doesn't involve much singin'. 'Least not on ours."

I gave Gerhard the wine as we entered the kitchen. His face lit up as he read the label. "From your father's cellar?"

"Of course! Only the best for you. Do you have a corkscrew?"

"In the top drawer next to the sink." He pointed. "And what have you brought me?" he inquired of Tex, indicating the portfolio still under his arm.

Tex handed it over with shy humility. "Just some of my photos. They're a mix of landscapes and candid portraits. I'd like to do something more interesting on the island, experimenting with the natural light and terrain. I need to ask around in town about how to get some supplies to set up a darkroom."

"Oh, Daddy might have left behind some things you could use," I offered. "He was considering getting into photography for a brief period, but I don't think anything ever came of it."

Gerhard set his short glass of brandy aside and carefully opened the leather flaps. He laid the photos before him, and I leaned over to see what Tex had spent so much time selecting. They were all exquisite. I smiled at him, trying to convey my pride in his talent.

"The shadows in this one are quite beautiful," Gerhard said, pointing to a seaside vista. "Do you always work in color?"

"Most of the time, yes. Unless the assignment calls for black and white, which is more likely on celebrity coverage or jobs with a quick turnaround. I'm still trying to carve out my own style, but I like working in color the best."

"And why is that?" Gerhard asked.

"It tells a better story. I can say that the hibiscus flower is pink, but unless you see it in color, you don't understand *how* pink. That it's the same color pink as a lady's drink or her swimsuit. Same with Caroline's eyes." He gestured to the photo of me he'd included. "It's the green that draws you in. Not that she's not beautiful in black and white, but she was meant to be seen in color."

"Daddy thought so too," I said. "I still have a portrait he painted of me when I was a little girl—*Ojos Verdes*. Green Eyes. I've gotten offers to sell it, but I could never give it up."

"Where is it now?" Tex asked.

"A bank vault in Paris. I'm just keeping it there until I have a home of my own one day."

Gerhard smiled, looking down at the photos again, then at Tex. "You've got talent. No wonder our girl is drawn to you." Finishing his brandy, he stood to collect more glasses. As he began to set the table for our olive oil tasting, I noticed the string of black numbers peeking out from beneath his sleeve, and my heart twisted at the ugly souvenir from his past.

Putting his photos back in the portfolio, Tex turned his head to our neighbor. "Do you still write, sir? Or do the olives take up too much of your time?"

Gerhard shook his head with a tiny smile. "It's not the olives; that's just a silly battle I've decided to wage against the island's soil. No, when I wrote my story down all those years ago, it was because I didn't want my wife and daughter, and so many other wives and daughters, to be forgotten. But after accomplishing what I set out to do, I find I'm left with only the simple hobbies of an old man. Nobody wants to read about that."

"Did you write before the war?"

"I was a literature professor at the university in Berlin. Several of my colleagues escaped early, back when the danger was merely a threat. But I stayed because I had such faith in my country. I didn't think for a moment that a tyrant could turn neighbor against neighbor, or that he had the power to erase my life and all the things I'd worked for. Some would say it was courage that kept me there, but there was a little bit of naivety too." Gerhard shook his head with wistful regret. "After it ended, I had nothing but my memories and a desire to tell the world what had happened. News reports weren't enough; most people just skim the headlines over their morning coffee. It had to be told in a way that would have an impact, so it would never happen again."

Tex broke off a piece of bread, dipping it in the oil. He looked like he was pondering something. "You know, that's still true today."

"What is?" I asked.

"The way people choose to ignore the details. They don't actually read newspapers anymore; they only glance at the pictures."

"Which makes your work even more important!" Gerhard exclaimed. "People need to be confronted with the ugliness of humanity before it spirals out of control. A photograph has the potential to shock them into action."

"Maybe," Tex conceded. "But take Vietnam. Cameras are documenting it all, every day, but it hasn't made it any easier to understand what's really happening or why we're still there. So maybe it's not the simple act of photographing something, but rather *how* it's photographed. Does it tell a story or make people feel a certain way? You can't just strap a camera to a soldier's back and hope he ends up with useful footage. We need more photojournalists over there to get to the real truth."

The conversation humbled me, making it even more apparent how narrow my worldview was. Yes, I'd visited many countries and spoke several languages, but it all fit within my tiny bubble of wealth and privilege. Did I know anything about the struggles that existed beyond the walls of those luxury hotels? And how did a person even begin to break through them and learn?

"Caroline, dear, you look distant," Gerhard observed. "Thinking about your father?"

I shrugged, knowing he was always swimming around the back of my mind. "I didn't realize how much of him was still here. His paintings and records and wine; even his old pocket watch was still on the nightstand when we arrived—the one with the Auden inscription inside: *The years shall run like rabbits.* Then, standing beside that shed again, in the spot where he . . ." I trailed off. Gerhard nodded, acknowledging what I couldn't say. "I know I need to go in eventually, but I can't do it alone. Do you think you could be there with me? You were his friend, and I think I need someone else who truly understands."

"*Mädchen*, I would be honored." He bowed his head, smiling.

Tex squeezed my knee under the table in solidarity. Sitting in Gerhard's cozy kitchen, a glass of red wine in my hand, I looked at the table's fourth chair and knew, even though I couldn't see him, that the seat wasn't empty. It gave me the courage to clear my throat and make an offering. "You said you wanted a song tonight. Is it okay if it's not one I wrote?"

Gerhard's face lit up. "Of course! It would be a joy to listen to whatever you wish to play."

I stood up and opened my ukulele case. "Eventually I want to start practicing on the guitar Daddy left for me. The tuning is different from what I'm used to on this." I plucked up the instrument by the neck and came back to the table, resting it on my crossed legs. Quickly, I adjusted the strings to my liking.

"Have the Beatles made it to Formentera?" I asked Gerhard.

"If this is a music group and not a blight on my olive crops, then no." He shook his head.

I laughed, plucking the opening notes of "In My Life." Launching into the song, I smiled at Tex when I got to the part about loving him more, closing my eyes as I thought about how true the song felt for me here, surrounded by people and things I'd known before. I'd been running from the memories for so long, but maybe I didn't have to anymore.

After I'd finished, Gerhard and Tex burst into applause. "Wonderful!" Gerhard exclaimed. "You have a gift. However long you're staying, use the time; make something of it. You must promise me."

I blushed, nodding. "I promise. Would you like another?"

"Heck yes!" Tex exclaimed, jokingly pounding on the table. "As many as you got."

I winked, finding the chords for "Streets of Laredo." And there, in the kitchen of a world-renowned author and amateur olive farmer, we had a good old-fashioned cowboy sing-along.

January 15th, 1967
Casa Kimball
Formentera, Spain

Dear Daddy,

   I'm sorry my letters have been so sparse; Tex
and I have been . . . busy.
   But don't think I've forgotten you—that's
almost impossible to do here.

   I see you
   In this house, that has always been my home
   In the strings of your guitar, like an unwritten poem

Love,
Caroline

FIFTEEN

OVER THE FOLLOWING weeks, Tex and I settled into a relaxed routine on the island. It was fun to spoil someone else for a change, to find a sense of accomplishment in ordinary tasks like making supper or picking up socks from the bedroom floor. Not that Tex *needed* to be taken care of—he'd been out on his own far longer than I had—but he let me serve him runny eggs and overcooked vegetables like they were the most exceptional meals he'd ever had. I even sent Valentina away after her second visit; I wanted to prove that I could make this house a home, and not just with my money.

Finally opening the case to Daddy's guitar was a big moment, one that I conquered with Tex by my side. The instrument felt heavy and awkward at first, but once I got it tuned and started to strum, an incredible sense of rightness washed over me, as though my hands were meant to grip it and never let go.

"Hey, that sounds pretty good," Tex said from the kitchen table. He'd found an old jigsaw puzzle in the closet and was currently assembling a conquistador's ship crossing a violent sea. "Is it weird with the extra strings?"

"A little," I replied, picking out some chords on the frets. "I looked for Daddy's old instructional album, but I couldn't find it with the others next to the hi-fi. It'd be nice to brush up on the basics again."

"Did you check the third bedroom?"

"Yeah. No dice."

"Would it be in the shed outside? Didn't you say he mostly used that for his studio?"

My fingers stilled. I hadn't ventured in there yet, and the very idea made my palms sweat.

"I guess it might be. He had another record player in there. I used to listen to music while he painted."

"Maybe it's finally time to check it out. I've been itchin' to see what photo equipment he may have left behind. Do you want me to get Gerhard, see if he'll go in with us?" Tex got up from the table and came to sit beside me on the arm of the couch. He stroked my hair, his thumb brushing my neck. It was a comforting gesture, but even his touch wasn't enough to lessen my anxiety over what we were about to do.

"Okay." I exhaled. "Take the scooter. I'll run down to the basement and get a couple bottles of wine. We'll need them."

He kissed the side of my forehead and stood up, walking to the bedroom to retrieve his shoes. As much as I wanted that box in my head to stay closed, I knew it couldn't anymore. Mother's secret had cracked it open, and light was starting to trickle in. There might be nothing in the shed but dusty equipment and rolls of canvas, but if there was anything else, any clue at all about why he'd left us, I owed it to Daddy to find it.

The rumble of a scooter coming down the road drew my head up. My back rested against the outside of the shed, my foot moving a pile of dirt back and forth. On the ground below me sat two bottles of wine and three tumblers. As the scooter got closer, I could see Tex in the front with Gerhard hanging on behind him, cane clutched in his hand. A knee injury sustained in the work camps prevented him from riding a bicycle, but he didn't have a problem sitting stationary. If I weren't so apprehensive, I would have laughed at the funny picture they made.

Tex pulled into the driveway, cut the engine, and helped Gerhard dismount. The old man found his balance, then shuffled over to where I stood.

"*Mädchen*," he said, looking at me with a somber expression, "I want to tell you something before we go in there. It is something I learned the first time I went to visit what remained of our apartment in Berlin. After sorting through broken glass and bricks, coming away with nothing, I realized the things lost in that building didn't matter. They were already here"—he touched my forehead—"and here." His hand lowered over my heart.

"I know," I said, blinking back tears, both for my father and for all that Gerhard had suffered. "Thank you for being with me."

Tex pulled the door open, stepping through to turn on a light for us. Gerhard took my hand, and together we walked over the threshold. The smells were the first things I noticed: turpentine, like in the third bedroom inside the house, but stronger out here;

wood from the stretcher bars my father had piled up, waiting for their canvases; the sour notes of alcohol, like someone had spilled a glass of wine and never cleaned it up; the faint whiff of leather, either from Daddy's brush bag or from the pair of boots still waiting for their owner's return. I'd thought I would walk in here and smell death, but that wasn't the case at all. This smell was his life.

"All right, Al?" Tex asked, looking at me, wary.

"Yeah. I'm okay." I walked to the record player sitting on a weather-beaten crate. Beside it was a stack of albums, *Beginner's Folk Guitar Guide* resting near the top. I picked it up and handed it to him. "Set that by the door, would you?" I looked under the plastic case covering the top of the player to see what was there— a 45 of Johnnie Ray's "Cry." Plucking the album from the center post, I placed it in a white sleeve. "This too."

Across the room, Gerhard lifted the flap on a box. "Brushes," he confirmed.

Peeking inside another, I found paints and little wooden figurines. I didn't know what I'd expected—the rope still hanging from the rafters? Mother had told me almost nothing about the day he died, and in the absence of any real details, I'd begun to imagine all manner of horrors. But in the end, it was just a shed. Just a shed filled with all the haphazard clutter of an artist.

Tex spotted something in the opposite corner and practically sprinted toward it. "Oh wow! A photo enlarger! It's pretty old, but it might still work." He started fiddling with the machine, extracting cables and twisting knobs to see if they turned.

Gerhard came closer, offering up a small box. "I think this might be for photography too. I can't be sure—the printing is faded."

Tex peered inside, opened a bottle, and sniffed. "Developer. I doubt it's still usable, but worth a shot at least." He dug further into the box, pulling out more materials. "Wow, this'll definitely get me started here. I can block up the windows, turn this into a makeshift darkroom." Then he looked back at me, excitement turning to hesitation. "As long as that's okay with you, Al. I'd understand if you didn't want anybody in here."

I smiled and shook my head. "No, I think you should use it. Daddy would love that. He wouldn't want this place to go to waste."

Gerhard walked to a wall where sketches had been tacked up. Reaching to touch one, he gave a short exclamation. "Oh! David, *der Witzbold*. Always the joker." He shook his head and turned around, his eyes red and misty. On the yellowed, curled piece of paper was a drawing of Gerhard's face, his body depicted as that of a comically strong man, muscles straining against the skin.

"After the war, I lived in a fog," Gerhard admitted. "Traveling from place to place, always a little bit lost. I found this island while searching for something else, but it ended up being a place of healing. I found purpose here, strength. Just like my friend did, for a little while." He shook his head, fond memories likely warring with sad ones, as they did in my own mind.

"Let's all sit and have a toast," Tex said, pulling wooden chairs to the center of the room. He went outside and grabbed one of the bottles I'd brought. I sat on his lap as he poured, offering a glass to each of us. "To Mr. Kimball." He raised his arm.

"To David, *der Witzbold*."

"To Daddy." We clinked our glasses together, and I savored the rich, earthy Garnacha.

"So what's up in the rafters?" Tex asked, looking above us. "Anything important?"

I shook my head. "No, just some old junk. Whatever wouldn't fit in the closets in the house." I scanned the area briefly before my attention caught on something directly over the center of the room. It was a flat item wrapped in an old blanket, but the corner had come loose to reveal a patch of cerulean blue. Pointing, I said, "Hang on, I want to see what that is."

Tex and I stood, and he dragged his chair over to where I'd indicated. He centered it under the object, then climbed up. Easily reaching the blanket, he brought the panel down to the ground. Gerhard and I worked the covering loose, letting it fall to our feet.

My breath caught at the sight before us.

It was obviously one of Daddy's paintings, with his typical abstract style in the background, but the foreground was something completely different. This was more photo-realistic, like something from a Dutch master. But instead of a bowl of fruit or a slaughtered fowl, it was a man, underwater, reaching toward the surface. His legs appeared motionless, as though they'd already stopped kicking. He wasn't pulling himself up, but rather waving goodbye. I touched my fingertips to it, feeling the oily texture of his brushstrokes, wishing I could climb right inside that painting and grasp his hand.

"There's a piece of paper taped to the back," Tex said from behind the image. He plucked the note loose and handed it to me. In Daddy's jagged script, I saw the words *Earth Angel*.

My lips parted in surprise. That was his nickname for Mother. I'd barely been a preteen when the song hit the charts, but I could still recall the dreamy look that came over his face when it played and he held Mother tight. Funny, I couldn't remember what her face looked like while they danced.

I knew it was wrong, and this wasn't my letter to read, but I didn't care. We'd come too far to turn back. Gently opening the folds, I scanned the words I'd craved for the last five years.

His final goodbye.

Darling,

I can't do it anymore. I'm sorry.
Between the two of us, you were always the strong one,
whereas I was always the fool (the fool in love with you).
Now you have to be strong again, for Caroline.
I beg you to give her the following things:
    -Air
    -Light
    -Water
    -Time
Let her grow tall and fierce like you. Keep her free of the
weeds that would serve to smother her. Help her see how
special she is, how she's the best of both of us. The one thing
we did right together.
Let all the memories be good ones.

Love you forever, and ever more,
David

My throat hiccupped as I finished the note, tears flowing freely. "Turns out he said goodbye. Just not to me." I handed the note to Gerhard, whose face turned ashen at the sight of my father's handwriting.

Tex took me in his arms, wrapping my body in his while I sobbed. This was all I'd wanted for so long, to know my father hadn't just left us without a backward glance. But I hadn't imagined it would feel like this—like someone had stabbed a fresh hole through my heart.

Gerhard shook his head. "I don't understand. This was here the whole time? Why did he hide it, and not put it where we would find it immediately?"

I pulled back from Tex's hold. "He must have placed it there right before he tied the rope, figuring someone would find it when his body was cut down. But no one ever did."

"Oh, *Mädchen*. I am so sorry I didn't see his pain." Gerhard's shoulders sagged as he sighed. "This is the thing about David—he gave all his joy to us and kept none for himself." He hugged me, and I took comfort in his frail arms around my back. We held each other as my tears dampened the fabric over his shoulder.

"What should we do with the painting?" Tex asked, once we'd regained our composure. "Take it back to the house?"

I shook my head. "I don't know. I don't think I can look at it every day, knowing it was one of the last things he touched. But I can't just leave it here to rot or be stolen. It's probably valuable."

Gerhard put his hand over his chest. "With your permission, I can take it to my house. It will be safe there, I promise. Let me ease this one burden for you."

"That sounds good, thank you." I tucked the letter into the pocket of my dress. I'd need to give it to Mother eventually, but I couldn't think about that right now. "No more tears today. He wouldn't want that." I poured another splash of wine for myself and raised the glass. "To Daddy and our memories—only the good ones."

SIXTEEN

AFTER OUR DISCOVERY in the shed, I found myself reading and rereading Daddy's letter to Mother. He'd asked her to give me air, light, water, and time—all the things I'd rediscovered on Formentera. It was clear to me now more than ever that this was where I was meant to find my voice. Yet it wasn't just this place that provided the soil to grow, but Tex as well. Being with him brought up all sorts of new feelings that colored my lyrics. I still didn't know if there was an audience for what I was creating, but I wouldn't let my fears and insecurities be smothering weeds. Not anymore.

I hadn't given much thought to my old life over the past few weeks, but a box from Daphne arrived the second week of February that made me remember the things I missed. Namely, my friends. The package contained records (a new band called Buffalo Springfield and the latest Simon & Garfunkel album), a tiny bikini Tex thoroughly approved of, issues of my favorite magazines, a copy of the *New York Times* with a feature on Daphne's

Blow-Up nemesis Veruschka (next to which she'd scrawled *THAT BITCH!*), and a letter:

Dearest, Darlingest Caroline—

Your alpine escape was the biggest shock I've had all year! (And yes, I know it's only January.) Always the quiet ones, they say. Naturally, I'm wild about the idea of you running off with your sexy photographer, reputation be damned. Your mother was rather calm about the whole thing when we spoke—maybe she expected it? I'm on a yacht in Montego Bay with—of all people—Dickie Waddlestone! Caroline, darling, I never thought I'd say this, but I'm in love! Dickie has talked of marriage, and he's even flying me to Palm Beach to meet his parents soon!!! Who knew taking an accidental trip would lead us both to such happiness? For the record, Dickie found out what happened with Roger, and he gave that rat a firm punch to the jaw. Who says chivalry is dead? Kisses to you and Tex, and write back when you can, c/o The Breakers Hotel, Palm Beach. Au revoir, mon cheri!

—Daphne

"Oh my god," I breathed, reading the letter a second time.

"What is it?" Tex asked from across the kitchen table. "Bad news?"

"I'm not sure. Daphne says she's in love with Dickie Waddlestone! She thinks they might get married."

He scrunched up his face. "That's a hell of a name. She'd be Daphne Waddlestone. Sounds like a cousin of Daffy Duck."

"The name isn't the point. She barely knows him! We met him New Year's Eve at that awful party. Now they're off sailing around Jamaica, and he wants to bring her to Palm Beach to meet his mother. This isn't like her at all." I shook my head. "We'll have to see if there's a phone in town with long-distance service. I've got to call Billy and find out what's going on."

Tex looked at me over the top of the newspaper. "You can't be serious. Do you even know where he is?"

"Well . . . no," I admitted. "But this is huge news! My best friend could be making the biggest mistake of her life, and I'm not even there to talk some sense into her."

"Let's see the letter," Tex demanded, taking it from me. He scanned it, processing her words. "She sounds happy to me. I'd let it go."

"*Let it go?*"

"Yes. Either he's the right guy, and he keeps on makin' her smile, or she gets bored of him and hops the next flight to Marrakesh or someplace else. Meanwhile, you've not done or said anything to bring her down, which means you're still a good friend. After all, isn't that what you were looking for when we first came here? An escape from judgment?"

Thinking back to that cold train station in Switzerland, I had to admit he was right. I hadn't told anyone we were leaving together, not even Daphne, because I didn't want to be talked out of such an impulsive decision. So who was I to dissuade her from doing basically the same thing?

"People have to be free to live their own lives. If I were you, I'd write her back, say you're surprised at her news, but don't give an opinion. Let her know you're there for her if she needs you. Tell her everything you've been up to here."

"Everything?" I flashed a wicked grin, remembering something we'd tried earlier that morning.

His hooded eyes darkened as he caught my meaning. "Well, maybe not everything . . ."

※

A few days later, Tex and I went in search of a secluded swimming cove we'd learned about in the village. After hiking down to the water, I pulled off my dress and jumped in wearing the new bikini from Daphne. Tex stayed on the rocks above, snapping photos while I swam. Once my limbs started to tire, I lay back and floated on top of the water, staring up at the sky. The silence was so peaceful; I imagined this was what it must feel like to be in utero, slowly forming, but not yet born.

Resting on a large, flat rock afterward, I let the sun warm my skin as Tex dug into the picnic lunch we'd packed.

"What are you thinking about?" he asked between bites of his sandwich.

"How this might be the most relaxed I've ever been in my whole life. You?"

He was silent for a moment more as he chewed. "Nothing worth gettin' into."

That piqued my curiosity. "Well, now you've got to tell me."

He sighed. "I'm thinking that I'm sitting here in paradise while guys younger than me are over in Vietnam just trying not to get shot today. I feel happy and guilty all at the same time."

I leaned up on my elbow. "What brought this on?"

He shrugged. "Maybe it was the newspaper Daphne sent. There was an article about the war, and about how more troops are being sent over. It could so easily be me. And why isn't it? What makes me so special?"

I turned onto my stomach and rested my torso on his legs, gazing up at his troubled face. "Well, first of all, you were born a little too early and missed the draft cutoff. Doesn't make you special, but it makes you lucky. What *does* make you special is that you shot your way out of Texas with a camera instead of a gun." I cleared my throat, preparing to say the words that had been in my head for quite some time. "And another thing that makes you special is me. Because somehow, you pulled off the impossible: you made a girl who wasn't sure she believed in fairy tales fall hopelessly in love with you. And if love isn't special, I don't know what is." I watched him absorb what I'd said. We hadn't uttered the words yet, and part of me had worried that saying "I love you" would be akin to diving off the cliff in Acapulco. But it wasn't that way at all—I felt like a jet leaving the runway, weightless and sure.

He sat, unblinking, before erupting into a brilliant smile and hauling me into his lap, arms snaking around. "Aw, Al, there you go, beatin' me to the punch. I've wanted to tell you I love you for weeks. And the feeling's only gotten stronger the longer we've been here. Seeing how brave you were, facing your father's death, playing the guitar, writing your songs . . . you amaze me."

Our bodies melted into each other, my hands clinging to newly bronzed shoulders as his tongue swept between my lips. We shared a scorching, soul-melting kiss, until the ache to feel him inside me became too great. Keeping our mouths fused, I reached around to undo the clasp in the back of my bikini. The strapless top fell between us, and my bare breasts pressed against his chest.

"Jesus, Al, tell me you want this as bad as I do," he panted.

I nodded, desperate. It had never been this frantic before, as though we might both come undone if the hunger wasn't sated.

Tex laid me down on the blanket, and I raised my arms above my head, reveling in his gaze as he pulled my bottoms off. I bared my naked body to the sky, wanton and alive. The rock was hard against my spine, almost painful, but it only sharpened the intensity of the moment.

My eyes rolled backward as he entered me, focusing on the cloudless sky, the unyielding sun. It beat down on us, warming my blood, stoking a fire that burned from the inside out. I was Icarus, racing toward the heat, higher and higher until that slow, delicious melting of my wings. Like molten wax I dripped, over the rocks and into the sea, drowning in my pleasure.

Afterward, as our heartbeats finally started to slow, Tex pulled back onto his forearms and looked down at me with wonder. We kissed again, understanding the magnitude of what we'd just shared. I knew for the rest of my life I'd never forget this moment under the blue sky of Formentera, when I'd given all of myself, body and soul, to Jack "Tex" Fairchild.

Minutes later, the spell was broken by a loud wolf whistle through the trees. I sat up, suddenly alert, as Tex moved quickly to shield my body with his. Emerging from the nearby forest, two long-haired couples in loose clothing smiled and waved at us. Tex cursed, scrambling to cover me with the picnic blanket while he pulled on his swim trunks. As the couples made their way toward our swimming cove, I clutched the blanket tighter and tried to pull my bikini bottoms on underneath.

"Sorry, we didn't mean to chase you away!" one of the women yelled out. "Live and let live, right?"

"That's okay," Tex called in response. "We were leavin' soon anyway."

As the group got closer, I noticed they were around our age, perhaps a little younger. Hippies, by the looks of their worn clothing. One of the men stuck his hand out to greet Tex. "Hey, man— good to see another American around here. Been awhile since we've heard English."

"I'm Tex, and this is Al," he introduced us, while I tried to pull myself together. "We've been on Formentera since January. How about y'all?"

"Just passing through. We were on Ibiza, and a fisherman said we should check this island out. So far, I dig it."

"Is the water warm?" his girlfriend asked, with a dreamy, stoned quality to her voice.

"Not really. But you get used to it."

"Far out." With relaxed grace, she pulled off her dress, and her friend did the same. Both were completely naked underneath. The men began removing their clothes as well, and I looked away. I knew I wasn't one to pass judgment, especially after what Tex and I had just done, but being confronted with a stranger's nudity still made me uncomfortable.

Tex cleared his throat. "We'll let y'all enjoy your swim. Maybe we'll see you in the café if you'll be stickin' around town. Watch out for the Civil Guard—you never know who's got eyes and ears here."

The tall man with shaggy blond hair shrugged and smiled. "Appreciate the warning. Peace, brother." He flashed the sign with his fingers, and the other three members of his party followed suit. I blushed, awkwardly returning the gesture.

Tex grabbed our picnic sack and put his arm around my lower back, steering us away. "You can put your clothes on in the woods," he whispered into my ear. As we climbed barefoot over the rocks, I turned back to watch the group of friends splashing in the turquoise pool. They were nomads like me, but they'd rejected all trappings of polite society. Now that I'd gotten a taste of that same freedom, I didn't know how I'd ever be able to give it up.

That evening, I reclined on the couch, tinkering with a new song. I'd finally worked up the courage to approach the owner of the Café Sirena about doing a small set in two weeks, and to my surprise, he'd agreed. It would be my first opportunity to play in front of strangers, and every time I thought about it, my stomach did a somersault. Gerhard had promised to come and clap the loudest, so at least my audience would be enthusiastic, if not large.

Tex sat at the kitchen table, looking over some negatives with a magnifying glass. My humming must have caught his attention, because a few minutes later I sensed him looming over my shoulder.

"Did you need something?" I asked, distracted as I tested out a chord progression. My fingers were still getting used to the additional strings of the guitar.

"No, just glad to see you so excited."

"You mean about something other than you?" I asked wryly.

"I meant, it's good you're workin' on something that makes you happy."

I shook my head, waving him off. "It's just a song. For a show that maybe three people will attend."

"Well, whatever it is, you're motivated, and I think that's great. Can you tell me what it's about?"

I hesitated, not sure if I wanted to put the idea out into the world yet. Once it left my lips, it was a concrete thing and no longer just a passing fancy in my head.

"It's about how my father found this island, on a sailing trip with Mother and some of their friends. How he saw it and immediately began painting a picture in his mind. It would turn out to be his most famous work."

"*Abstract No. 7*? That's Formentera?"

I nodded. "It was the color of the sea that inspired him. It was a living, moving thing, but just as it could pull you in, it could also suck you under. Savior and executioner all in one."

Tex sat down and brought my ankle up into his lap, massaging my foot. "I think you're really on the right track with this," he said, putting pressure on my arch. "And hey, maybe when we leave here, you can audition for some of the clubs in New York. Your stuff's ten times better than anything I've heard at the Bitter End."

My insides twisted at the thought. I hadn't let myself consider the day when decisions would have to be made and he'd be forced to return to his old life. Would I have a place in it? And what about *my* old life? Was I ready to give it all up?

"Will you go back to magazine work?"

He frowned. "I don't know. A few months ago, I would have said yes. Now, it just seems so silly. Photographing all these pretty places, and pretty people, when there are bigger stories that need to be told. I'm not sure if I'm capable of telling them, but I've been thinking more and more about taking a shot at it. Maybe you're not the only one who's trying to find their voice."

"What kinds of stories? Like civil rights?"

"Maybe." He shrugged. "It just seems like everywhere you look, things are on fire. People are angry, the world's gone to pieces, and I want to understand why. Even on Formentera, it feels like we're hiding from the truth. Franco's still on the mainland, people are still afraid to speak out against him, but here we are, livin' it up at the beach. I'm grateful to be here with you, but remember what I said when we first met about feeling like I'd be wastin' my life if I sat around doing nothing? Turns out it only took about six weeks."

I set the guitar down and swung my legs from his lap. Walking to the hi-fi, I selected a Chet Baker album from the stack and dropped the needle onto one of Daddy's favorite tracks. "My Funny Valentine" began to play, its melancholy notes calling out to us. I didn't want to think about the future, and the fact that part of me was starting to have the same worries. It was like Daddy's guitar had flipped a switch I couldn't turn back off. But how my dreams and desires fit with Tex's, I still didn't know. For now, I just wanted us to hold one another.

"Dance with me?"

He smiled and stepped toward me, wrapping his arm around my waist, his left hand cupping my right palm. The rain pattered steadily on the roof while the fire in the hearth crackled and popped. We swayed to the music, and I rested my head against his shoulder.

"Did you put this on because my looks are laughable?" Tex joked. "Unphotographable?"

"I put it on because it's Valentine's Day, according to the day planner I try not to look at. Though, come to think of it, your nose *is* pretty crooked." I smiled against him.

"Riding accident when I was twelve. But I'm okay being your funny valentine, as long as I'm your favorite."

"Always," I whispered.

The candles flickered against the stucco, and the lonely wail of a trumpet reflected the longing and sadness of my heart. *Stay, little valentine, stay . . .*

"You think your mom and dad used to dance to this song and feel like we do?"

I frowned, thinking about their relationship. I hadn't told Tex what I'd discovered about Mother and Maria, but maybe it was time. He'd seen the letter; he knew their marriage had had problems. "Maybe Daddy did," I said finally. "For Mother, it's a different story."

"What do you mean?" He searched my face, suddenly curious.

"She's . . . Tex, I saw something on New Year's Eve. Her and Maria. They were together. And not in the way that good friends are together, not like Daphne and me. It was more like . . . you and me."

His eyes widened in shock. I knew from our talks about Billy that he was open-minded, but that didn't mean he could have predicted this. I sure hadn't. "Holy hell," he said finally. "Did you know before?"

I shook my head. "No. Maybe? I don't know. They've always been close, and held hands, touched each other, but I never imagined it was anything like this. I don't know if it was going on when Daddy was alive, but something tells me it was. Now everything I thought I knew has been turned on its head. I'm not sure which of my memories are real, and which are just lies my mother told to keep up appearances. It's like when you showed me how a camera worked, and how changing the depth of field would change the image. The truth was always there, but my focus was too shallow to see it."

"Is that why you wanted to leave Switzerland so suddenly? Were you running from her and Maria?"

"In part," I admitted. "Also, I couldn't stay away from you. That first dance we shared in Acapulco, it's like I just knew—this is where I'm supposed to be. In your arms. But the rest of the world had to evaporate before we could be together."

"I promise, Al, with me, what you see is what you get. Just a simple guy who loves you. No secrets, no lies."

I hugged him tighter to me, allowing his words to seep through my clothes and skin and muscle, directly into my bones. Allowing them to fill the empty chambers of my heart. We wouldn't be like my parents; we couldn't be. I loved Tex with my whole heart, not just a piece of it. And feeling the steady beat of his as we moved, I knew he felt the same.

February 28th, 1967
Casa Kimball
Formentera, Spain

Dear Daddy,

Tonight, I'm performing at the Café Sirena. I've been practicing, trying out tunings on the guitar you left me. I've got some folk songs memorized, but I also have one of my own, about the island . . . and you.

Tex keeps insisting I'm ready, but I've had to remind him that you can't tell by looking at a person whether they'll sink or swim—you just have to throw them in the water and see what happens.

Love,
Caroline

SEVENTEEN

PAUSING OUTSIDE THE door to the Café Sirena, I took a deep breath, willing myself not to throw up. Behind me, Tex rubbed my shoulders. "You've got this," he whispered. As we stepped inside, my eyes adjusted to the interior lighting, and I saw several patrons huddled around tables. Maybe I wouldn't be the laughingstock of the entire island—just a tiny corner of it.

"*Mädchen,* you are here!" Gerhard exclaimed, shuffling over with his cane. He kissed me on the cheek before leading me to his table. "Come, I have ordered courage for you."

My brows knitted together as I followed him; his English phrases sometimes needed a translator. But when I saw what awaited us, I burst out laughing. Next to one of the empty chairs, there was a glass of wine, a glass of brandy, and a glass of pastis. "Gerhard! Are you trying to get me drunk?"

He patted my hand. "Just trying to relax you. If you drink all of those, you will not care if people are listening to your music."

"I also won't be able to *play* my music." I shook my head,

handing the brandy to Tex. "Here, you take this one, I'll drink the wine, and we'll save the pastis as a reward for the end. If I make it that far."

"You'll make it," Tex said. "And I hope you prepared extra songs, because we'll be callin' out for an encore."

I rolled my eyes, though I secretly loved how much he believed in me.

"Carolina?" the café owner called from behind the counter. "¿Carolina, está aquí?"

"Oh, that's me," I said, getting up.

"Carolina's her stage name," Tex explained to Gerhard. "Just one word, like Donovan or Cher."

I'd thought it was silly when Tex suggested coming up with a stage persona, but now I was grateful. Caroline was a person who lurked in the shadows, in her satin gloves and diamond earrings, waiting for her life to start. *Carolina* was a person who walked into the spotlight, in a simple sundress and plastic hoops, grabbing her future like a sailor hoisting the jib. Maybe Mother had been right all along in regard to my name—something I dreaded having to admit to her one day.

I checked in with the café owner, noting the lone stool set in a small alcove along the side wall, but thankfully there was no raised stage to make me even more nervous. No microphone either, but it was a small place; my voice would carry.

With the guitar strap secure around my neck, I walked to the stool and sat down, taking another deep breath. I strummed a few chords, testing out the tuning. Quickly, the ambient chatter died down as people turned curious glances to the girl with the guitar. I locked eyes with Tex, and he winked. Gerhard raised his brandy and gestured to the wineglass he'd set on a nearby table. I smiled and took a heavy sip. *Courage.*

"This show will be in English; I hope that's all right. A song is magic in any language, I've always thought. Maybe you already know this one: it's called '500 Miles.'"

And then I began. Immersed, I snuck a glance at Tex, our eyes meeting over the sounds and intonations that turned simple poetry into music. My voice was clear, fingers nimble on the strings. There was an unbelievable sense of rightness, of knowing this was what I was supposed to be doing. Singing about being far from home, not sure if you could ever go back. And worst of all, having left without the person you loved. This folk song I'd heard Peter, Paul and Mary sing dozens of times suddenly felt so personal, I ached inside.

As the final downward motion of my hand against the strings resonated, I raised my head and looked into my small audience. It took a second, but then Gerhard and Tex leapt to their feet, clapping and whistling. The other patrons followed their lead, cheering me on over cups of coffee and digestifs.

Blushing, I thanked them and started quickly taking my guitar out of standard tuning. Feeling emboldened by the applause, I felt ready to share the song I'd been working on for the last two weeks.

"This is one you haven't heard yet, but it was inspired by the beautiful island we find ourselves on. It's a little song I wrote for my father, called 'Blues Rushed In.'"

I closed my eyes and strummed the opening chords.

Churning water 'neath your feet
Ribbons of sun slashed through the wake
'Twas an abstract, a life renewed
With a beauty none could fake

Navy, turquoise, cerulean blue
Was this how it looked to you?
A god-made painting for anyone's taking
At long last, something true

Hands, tighten the sail
Hold back that violent wind
You were happy for a second
Till the blues rushed right on in

I made it through the first chorus before my finger slipped. An errant chord, jarring and out of place, made me look down in shock. That was all it took, just one mistake, before the song became a complete and total failure.

Trying desperately to press on, I focused on Tex's sympathetic, encouraging eyes, as though he could get me back on track just by wishing hard enough. But then I saw all the other faces in the room, patrons who now grimaced and looked on with pity, wondering when I'd do them all a favor and leave. And though I knew it was impossible, I thought I saw Mother's face in the crowd, wearing its trademark smirk, silently mouthing *I told you so*.

I started to forget words, then notes, and the room became blurry through my tears. With my face on fire, I finally reached the end. Not stopping to apologize for what had just happened, I felt my legs carrying me off the stool, through the crowd, and out into the cool winter air. I fell back against the stone exterior of the café, slipping the guitar off into the dirt beside me. The instrument landed with a thud, the discordant notes a perfect coda to this embarrassing night.

Beside me, the door swung open and Tex ran outside, his eyes wild with worry.

"Al! Are you okay?" He grasped my upper arms as I gulped oxygen into my lungs.

"She was right," I finally managed. "Everything Mother said was true. I'm ridiculous. A joke."

He shook his head. "No. You just got nervous. Your first song was great! The crowd loved it!"

"But it wasn't my song. When it came time to say *my* words out loud, I choked. I can't do this. Please take me home." I'd started to cry, and he pulled me against him, letting me soak his shirt as he cradled the back of my head. I heard the door open again and, looking up, saw Gerhard coming out.

"Oh, *Mädchen*," he sighed when he spotted me. "I am so sorry. You will get them next time, I know it. The astronauts still haven't hit the moon, yes? Art is no different than science. It takes work and practice, and above all failure. The only ones who succeed are the ones who never give up."

"I'm gonna take her home," Tex apologized. "We'll stop in and visit tomorrow."

Gently, he picked my guitar up and slung it behind my back. It felt like an albatross as I climbed onto the scooter, wrapping my arms around him. As we took off gently down the road, I raised my head to the sky and let the cold wind dry the tears from my cheeks.

Back at the cottage, I grasped my guitar by its neck and lifted it off my shoulders, the strap brushing the stones of the front path as I walked to the door. Tex followed close behind.

"You want a drink?" he asked once we'd stepped inside.

"How about a dozen?"

On the counter was a bottle of whiskey, and he poured a generous amount into a glass. I gratefully took it from him before collapsing onto the couch in defeat. He sat down beside me, not saying a word. Giving me time to speak first.

"I'm so ashamed," I finally said. "How am I ever going to show my face in that café again?"

"Don't. Don't go feelin' sorry for yourself. You're better than that. What Gerhard said was true—it's not about being perfect right out of the gate. It's about failing and learning from your mistakes. You think my first photos were any good? They were trash. Maybe I should be embarrassed for ever showing my sorry excuse for a portfolio around New York City, but I'm not. Because the rejections I got from editors and agencies made me want to try even harder. Hell, I'm still tryin'. Real artists never stop."

Tex took my empty whiskey glass from me and set it on the coffee table. "Look," he continued, "did tonight go how we thought it would? No. But think of that first song you sang, how you held the audience in the palm of your hand. Remember *that* feeling. Maybe you weren't ready to sing your own stuff yet; that's fine. But someday you will be."

I sighed, my head resting on the back of the couch. "It was like Daddy's final painting. Up there, on that stage, I felt like I was drowning. I couldn't breathe."

Tex stood up, reaching out for my hand. "Come with me. I want to show you something."

I let him pull me toward the back patio, to the pool illuminated from below. Following his lead, I removed my clothes with heavy arms. I wanted to lose myself in him, just for tonight. Once we were both naked, he took my hand and led me to the water, flinging us over the edge, landing with a loud splash. Legs pumping, we grasped for one another, straining against the frigid water lapping at our skin. Tex pulled us toward the shallow end, backing me up to the edge. It felt like that night in Acapulco all over again, but this time, I didn't hesitate to find his lips, to press my mouth to his, to run my hands over his back and shoulders, clutching him to me. He wasted no time in cupping my jaw, taking me roughly against the cement wall, our tongues tangling and teeth scraping.

"You ever think you're gonna drown, remember how it feels to jump into the deep end," he whispered against me. "Your legs want to kick; you just have to let them."

"What if you're not there to pull me to the shallows?"

"You'll get yourself there on your own. My siren." He gently grasped my neck, stroking his thumb over the hollow of my throat.

I pulled back to look at him, his eyes burning black coals. My pulse throbbed against his fingers, and my bruised lips begged for more.

"Sing again. Sing for me now," he demanded, reaching down to find my center, that place where life and love began. Grasping his shoulders, my head tilting in rapture, I stared up at the ocean of stars and did as he asked. It was a song of no words, but a ballad all the same.

EIGHTEEN

ON MY WAY back down the road from Gerhard's house in early March, my feet stilled the moment I noticed a sporty red car parked in our driveway. Curiosity turned to dread as a gloved hand extended from the passenger-side door—Mother's. Maria got out the driver's side, cat-eye sunglasses obscuring her face. I fought against my instinct to hide in the bushes before they saw me, reminding myself that I wasn't a scared little girl. I'd have to face them sooner or later.

With my legs dragging, I approached as Maria unloaded bags from the car. I knew the instant Mother spotted me, because her spine straightened. I hadn't forgotten how we'd left things in Switzerland, and I knew she hadn't either.

"*Ciao, piccola mia*," she called as I got closer. "I almost didn't recognize you."

I glanced down at my denim pants and plain white t-shirt, tucking an errant lock of hair behind my ear. "Hello, Mother." I leaned in, quickly air-kissing her.

"Caroline! Is good to see you, my darling!" Maria exclaimed, wiping her palms on her red shirtdress before bringing me in for a warm hug. "You look well. Your cheeks—they have color again."

While part of me was glad to see the woman I'd always thought of as a favorite aunt, I couldn't shake the anger and hurt that came with knowing I'd been lied to my whole life. *She* had lied to me. I lightly patted her back, shrugging out of her embrace. "I didn't know you were coming," I said to both of them.

"How could you? Your father never installed a long-distance telephone line." Mother rolled her eyes with disdain. "I considered wiring, but then decided a surprise might be more fun." Her sarcastic tone implied not all had been forgiven. "And where is that young man of yours? What's his name? Nevada? Dakota?"

"Tex," I answered through gritted teeth. "He's out taking pictures. I was just up the road visiting Gerhard."

"The old man is still here?" Mother clutched her necklace in surprise.

"Yes, and he's become a very good friend."

"Careful with that one," Maria interjected. "Ema and I always suspected there was more to his story here than just olives."

"Like what?"

"I don't know, but I've always said, never trust a man with too much idle time," Mother replied.

"You seem to like dressing them," I pointed out. "Maybe fit him for a suit and see if you feel differently."

She waved me off, set in her crackpot theories. "We should get inside. Perhaps you can help Maria with the bags?"

I hesitated for a moment, then came out with it. "Just to warn you, Tex and I are in the main bedroom. Together. The second one is mostly usable, but you might have to move some things around."

"I see," Mother replied after a pause. "Well, we won't disturb the happy couple. Maria and I can manage just fine." Stone-faced, she turned and walked into the house.

Maria squeezed my arm in reassurance. "She *is* happy to see you, *principessa*. Just give her time. This place . . . it is not all happy memories for her."

I nodded, grabbing one of their many suitcases. Our little slice of paradise had just gotten a lot more crowded.

※

Later, I was helping Maria arrange cushions on the patio furniture when Tex returned on his bicycle. I waved and ran to meet him before he got to the house.

Stopping at the bottom of the driveway, he pointed behind me to the car. "You get tired of the scooter, or do we have company?"

"The latter, unfortunately. Mother and Maria got here about an hour ago. I had no idea they were coming, which was the point, I think. Mother loves a surprise."

He chuckled, smoothing my hair back behind my shoulder. "I've met Emanuela. She doesn't scare me. I can take care of myself. And you."

I leaned into his touch, resting my neck against his hand. "God, I want that to be true."

"Did you show her the note yet? The one from your father?"

I shook my head. "Still working up to that."

We walked his bicycle to the shed, then went to face the inevitable. Stepping inside, I noticed Mother had already covered the kitchen table with drawings and fabric samples. As a little girl,

I'd been fascinated by her design process. For all her faults, she was a gifted artist. But for some unknown reason, she didn't think I could be one too.

"Mother, Tex is back," I called toward the bedroom. He set his camera down, leaning over her sketches to get a better look. I turned on the stereo, letting it cycle through Daddy's 45s on the autochanger.

"These are good," he commented, picking a drawing up. "Your mother does all these herself?"

"But of course," Mother said, entering the room, fresh from a bath. Her hair was pulled up in a silk scarf, and she wore a matching housecoat. "How else to communicate my ideas?" She glanced over his shoulder to examine the drawing he held. "A true artist never lets others do the work for them."

"What about Warhol?" I asked. "Don't his assistants do the paintings now?"

"*Pfft!* Soup cans and Brillo boxes? Not a true artist."

"Emanuela, I like a gal who knows her mind," Tex laughed. He leaned down to kiss her cheek, as he'd often seen me do with others. It wasn't his way, but he knew it was Mother's. "Pleasure to see you again, ma'am."

She took a drag from her cigarette. "How are you finding the island, Mr. Fairchild? I see you've gone quite natural with your appearance." Her finger pointed at the beard he'd started to grow, and the shaggy hair that now fell past his ears. I hadn't thought he could get any sexier, but in two months here he'd proven me wrong.

"It's incredible! I'm hoping I can talk *Life* into a story about this place. The landscape, the water, the remote beaches; it's unlike anything else I've shot. I can understand why Mr. Kimball bought a house here."

"I would have rather he settled on Bermuda or Capri, but David hated crowds. He rarely got any visitors on Formentera. Until his funeral, of course." Mother looked off to the side, frowning. I'd never seen her cry over my father, not once. Knowing what I did now, about her and Maria, I wondered if she'd ever grieved him at all.

"Enough of this talk." She waved a hand to chase away the gloom. "Caroline, have you heard the news about Daphne?"

"You mean about her and Dickie Waddlestone?"

"They were the talk of Montego Bay. And now Palm Beach. I wouldn't be surprised to get a wedding invitation by the end of the year."

"Yes, she wrote to me. Seems she's madly in love. I just hope he's worthy." For all her flamboyance and wild ways, my best friend's heart was the biggest one out there. It would take a special person to match it.

"Oh, are you talking about Daphne?" Maria asked, coming into the house. "We saw her with her *ragazzo* in Paris just before they left for Jamaica. I've never seen her look so happy."

Just then, the first record ended and the next one started. "Cry" by Johnnie Ray. The opening notes played through the speaker, and Mother looked abruptly at the turntable. "That song . . ." she said, walking toward it as though possessed. "Where did you get this?" She flashed a stricken face at me.

"In the shed. Tex set up a darkroom in there, so I moved some of Daddy's things to the main house."

Mother's skin had gone pale. She turned back to the record and removed the needle with a harsh scrape.

"Never play it again."

"I'm sorry, I—"

She silenced me with her hand. "I'm going to the cellar to choose a bottle of wine. Maria, I need your help."

The two of them left, and I frowned up at Tex. "She looked like she'd seen a ghost."

"Maybe she just heard one."

I rubbed my arms against the shivers. All the warmth Tex and I had made in this house over the last two months had suddenly vanished.

After supper, we remained seated around the outdoor dining table, watching the candles burn lower and lower. Two empty wine bottles sat between us, with a third slowly disappearing. Tex had grilled the meat we'd picked up in town the day before, and Maria had contributed a salad of fresh herbs, vegetables, and some of Gerhard's olive oil. The meal was pleasant enough, conversation circling around the gossip from Paris and London, Mother's criticism of Oleg Cassini's latest collection, and the unusually warm winter we'd had on the island. I'd started to think we'd managed to avoid conversational land mines altogether when, after four glasses of wine, Mother turned to Tex. Her face was a mask of determination in the dancing candlelight, and I knew the scorpion was preparing to bite.

"Mr. Fairchild, I feel I am at a disadvantage. You've seen so much of our life, capturing it with your camera, whereas we know nothing about yours. Tell us—what is your life like back home? And where is home exactly?"

He smiled, probably assuming she was making innocent chit-chat. "New York City, ma'am. I have an apartment in Greenwich Village. It's not much, but a lot's happening in the area. Especially right now."

"Ah yes. The protests, the marches, the music of Bob Dylan—what a fascinating time to be an American, no?"

"You said it. That's something I miss here; we're so isolated from what's goin' on in the world."

I hated when he brought this up. It made me feel like I wasn't enough for him.

"So, this apartment," Mother continued, still focused on Tex. "Do you live there alone?"

"No, ma'am, I have two roommates. One writes for the *Times*, and the other's a photographer like me."

"My, that does sound cozy," she tsked. "Particularly if you bring my daughter back with you. I assume you won't be going your separate ways when your little vacation here comes to an end?" She glanced between us. Maria stayed silent, her eyes directed down toward her glass.

"We haven't made any decisions yet," I answered coolly.

Tex looked at me, unsure of what to say when faced with the Inquisition.

"Hadn't you better decide soon? I assume Mr. Fairchild has responsibilities back in New York. Unless, of course, you'll be handling the bills?"

"No, ma'am, I'd never take advantage of your daughter that way. I provide for what's mine. And just so's we're clear, she's mine now." His jaw locked tight, and he reached for my hand under the table.

"I can't pretend to know what photographers make these days," Mother responded, lifting her palms in surrender. "But if you believe you can keep my daughter in the type of life she's accustomed to, I think that's wonderful. I have a real estate acquaintance who would be happy to help you find a suitable apartment. Perhaps something on the Upper West Side, near the park. I'd offer my own assistance, but it's been quite some time since I've called New York home."

"Mother, if he likes his apartment in the Village, then I'm sure I will too. After all, an artist's life was good enough for you when you married Daddy."

She raised an eyebrow as if to say touché. "You're right. David was a painter when I met him, and his creativity was very exciting at the time. But your father was not *just* an artist. He was also the heir to an oil fortune, with a three-story townhouse deeded in his name. Not a small apartment shared with two other men."

"I can get used to it." My words sounded hollow even to my own ears.

"You shouldn't have to 'get used' to anything," Tex said. "If you want a nicer place, I'll find a way to make it happen. I've saved money over the years, and I can try harder to get a permanent staff job at a magazine."

I didn't want to contradict him, even though I doubted he understood the kind of money it would take to set us up in the manner I was used to. "Being with you is what matters most. We don't have to figure this out tonight."

"Yes, you have—what?—a week? Two? How long were you planning on staying here?" Mother persisted.

"We're still deciding," I responded, my voice icy. "And on that note, Tex and I are going to turn in. It's been a long day." I pushed my chair back from the table, collecting our wineglasses and the empty bottles.

He hurried to follow, desperate not to be left alone with Mother and Maria.

"Of course. Good night, children," Mother said, reaching for her cigarettes.

"'Night, ma'am. Maria."

"*Buona notte*," Maria replied with an apologetic smile.

Leaving our dishes in the sink, I steered us back to our bedroom, the only safe haven we had left. Once the door closed, Tex turned to me and exhaled, tension releasing from his shoulders. "I feel like I just went ten rounds with a firing squad."

Flinging myself onto the bed, I covered my face with an arm. "I tried to warn you. She finds the one thing she knows will cause trouble and just picks and picks at it. I'm so sorry."

"Hey, nothing to be sorry about," he said, lying down next to me. "I hate to admit it, but she *is* right. We have to make some decisions soon. Maybe it'll be easier with her crowdin' us out of here. At this point, I think I'd follow you anywhere."

"How do you feel about Saskatchewan?"

Chuckling, he began to kiss our troubles away, until the worries and doubts flooding my mind faded to the background.

※

The next morning, our strained coexistence came to an end with a knock on the front door. I heard it from our bedroom just as the island birds were beginning their morning reveille. Assuming Mother and Maria were still asleep, I covered myself with a sweater and dashed to the foyer. On the front step, I discovered a boy, roughly ten or eleven years old, holding an envelope out to me with supreme authority. Grabbing some change from the nearby table, I tipped him and watched his brown eyes widen with delight as he scurried back to his bicycle.

Shutting the door, I tiptoed back to the bedroom.

"Who was that?" Tex asked, his voice muffled by the pillow he spooned.

"A messenger. Somebody's sent a telegram." Sitting on the bed, I sliced a fingernail through the fold and pulled out the Western Union correspondence:

> *Dearest Caroline. Dickie proposed. Wedding in Palm Beach.*
> *Three weeks. Come at once. Maid of honor, darling.*

Tex moved closer, alarmed by my sudden gasp. "What's it say?"

"Daphne's engaged! She's getting married in Florida and wants me to fly there immediately."

"I'll be damned. That girl moves fast," he marveled with a whistle. "So, you gonna go?"

"I don't see how I can refuse. She's my best friend. But it means leaving here . . ."

"It had to happen eventually," he said, rubbing my back. "As much as I disliked your mother's line of questioning last night, she wasn't completely off base. I *do* have a life to get back to in New York."

"But what about us? Can't you stay with me a little longer and be my date to the wedding?" I asked hopefully.

He smiled and brushed his lips against my shoulder. "Of course I'll be your date. But I should go home first, deal with some business. I've got some retouching that needs doin', and I can't finish it in that little darkroom here. Besides, you ladies don't want me taggin' along while you look at dresses and flowers."

I knew he was being sensible, but I couldn't shake an ominous feeling. My father had abandoned me for reasons I still didn't fully understand; without the constant daily nurturing of our love, would Tex do the same? Would he get sucked back into his old life and forget about what we had here? Would I?

"All right. As long as you promise to meet me in Palm Beach as soon as you can." I nuzzled against him, memorizing his scent.

"I promise, Al. Now hurry up and take off that nightgown. We've got to make the most of the time we have left together."

I giggled as he pulled me under him, letting myself be distracted from the knowledge that someone had finally righted the hourglass. On the nightstand, I could've sworn I heard Daddy's pocket watch tick once.

NINETEEN

STARING AT THE suitcases on the bed the following day, it finally hit me—we were leaving. I fingered the edge of Daphne's telegram, reminding myself why we had to go. Tex planned to take a boat to Ibiza that afternoon, and from there, sail to the mainland to get a flight to New York. I was scheduled to leave the next morning with Mother and Maria, eventually catching a ride on Birdie Fitzwilliam's jet. Heiress to an old railroad fortune, Birdie was headed to Nassau but had agreed to drop me off in Palm Beach on the way. It felt wrong not to go with Tex to New York, but I was desperate to see my best friend before she became Dickie's wife.

"You ready to say goodbye to Gerhard?" Tex asked, stepping out of the bathroom.

"I guess." My voice was glum. "He sleeps late, but I hate to wait any longer."

Tex and I were silent as we headed down the dusty road, our fingers laced together as though knowing we had to savor every second of contact. It would have to be enough to last us the next three weeks.

We stepped onto Gerhard's front porch and knocked twice. Eventually, the door opened to reveal a hastily dressed old man, hair still rumpled from sleep.

"*Guten Morgen!* What are the two of you doing up so early?"

"We've come to say goodbye," I explained. "I'm sorry if we woke you, it's just that we couldn't leave without seeing you one last time."

"Leaving! Oh dear, come in, come in." He shuffled aside to let us pass. Tex and I walked through to his kitchen with Gerhard following, his cane dragging on the tile floor.

"Would you like me to put some coffee on?" I pointed to his percolator.

"Yes, that might be a good idea. I don't often see this hour of the day." He yawned as he sat down at the table.

"Like Caroline said, we're sorry for wakin' you. But I'm headed to the mainland today so I can fly back home. She's leaving with her mother tomorrow."

Gerhard squinted at us, his forehead wrinkling. "Not together? And why so sudden?"

"My best friend is getting married in Florida, and she's asked me to be the maid of honor. It's a very short engagement, and she needs help with the planning. Tex will join me in a few weeks. Believe me, we both wish we had more time here on the island with you."

Gerhard raked his hand through his gray hair, smoothing out the kinks. "I'm glad you came, even if it was to share sad news. But perhaps you will consider returning to visit your old friend someday?"

"Of course we will! Gerhard, you've become like family to us.

As soon as I know where I'll be after the wedding, I promise to wire you with the address. I want us to stay in touch."

"That is a promise I hope you'll keep." He pointed his crooked finger at me, smiling. "After all, I'm still on duty to guard your father's painting."

I smacked my forehead. "Oh my god, the painting! In all this rush to leave, I completely forgot. Do you mind hanging on to it a little longer? I just—I need more time to think about what I should do with it."

"That is perfectly fine, my dear. Take all the time you need." Then he turned to Tex. "And you, young man—headed back to New York?"

"Yes, sir. I've got to find out what's become of all the pictures I've been taking here. See if there's anything true in them."

"Ah. I hope you've taken many photos of our girl." Gerhard gestured to me.

Tex grinned. "Too many to count. That's the only thing that's making it easier to say goodbye to her: knowin' I'll still see her face every day we're apart."

His words poked at the anxious part of my brain, reminding me I didn't even have the bare minimum of a photograph of him to take to Florida.

"But speaking of photos," Tex continued, "I'd love it if I could take your picture. Who knows, maybe you'll need it for your next book jacket."

Gerhard waved him off. "I don't know if I have any more books left in me. There are stories, but none I want to share yet. However, a photo of one friend taken by another—*that* I will allow, if you promise to send me the very best one you've got of our Caroline."

"Deal. I was thinking maybe outside, near your olive trees. The light is just about perfect this time of day. Does that sound all right?"

Gerhard shrugged. "I am at the mercy of the artist."

I stood up to go. "I'll leave you men to it. This should be a private portrait session."

"Are you sure, *Mädchen*? You are welcome to stay."

"No, it's okay. I've still got some packing to do, and I'm sure Mother needs help. I'll just say goodbye now."

Gerhard rose to hug me, and a lump formed in my throat as his thin arms closed around my back. "Special girl. Don't ever stop singing. That is your gift to the world," he whispered into my ear. I tightened my hold around his shoulders.

When we finally separated, I wiped the tears from my eyelids. "I'll miss having you so close. But we'll write, and someday I'll make it back here."

Gerhard nodded, his eyes misty. "So this is not *auf wiedersehen*. This is . . . *bis dann*. See you later."

"*Bis dann*." I kissed him once on the cheek, then headed to the front door, leaving a tiny piece of my heart behind in that kitchen.

Returning to our house alone, I found an unfamiliar car parked next to Mother's. Inside, she and Maria were speaking rapid Italian to a man with a clipboard. He wore narrow wool trousers, a pink tailored shirt, and a polka-dot-printed ascot—obviously not a native islander.

"What's going on?" I asked, stepping into the living room. Their conversation halted, and Maria looked at me with a guilty face.

"Darling. Allow me to introduce Alberto Francesco de la Monteforte. An old friend in real estate." Mother swept her fingers gracefully toward him. "Alberto, this is my daughter, Caroline."

"Charmed," Alberto greeted me, moving to where I stood rooted near the fireplace. He took my hand and kissed it with panache, bowing slightly. "Your mother was just giving me the tour. Such a fabulous property; it should go quickly."

"Go? Where is it going?" I didn't need this nonsense today. We had enough happening as it was.

"I've decided to sell," Mother explained. "It's too much work to maintain, and it's very inconvenient to get here. Maria and I feel our time would be better spent elsewhere."

"But you can't sell," I reminded her, indignant. "Daddy left it to both of us."

She frowned. "I am aware. Perhaps the two of us should speak alone. Maria, would you be good enough to show Alberto out to the pool?"

"Of course. Right this way." She herded him toward the door next to the kitchen.

As soon as they were gone, I turned back to Mother. "You can't do this. This is as much my house as it is yours. I'm not giving it up."

"Sit, please." She pointed to the sofa. Claiming a spot at one end, she lit a cigarette and moved the ashtray on the coffee table closer.

I sat as far from her as possible, arms crossed over my chest. As I opened my mouth to speak, she held up a finger to silence me. "What I have to say is not easy. Just give me a moment." She took a drag and stared at the fireplace. Finally turning back to me, she exhaled. "We don't have a choice. We *must* sell the house."

I shook my head. "There's always a choice. We can tell Alberto to go home right now."

"We cannot do that. You see, my darling, we're broke."

Her words bounced off me like a child's rubber ball. Surely I'd misheard. "Broke? What do you mean broke? That's impossible. Daddy left us a fortune. Between his paintings and his family money, we'd never be broke."

"I am very sorry. I'd hoped to spare you from the pain of what I went through as a young woman. But it's true. I invested the money in my business, and we've had some setbacks. Maria did what she could, but the House of Leoni is in trouble. The money is gone."

Confusion and anger burned inside me. Her words were a contradiction to everything I'd been raised to believe. We had money; we would *always* have money. "But Daddy left me a trust that's mine alone."

"A trust that you do not have sole control over until the age of twenty-five. I am the executor, and at the time, I deemed it necessary to divert the funds to the company. We had an exciting new collection planned, and I thought I could pay it back with interest. But rising labor costs and abysmal sales for the last three quarters have made that impossible."

"Is there anything left?" I shook my head, my voice bleak.

"A few thousand. Unless, of course, you decide to sell *Ojos Verdes*."

I tightened my lips in defiance. She knew damn well I'd never give it up.

Mother cleared her throat, gazing at me with wary eyes. "I've . . . had a proposition. One that would save the company and ensure your security forever. You wouldn't have to sell anything of your father's, and all of us would be taken care of. You, me, Maria, and Leoni."

"What sort of proposition?" I asked, my hackles already raised.

"It seems Henry was quite distraught after Switzerland. His father contacted me to see if there was a chance of repairing your relationship."

"What does Henry have to do with anything? I'm with Tex now. We're in love."

Mother's face twisted with pity, and she shook her head. "My darling girl. Don't you see? A future with the photographer is impossible now. That's what I was trying to suggest the other night. He cannot support you in the manner to which you are accustomed. But Henry, and his family, can."

The blood drained from my face. "What did you do?"

She took a deep breath. "Henry's father has agreed to an immediate investment of one hundred thousand dollars if you take his son back. Two hundred thousand if there's a marriage."

"No!" I stood to pace in front of the fireplace, rage coursing through me. "I don't need your money, or Daddy's money, or Henry's, or even Tex's. I'll find a way to take care of myself."

Mother leaned back, taking another drag of her cigarette. "Caroline. Don't be stupid. What skills do you have? Perhaps you could model, but how long before your looks fade or tastes change? You must think about the long term. I'm sorry, but this is the way it is. We are women; our choices are not our own."

"Maybe that was true for you, but it's not for me," I argued. "Did you notice the guitar in the corner over there? I've been playing it, and with enough time, I think I could be good, Mother. Really *good*."

"It takes more than talent and hope to make it in this world. If that were all a person needed, I wouldn't have had department store buyers and wealthy women turning their noses up at the young immigrant with the sewing machine. No, I found out first-hand that success requires power, and connections, and money. What will you do with this guitar when you leave the island? Play dirty clubs and street corners, surviving on tips? The life you think you want—singing, Tex—it means sacrifice, and I don't think you have any clue what you're in for. I certainly didn't when I was your age."

"Is that what you meant when you said you'd been in my situation before? You were broke, and that's why you married Daddy?"

"In part," she acknowledged. "My family was in a precarious position under Mussolini. I was also in love with someone I knew I'd never be able to be with. So when my parents sent me to America with instructions to find a husband who would keep me safe, I agreed because my freedom of choice had already been taken away long before. At least, by marrying your father, I would be wealthy enough to support what truly mattered to me."

"Maria."

She gave a slight nod. "Also, my designs. I knew with his pedigree behind me, my work would be taken more seriously. And I was right."

"Did you ever love him?" My throat cracked, and I turned to face the mantle. I wouldn't let her see me cry.

"Of course I did." Her voice was sharp, surprising me. "Is it the way you love this 'Tex'? No. But it's the way you could love Henry if you gave him a chance. A love based on respect, admiration, and gratitude. And if you are very lucky, he will make you laugh to spite all the world's cruel unfairness. Give you new dreams to replace the ones you left behind."

"Tell me about the day Daddy died," I choked out. "You always refused to answer my questions, but I need to know."

I turned as Mother's face paled, her shoulders sagging under the weight of her secrets. Then she sighed, as if realizing she couldn't hide the truth from me any longer.

"In the beginning," she finally said, "I needed a husband to gain entry into society and hide my relationship with Maria. David was obsessed with me, and I used it. He loved me too much for his own good. Maria and I were always careful for so many years, but one night he discovered us together. It was the beginning of the end. His mood swings got worse, his work frantic and violent. Eventually, I decided it would be safer to send Maria away."

I shook my head in disbelief. This picture was nothing like what I remembered. "When did all this happen?"

"You were at boarding school. I was grateful you didn't have to see the wine- and urine-soaked sheets he woke up in, or the canvases slashed to bits, like a tiger had been set loose in the studio. The winter you were seventeen, I sequestered him on the island, attempting to keep his illness a secret. Not even Gerhard knew how bad he'd gotten. I tried to talk him into seeking help. Perhaps some time away at a sanitarium would do him good, I suggested, when he hadn't left his bed in days. He said he would think about it and sent me into town for cigarettes. I came back an hour later to an empty house. I searched outside, then went to the shed." She looked away, lost in the trauma of that night.

"I heard the music first," she continued. "That awful Johnnie Ray ballad, made grotesque by the sight of David hanging from the rafters. His neck was at an unnatural angle, and I knew immediately he was gone. I crumpled to the floor and stared at his body, wondering how he could do such a thing to us. Oh, I knew how he could do it to me, but not to you. I can't say how long I sat there, that stupid record repeating over and over. Was this his revenge? Did he understand what he was doing, or was he too sick? I'll never know."

With a shaking hand, I reached into the pocket of my dress and pulled out the note I'd kept with me every day for the last month. "Tex and I found this in the shed. It was up high, easy to miss." I still didn't tell her about the painting. "I know it's for you, but I read it anyway. I'm sorry."

She took the letter from me and opened it, her fingertips covering her lips in shock. I saw tears fill her eyes at the sight of my father's handwriting. Shaking her head back and forth as she read, she whispered, "Oh, David. You beautiful fool." Reaching the end, she looked up at me, her expression raw. "I'm grateful he left something, however small. He's right—you are the best of both of us. And despite what you might think, I *am* being strong for you. I push you toward Henry because I want you to have the entire world at your fingertips. His money and contacts will give you every opportunity. He is not troubled like your father was, and despite this dalliance with the photographer, I know you truly care for him—your story can have a happier ending than mine."

As I opened my mouth to argue the point that a marriage with Henry might also become a prison, the door from the patio opened and Maria started back in with Alberto.

"Ay, I am sorry." She stopped short, confronted with our grief-stricken faces. "I do not wish to interrupt. I can show Alberto to his car, perhaps."

"No, it's fine, Maria. We're through." My mother sniffed and carefully folded Daddy's note, placing it in her pocket. "Caroline has all the information she needs."

I wiped my cheeks. "Excuse me, I need to finish packing. Tex will want to leave for the harbor as soon as he gets back." With my head down, I walked to the bedroom and closed the door behind me. I shoved the suitcases out of the way and flung myself onto the mattress, my sobs filling the tiny room.

※

Gazing into the mirror over the dresser, I barely recognized the face reflected back. Even though I'd taken time to fix my hair and apply some light makeup, inside I felt like something had died. Tex and I were quiet as he organized rolls of film, notes on what he'd shot, and the few clothes he had. I hadn't told him about my conversation with Mother; I still didn't want to think about what she'd said.

Once his things were packed, we carried his bag and satchel out to her car, and I got in the driver's seat.

"Shouldn't I say goodbye to Emanuela and Maria?" he asked.

I waved the idea off. "I'll give them your regards. Come on, you don't want to be late." I stared straight ahead as he settled next to me, hearing him close the door with a soft thud. The slightest touch or sideways look would shatter my control, and I didn't want to make this harder on either of us.

As the car traveled down narrow dirt roads, a warm breeze blew through the open windows, swirling my hair. I absorbed the earthy air of Formentera, breathing in the scents of pine trees, brackish salt, and juniper. Tex had his arm resting on the windowsill, one finger held up as if to let the island flow over him. Soon the harbor came into view, and I spotted a boxy fishing boat anchored to the dock. There were several people milling about, smoking and waiting for the crew to finish their preparations.

"There's a space over there." Tex pointed toward the edge of the dirt lot. I parked and turned off the ignition, a sense of déjà vu washing over me. I hadn't been behind the wheel since we'd left Gstaad, and I recalled the anticipation I'd felt before meeting him at the Hotel Olden. It seemed like a lifetime ago.

"We'd better get your things."

He nodded, stoic. Stepping out of the car, he retrieved his bags from the trunk and set them next to his feet. He took my hands in his, and it was all I could do not to start sobbing again.

"You don't have to be strong, Al," he said, stroking my hand with his thumb. "Lord knows the thought of gettin' on that boat without you is killing me."

"Really?"

"Of course," he said, his eyebrows pulling together. "I love you, remember? Even if we're only apart for three weeks, that's three weeks too long."

I pressed my forehead into his chest as his arms wrapped around me. We latched onto each other, already mourning the island and the halcyon days we'd spent here. I didn't have the heart to tell him we might never be able to recapture them. Not now.

"Damn you for changing everything. For changing me," I blubbered into his shirt.

He rubbed my back, soothing me. "How do you mean?"

"You made me start wanting things. Music, love—all the messy, complicated stuff that can lift you up, then wreck you once it's gone. That's why I'm terrified of you getting on that boat, and why I lived so long the way I did. Flying from place to place, running away from anything that gets too serious—it's safer that way. You can't lose what you never had to begin with. But now it's all different. *I'm* different. I let you in, and now I have to let you go."

"Hey, now, you talk like you'll never see me again. But I swear to god, I'm coming to Florida," Tex promised. "No matter what, I'll be dancing with you at that wedding."

His words reassured me, though they didn't completely remove the anxiety churning in my stomach.

"And here, I've written down my phone number in New York." He slipped a scrap of paper into the pocket of my dress. "You call that whenever you want, no matter what time it is. And before you know it, we'll be back together again." His voice broke at the end, and when I met his eyes, I felt the desperation in them. He wanted to believe this was just a temporary separation as much as I did.

A foghorn sounded, signaling that it was time to board. Tex hugged me tighter, crashing his lips into mine. Our kiss was ecstasy and agony all at once.

Breathless, he pulled back and said, "I love you to the stars and back. Keep singin' so I'll always be able to find you."

"I will, I promise. I love you too."

He stepped away, and with one last woeful look, turned to the boat. I watched him go, wishing I could follow him down the gangplank, knowing it was impossible. As the vessel began to pull away from its mooring, he reappeared on the stern, seeking me out in the small group of well-wishers. I raised my arm to wave, blowing him a kiss. He lifted a hand to catch it, and I didn't look away until the boat and Tex had become just a tiny speck on the horizon.

Minutes passed, and my body remained there long after the others departed, waiting for something I couldn't put a name to. Beyond the dock, the water glistened in the overhead sun, shadows of seagrass lurking below. Daddy's ashes were part of that world now, part of that strange underwater landscape that grew and prospered in briny, filtered light. I walked to the end of the boards, grasping a wooden pylon. Anger battled with sorrow, turning my vision blurry.

With an animal rage I hadn't known I possessed, I closed my eyes and screamed. I screamed for the father who'd left me, and the mother who'd betrayed me. I screamed for the circumstances that kept pushing Tex and me farther apart. Most of all, I screamed for myself: the chessboard pawn who never managed to advance.

Sucking air over raw vocal chords, I dropped to my knees, the pieces of my broken heart pounding inside my chest. In that moment I understood how my father could have given in to such dark temptations. The real world was waiting, calling to me from the other side of the looking glass, but what I wouldn't give to stay on the island of make-believe forever. To sink down into the grass and never again be the one who was left behind.

PALM BEACH

March 9th, 1967
Palm Beach, Florida

Dear Daddy,

Time is moving again, but there's been a mistake. Somehow, the clock hands are going in reverse. I'm back in the world of pink hotels and polo matches, but it may as well be the surface of the moon. Nothing feels familiar; not anymore.

Is this what it was like for you every time you left Formentera? Like you had two separate lives— the real one and its abstraction? Which one is even real?

Send me a clue?

Some sign of what I should do?

Love,
Caroline

TWENTY

STEPPING ONTO THE patio of the Wentworth-Waddlestone mansion, I raised a hand over my eyelids, blinking against the bright Florida sunshine. Opulence spread before me like a mirage—Greek revival columns and balustrades ringing the manicured yard, yellow umbrellas shading coordinating table and chair sets, and crisply tailored black-and-white-striped chaise cushions next to the oversized swimming pool. The air was thick with the cloying fragrance of roses and privilege.

"This way, miss," a maid said, gesturing to one of the tables beside the pool where a group of ladies sat.

A shriek pierced the quiet morning as a blur of tanned skin and blond hair hurtled toward me.

"Darling, you're heeeere!" Daphne wrapped me in a hug, as though it had been years, not months, since we'd parted in Switzerland. She stepped back and held me at arm's length, taking in my appearance. My hair had gotten longer, and I hadn't been motivated to put on much of a face. Freckles be damned.

"You have no idea how much I've missed you!" she exhaled in relief. "Dickie's mother has been driving me crazy, *my* mother is only interested in rubbing her latest lover in Father's face, and his infant wife has been acting like my long-lost sorority sister. Billy's been keeping me sane, barely. And, of course, Dickie." Her smile widened at the mention of her fiancé.

"I still can't believe it," I admitted, shaking my head. "You're engaged! How did that happen? To you of all people?"

"He swept me off my feet! I didn't think I was the marrying kind, but Dickie convinced me otherwise. I would've said yes even if he hadn't coughed up this enormous rock." She displayed her hand, stunning me with the size of her engagement ring. "But a little jewelry never hurt anyone."

"I can't wait to get to know him better." I linked my arm through hers as we walked down the steps. "I probably didn't make the best first impression."

"Oh, darling, don't you worry. Dickie still feels awful for letting you go off with that disgusting Roger."

I shivered internally at the memory of Roger's hand on my thigh. I'd tried hard to put it out of my mind, but I doubted I'd ever be able to forget the bone-deep feeling of panic I'd experienced in that hallway. "So what happened to you after I left? You never gave details in your letter."

Daphne sucked in a breath before launching into her story. "Well, once he realized I was incapacitated, Dickie put me in his room, then went to find you. When all he could find was your purse, he left it with the front desk, then came back upstairs to take care of me. Other men might have taken advantage of the situation, but not Dickie. He stayed awake on the couch the whole night, watching over me. When I finally came out of it, there he was with a cool towel for my forehead and the most lovesick expression I'd ever seen." Her eyes got soft at the memory.

"I really am happy for you." I squeezed her arm affectionately. "And just look at all this! When the taxi driver dropped me off, I thought I must have given him the wrong address. It has to be the largest mansion in all of Palm Beach."

"Second-largest, after that tacky monstrosity Mar-a-Lago," replied a sour-faced woman with leathery skin and a platinum-blond bob as we got closer. She looked like a constipated doppelgänger of Doris Day.

"Mrs. Waddlestone, allow me to introduce my maid of honor, Caroline Kimball, daughter of David Kimball and Emanuela Leoni. Caroline, this is Dickie's mother, Elizabeth Wentworth-Waddlestone, of the publishing and media Wentworths."

"Bitsy, please," Mrs. Waddlestone said, extending her slim hand to me. I was familiar with the Wentworth media conglomeration, which started out in newspapers, books, and magazines before transitioning toward WBS—the Wentworth Broadcasting System of television and radio. Meanwhile, the Waddlestones were best known for having patented the technology that fueled those new industries. "I met your mother once at a party. Fascinating woman."

"Ah, small world." Too small. "She's in Nassau with Birdie Fitzwilliam at the moment, but she plans to be here for the wedding."

"Yes, darling, I *do* hope your mother understands that while I would've loved to have had her sartorial guidance on my dress, we all decided something more traditional might be better suited to the occasion," Daphne apologized.

"Of course." I'd already gathered that Bitsy would be the one calling the shots over the next few weeks. "Listen, as eager as I am to talk about what's been planned so far, it might be best if I got settled in at the hotel. I'm a little jet-lagged." This was putting it mildly. After a ten-hour flight and a six-hour time difference, I didn't know which way was up.

"Don't be silly, Caroline, you're staying here. Right, Mrs. Waddlestone? I mean, Bitsy?"

"Yes, I've already had Mabel make up the room next to Daphne's. It will be much more convenient for us all." Waving to the pretty young woman standing in the shadows, she directed, "Please show Miss Kimball to the lavender room. On the northeast side."

Privately, I was relieved not to have to spend what little funds I had left on a pricey hotel. "Well, all right. And thank you, Bitsy, that's very generous."

"Of course. Just tell Mabel if you need anything special for your stay. We serve cocktails at five. I hope you'll join us." She lowered her sunglasses back down, the conversation evidently over.

"Come on, race you up there." Daphne tugged my hand as she dashed toward the house. Turning my head, I saw Bitsy's mouth tighten into a frown as she shook her head at the retreating back of her soon-to-be daughter-in-law. Surely nobody would ever accuse Dickie of having an Oedipus complex.

With Diana Ross crooning from the bedside radio, I unpacked my things into the antique chest of drawers. My guitar case rested on the floor, along with the smaller ukulele. I had some clothes from Formentera, but I'd need to go shopping to blend in with the fashion mavens down here. Lilly Pulitzer's boutique would be my next stop, after Daphne's closet.

"We got your care package. Thanks for sending it," I said, shaking the wrinkles out of a sundress. "Tex liked the Buffalo Springfield album."

"I thought he might." Daphne lay reclined on the bed with a bridal magazine. "So, he didn't come down here with you?"

"No." I shook my head sadly. "He had to go back to New York to sort through his slides and check in with editors. He'll be down here for the wedding, though. He promised."

"Do you think he'd be interested in being the wedding photographer? Mother and I haven't chosen anyone yet, and I'm sure she'd be willing to pay handsomely. She'd love the idea of hiring someone who shoots for *Life* and *Vogue*."

"I'll give you his number so you can ask him, but I'm sure he'll say yes. We'll need the money."

"We?" Daphne looked up from her magazine. "So there's a definite 'we'?"

I didn't know where to start. "It's complicated. I know I said before that I didn't know how he fit into my world, but for two months it was like we made our *own* world. But now I'm here, and he's there, and I guess I'm back to being uncertain. Almost like this winter was just a dream, and we finally had to wake up."

"Is it just the money? I know it's a bit awkward that you have it and he doesn't, but that could change. Just look at David Bailey. Photographers, good ones, are in high demand now. You never know where Tex could end up."

I bit my lip, desperate to confide in someone. "No, it's not that, but for the record, I don't think he'd be put off by my ability to support him. Thing is, I can't support him now, even if I wanted to. My inheritance is almost gone."

I heard an audible gasp across the room. "Gone? What do you mean gone? Did you and Tex have a stopover in Monte Carlo and lose it on the roulette wheel?"

"I wish. That would have been more fun." I paused for a moment, before reminding myself that Daphne was my best friend. I could trust her. "Mother invested it in her company, which is now going belly-up."

"Oh, darling, how dreadful!" Daphne exclaimed with genuine sympathy, getting up to hug me. "You know if you need any help, you just have to ask. Dickie's very generous; he'd do anything for my family or me. And *you're* my family. Besides, I've got plenty of my own money socked away for a rainy day. It's yours in a second."

"No." I shook my head vehemently. "I couldn't take a handout. There's no need to worry, I'll figure something out. But if you really want to help, you can let me borrow some clothes while I'm here."

"Done. My closet is yours." She squeezed my arm and sat on the bed again. "I can only imagine how that conversation with Emanuela went."

I barked a sarcastic laugh at the memory. "Oh, just peachy. Particularly when she told me she'd sold me to the Halliday family for a cool hundred thousand."

"WHAT?!"

"Yes, it seems Henry isn't handling our breakup too well. His father agreed to invest in Mother's company if I take him back. And given my irrational need for approval from her, I didn't immediately say no."

"Bloody hell. And I thought *my* family was full of nutters."

I shook my head. "Mother's got 'em all beat. Except I'm not much better—I told her I'd think about it, even when I know deep down Tex is the love of my life. I just feel like I'm suddenly on this speeding train, and I don't remember buying a ticket. Tex is telling me to come to New York and pursue my music, Mother's telling me to marry Henry and keep the life I've always known, and neither one feels a hundred percent right. Even though I love Tex, I can't turn my back on Mother. Plus, I don't know if the New York scene is where I'm meant to be."

"Not to make things harder on you, but I have some news concerning Henry." Daphne sucked in her lips, looking apologetic. "You see, it turns out he and Dickie were both in the Porcellian Club at Harvard. With Roger out of the picture, Dickie needed a best man, and well . . ."

I didn't know whether to laugh or cry. It made sense, of course—everybody knew everybody in our tiny world—but just once I wished it could be a little less incestuous. "It's not your fault. I'd have to see him eventually, right? I didn't imagine we'd be thrust together in a wedding party, but I'll manage. When does he arrive?"

"Saturday, according to Dickie. He's finishing up a deal in LA with an artist he wants to sign, but he'll be staying at the Breakers when he gets here. Billy's there too. Oh, and did I tell you we're having the reception in their ballroom? The guest list is enormous—Bitsy's doing, not mine. Dickie and I would have preferred a small ceremony on the beach, but she's insisting on a church wedding. And, well, we couldn't have the reception at the Everglades because of some Jewish relatives on Father's side."

"Why do you care what Bitsy wants? It's your and Dickie's day. You should have the wedding of your dreams."

Daphne just shrugged. "Dickie loves his mother and doesn't want to disappoint her. He's already done that by showing up with me, so the least I can do is give him this. Besides, it's just for a few more weeks. After that, we'll be off on our honeymoon, then starting our life together in London. That's where we want to settle."

"*Settle*," I huffed, shaking my head. "I never thought I'd hear that word coming from you."

"Oh, we're not talking about me pushing a pram down Kensington High Street," she clarified. "No, London just seems quite exciting these days. Paris is too revolutionary, LA too polluted, New York too violent. But things are still swinging along the Thames. Dickie wants me to pursue my acting career, which I can do from there."

"It sounds like you've got it all worked out. I'm envious." She had no idea just how much. But jealousy wasn't a good look on anyone.

"Not everything is worked out. I still need *the dress*." Her face lit up at the prospect of an afternoon spent trying on gowns. "Come, then, put your shoes back on. Worth Avenue beckons!"

✳

My tired feet were crying in protest when Daphne finally suggested we stop at a café near Via Amore to rest. Finding a table along the crowded sidewalk, we plopped our bags onto an empty chair and relaxed against soft pink cushions.

"Good grief, how can one street be so long?" Rolls-Royces and Cadillacs meandered down the avenue, a shopper's paradise full of high-end boutiques and ladies who lunch. Women and daughters in matching Lilly Pulitzer dresses stopped to admire the windows, while men flitted in and out of Cartier. In this rarefied world of style over substance, who you wore eclipsed who you were.

"Shopping is a competitive sport here," Daphne declared. "But look at what we accomplished! A bridesmaid dress for you, shoes, bikinis, and cocktail attire. You should be all set now."

"I wish you'd have let me pay for some of it. I'm not destitute. At least, not yet, anyway. And I thought we were here to pick out a dress for *you*." Finding something that would please the bride, the groom, and most of all Bitsy was turning out to be a tall order.

She waved me off. "I'm not worried. Bitsy said someone in her gardening club can get me an appointment with her local couturier. And Father can pay anybody enough to do anything quickly." A white-jacketed waiter with a black bow tie approached with two menus, which Daphne declined. "We'll have a bottle of your best prosecco, two glasses, and one piece of coconut cake. We're celebrating."

He smiled in response. "Very good, miss. Right away."

"Oh god, you may have to carry me back to the car after this. Couldn't we wait until we're back at the house to drink?" I stifled a yawn.

"Christ, no. Bitsy's cocktail hours are horrendous. Dry martinis. Dry white wine. Dry conversation. Little cheese straw things that taste like sawdust. I'd like to actually enjoy myself, thank you very much."

Our prosecco finally arrived in a silver ice bucket with two crystal flutes. The cake and two forks were set between us, and we both salivated over the mountain of white frosting and coconut shavings. The waiter poured us each a glass, and we toasted to our friendship.

As Daphne's drink reached her lips, her eyes widened at something behind me. "Dickie!" she shouted, waving her arm. "Over here!"

I turned to spy gangly Dickie Waddlestone walking toward us. He looked much the same as he had in Gstaad: glasses, long hair flopping over his forehead, arms and legs not quite in proportion to the rest of his body. But he wore a brilliant smile at the sight of his fiancée that turned average into handsome.

"Buttercup!" He leaned over the iron railing, giving Daphne a quick peck. "We were just driving down the street when I spotted your beautiful face. And Caroline!" He pivoted to me, smiling. "How wonderful to see you again! This one's been talking my ear off for the last two months about how much she misses you. I had to propose just to give her a good excuse to get you back stateside." His joy was contagious, and all my doubts about the speed of Daphne's engagement evaporated. The man was smitten.

"Who are you here with?" Daphne asked.

"That's the best news of all! Henry arrived early! I told him Caroline would be here this afternoon, so he hurried up and finished his business in LA. He's just parking the car now. It was meant to be a surprise at dinner tonight, but we saw you both here and figured we'd move the reunion up a bit."

The blood drained from my face as I looked to Daphne in a panic. She grimaced, mouthing the word *sorry*. I took a hefty swallow of prosecco.

"Oh no, is something the matter?" Dickie asked. "We thought you'd be happy. The gang all back together, so to speak."

"Dickie, you know very well where Caroline's been the last two months. And who she's been with . . ."

"Oh, *that*. Don't worry, I know it was all a bit of fun. Caroline, I completely support the women's liberation movement. Why shouldn't you sow some oats before settling down, just like men do?"

Daphne groaned over his square expression.

Dickie, ignoring his fiancée's embarrassment, continued, "Henry's been so upset about how you left things in Gstaad, and I thought seeing you, being part of the wedding, might give you both a chance to patch things up."

"I appreciate that, Dickie," I replied, trying not to laugh at the idea of "sowing my oats." "Really, I do. I wasn't happy with how we left things either. If he's changed his mind about wanting to be friends, then I'm all ears. I just don't want anything to distract from what should be the happiest day of your lives."

"Ah, speak of the devil," Daphne cut in. "Hello there, best man!"

Henry waved to our small group and came jogging across the street. He looked largely unchanged since we'd last seen each other in Switzerland. To hear Mother tell it, I'd half expected him to arrive emaciated and sporting a five o'clock shadow. But his cheeks were freshly shaven, his hair perfectly styled, and his blazer casual but expensive. He looked like he belonged here, on this street made of wealth and image.

"I almost couldn't believe it when Dick spotted you two," he said, reaching us. "Must be meant to be. Caroline, you're looking well." He leaned down to brush his lips against my cheek, then said into my ear, "We need to talk. Soon."

I nodded discreetly, my conversation with Mother still fresh in my mind.

As they ducked around the iron fence separating the café from the rest of the sidewalk, I scooped up the spoils of our shopping day and placed them under the table.

"Brace, darling," Daphne whispered.

I reached for the prosecco and topped up my flute.

Dickie took the chair next to his bride, and Henry settled next to me, placing his arm around the back of my seat. Last year I wouldn't have thought twice about it, but now the walls were closing in.

"Is that coconut?" Dickie asked, pointing to our cake.

"Yes, and it's *divine*." Daphne speared a piece onto her fork. "Here, try some." She brought it to his mouth, and he moaned in ecstasy.

"Don't they just give you a toothache?" Henry said to me. "When Dick called with the news that he was engaged to Daphne DeVossier, I assumed he was joking. But when you see them together, it makes a weird sort of sense."

"Absolutely," I agreed, relieved to put the focus back on our friends. As the waiter brought more glasses to the table, I turned to face Henry. "I didn't even realize you and Dickie knew each other until today."

"Oh, sure—we go way back. When he asked me to be in the wedding and mentioned you were the maid of honor, how could I turn him down?"

I couldn't tell if he knew about the bargain our parents had made, but I wanted to believe he didn't. Henry had never been cruel, and no matter how badly he might want to reconcile with me, I didn't think he'd resort to bribery. No—that was a move straight out of his father's playbook.

I took another sip of prosecco, trying to act like this was just an ordinary day where four friends met at a sidewalk café and rejoiced in their unexpected reunion. But that picture didn't tell the whole truth. In reality, I felt like I was outside the frame, a voyeur to a life I wasn't part of anymore. And the girl in my seat, though she might look like me, was playing a dangerous game of pretend.

TWENTY-ONE

TWO WEEKS WITH Daphne passed quickly as we met with florists, caterers, bakers, and dress designers. As she got swept up in wedding fever, I savored these last days with her before she became a wife.

Often, I caught Daphne and Dickie staring at each other like two lovesick teenagers, and my chest constricted with thoughts of Tex. The ache only intensified the longer we went without speaking. I'd called him twice since arriving in Florida, and both times one of his roommates told me he was working late. I knew he'd agreed to take candid photos at the rehearsal dinner for use in the society pages, and Daphne's mother had arranged a flight for him. But even the knowledge that we would reunite in a week failed to soothe me.

Complicating matters was Henry. He'd been attached at the hip to Dickie, and thus to me every time Daphne and I took a break from planning. I knew I needed to speak to him about Mother's predicament, but it seemed there was never a time or place we could be alone. And truthfully, I didn't go out of my way to find one.

Things finally came to a head one night after dinner at the Wentworth-Waddlestone mansion. Daphne and Dickie had been discussing their plans for an extended honeymoon in Tehran, at the invitation of the Shah and his glamorous wife, Farah. They'd also make a brief stop in Cannes so Daphne could appear at the festival in support of *Blow-Up*, already a sensation in the US. She'd been in talks with the director for his next picture, shooting in the desert outside Los Angeles. Bitsy, already two and a half martinis in, frowned in disapproval. She was of a generation that believed the wealthy should stay out of the spotlight; the very idea of celebrity was considered gauche. If Daphne noticed her pinched face, she didn't let on.

Following dessert, most of our party dispersed to head back to the Breakers or to bed. As I pushed out my chair, Henry turned to me and asked, "Join me for some fresh air?"

I nodded, taking his hand. We stepped through the sliding glass door onto the patio.

"Wow, the sky is so clear tonight," I remarked, looking up. "I'll bet the moon is beautiful over the Atlantic."

"Come on, let's go see." Still holding my hand, he walked us down the steps, past the pool lit from below like a giant turquoise jewel box. Henry led me into a raised open-air pavilion centered on the edge of the lawn, which offered a perfect view down to the ocean. The sea was calm, the bright crescent moon reflecting off the inky water.

"I hope Daphne has good weather like this for her wedding," I said, leaning against a stone pillar.

"She wouldn't have it any other way." He stepped closer to me, close enough that I could smell the bay rum in his aftershave, see the tiny anchor pin holding his tie in place. It was all so . . . Henry.

"It's been great having time with you this week," he said, interrupting the silence. "I've been carrying a lot of regret about what I said to you on the mountain. You were right—there's too much history here. Losing you forever would be like losing the ability to breathe. It's only been three months and I'm already wheezing." The side of his mouth tipped up in a tentative smile.

"What you said to me, about not wanting to be my friend anymore—it really hurt," I admitted.

"I was angry. And jealous. Sometimes I wish I'd never gone to Switzerland in the first place. Maybe then you and I would still be a couple. Maybe we'd be on a path toward something even better."

"Henry, I—" The words caught in my throat. I had to get them out, no matter the consequences. "The truth is, I haven't been alone the last few months. I went to Formentera with Jack Fairchild. We were . . . together."

He inhaled deeply, exhaling as he closed his eyes. "I know."

I was surprised, although I guess I shouldn't have been. Gossip traveled fast in our circle. "How?"

"Daphne let it slip one night. She probably doesn't remember, but she said something about sending a box to you and your cowboy. I put the pieces together."

I stepped closer, to better see the look on his face. To see whether it was one of hurt, or acceptance. Curiously, it was neither—Henry was a frustratingly blank canvas.

"So you know I was with him. Do you also know about the deal our parents made? The one where I give up Jack and take you back?" My heart thudded in my chest. Just saying the words made me anxious.

He gazed out at the ocean, giving a curt nod. "I do. I know because I'm the one who asked Father to make it."

I sucked in a breath, shocked and betrayed. To think, I'd actually felt guilty for being so torn in Gstaad. "I don't understand. If you knew I was happy with someone else, why would you think I'd want to get back together? How could you possibly think bribing me could fix our relationship?"

"Caroline, we both know this guy is just a mistake you needed to get out of your system. He's not the type of person a girl like you would actually *marry*. He's a nobody, from nowhere. He could never offer you what you're worth."

With that, Henry reached into his pocket and pulled out a little velvet box. He grasped my hand and placed it in my palm. As he opened the top toward me, a large diamond solitaire winked in the moonlight. Blood pounded in my ears at the sight of a ring. It was finally real—that thing I'd been so afraid of for years. Marriage.

"What's this supposed to be?" My voice sounded strangled in my throat.

"An engagement ring, of course. Didn't your mother already explain everything? I just assumed you'd want to skip straight to the two hundred thousand. Not much point in dragging this out when we both know it's the best thing for everyone."

I looked at him, this person I thought I knew so well, but had clearly underestimated. He was no better than Roger, shoving his hand up my skirt in a hallway. Except Henry was smarter than that—he'd played the long game, lulling me into a trap I couldn't so easily escape.

"So, what now?" I huffed. "I'm just supposed to say yes, give up Tex, give up music, and then what? Play the happy little wife beside you? Do you expect me to *thank* you?"

Henry snapped the box shut, his expression growing irritated. "This doesn't have to be so hard, and I don't know why you're being dramatic. We were always going to get married! That's what everyone expected—you, me, our parents, our friends, everyone who matters. We didn't talk about it explicitly, but it was understood. You've had your fun—plenty of it, by the sounds of things—and now it's time to grow up. You're not going to run off with some starving artist and leave people to wonder what's wrong with poor Henry that Caroline Kimball would choose a piece of trash over one of the most eligible bachelors in New York City. That's not how this works. You're going to say yes because you want to protect your mother, and because you know deep down this is the way it was always supposed to be."

My anger intensified on hearing the insults hurled at Tex. For years, I'd put up with Henry's little digs and slights against my friends, thinking he just didn't know them well enough, but now it was clear: he wasn't interested in who people really were beneath the surface. All he cared about were appearances.

Sensing he'd pushed too hard, he backed off slightly. "I'm sorry, this isn't how I wanted it to go, but you've left me no choice. We're just lucky not many people know about your little indiscretion in Spain. And look, I'll even make you another deal separate from the one with your mother. No matter what happens, you keep that ring. There's proof I'm not the villain you think I am, Caroline. I just want what's best for both of us. I want to give you the world."

I shook my head. "No, you want to give me *your* world."

Henry stepped toward the edge of the pavilion, gesturing to the beauty around us. "And is that so bad? It looks pretty swell from where I'm standing."

I fisted the ring box, wishing I could chuck it into the ocean but knowing I couldn't do that to Mother. Her business was everything to her, and in its absence, what would she be left with? Would she be strong enough to carry on without it, or would the same despair that had claimed Daddy come for her too? I wasn't naive enough to believe that I, or even Maria, could ever be enough for her—she needed Leoni to survive. And I . . . I needed her. A daughter would always need a mother, even a frustrating one. Frustrating was better than gone.

"For the record, I hate that you put me in this position. But you're right: no point in dragging things out. You'll get your answer before the week's over." Turning my back on Henry, I stormed toward the house. As my feet crunched over the cool grass, I wanted to yell back that he'd forgotten the only word that should have mattered in this farce of a proposal—*love.*

After a restless night, I got out of bed early, itching to spend some time alone with my songbook. Not wanting to burden Daphne, I'd decided not to tell her about Henry's proposal. How could she even begin to empathize with my predicament? She still had a trust fund; the world still overflowed with possibilities for her. Whether Dickie was rich or poor was of no consequence. But Henry's status, and conversely Tex's, mattered. I knew it shouldn't, but it did.

Giving in to temptation, I tried on Henry's ring while sitting at my dressing table, extending my fingers to admire how the light reflected off the flawless stone. It sparkled, previewing the shine of a worry-free life. Hopelessly conflicted, I put it back in the box, nudging the lid shut with a quiet thud. Out of sight, out of mind.

With my notebook tucked under my arm, I ventured outside to sit next to the pool.

Dear Daddy,

I can't stop thinking about your final painting. Were you picturing Caló des Mort when you made it? That was your favorite cove, and I never realized the meaning of the words until recently. Des mort . . . "of the dead."

What must it feel like to let your lungs fill with water and slowly allow your body to stop fighting? Is that what marrying Henry would be?

Picture her floating
Adrift under the waves
Mermaid's hair flowing and tangling
A siren, wild and free

Legs, keep on kicking
Arms, keep on reaching
Eyes, what do you see
Is it the darkness, or is it me?

The words practically poured out. Focused as I was on the lyrics, it wasn't until a patio door opened that my concentration finally broke. Bitsy appeared in a gauzy caftan, trailed by a maid with coffee service.

She waved as she approached. "Don't mind me," she called. "I'm an early riser."

I turned down the page so I could come back to it later.

Lowering herself onto the chair next to me, Bitsy opened a newspaper, her family's name on the masthead. The maid poured her a cup of coffee and a glass of orange juice from the carafe.

"Another beautiful morning," she remarked, scanning an article.

"Yes, and your pool is so lovely."

"I used to love swimming as a little girl. Father would bring the family down here for the season, and it was a nice break from New York."

"I can imagine. My"—I stopped myself before saying the word *boyfriend*—"friend Tex is there right now, likely shivering. Daphne's mother is flying him down here to take candid shots during the rehearsal dinner and reception. That's more his style than the formal posed pictures."

"Ah, yes, the *other* photographer. The artist. Though he's more than just a friend, no?" Her eyes met mine over the newspaper.

I blushed at her observation. "You could say that."

"I've heard my son and Daphne speaking in hushed tones about him. But then I saw you with Henry, and I wasn't sure of the situation. He's besotted with you. Henry, that is."

"Yes. It's . . . complicated."

"Things usually are when they involve matters of the heart. In my day, it was easier. There was a basic understanding that, when you belong to a certain world, your affections aren't solely your own to manage. There are mergers in business and in families. Publishing isn't doing so well, you need more technology to venture into new areas of entertainment, so you strike a deal. That's life."

I nodded, surprised by her honesty. "Let's just say I'm not sure whom this particular merger would benefit. If anyone."

"What does your mother think?"

"She's all for the combining of resources." I leaned back in my chair. "Except there's the thorny matter of my feelings to consider."

"And that's the unfortunate thing about young ladies today," she said, frowning. "Modern films and books have told them they have choices, but do they really? Until a woman has the desire and ability to stand on her own two feet, her life will never be truly free."

"Tex says sort of the same thing. That I should figure out what I want to do and make a go of it. Build a life of my own, pursue my passion. Maybe spend less time sitting next to swimming pools."

"He sounds wise," Bitsy acknowledged. "Though I've always found swimming pools to be absolutely essential."

I smiled, surprised at our camaraderie.

She took a sip of coffee and glanced at my notebook. "And what have you got there? A diary?"

"No. Well, sort of. They're song lyrics. That's what I really want to do—write and perform my own songs. I just don't know yet how to make it happen."

"A musician! You surprise me, Caroline. I assumed you wanted to be an actress like your friend." She said the word *actress* like it was dirt on the bottom of her shoe. "At least what you want to do takes some measure of talent. You're not just repeating words someone else told you to say. Or taking your dress off for the 'art' of it all."

"Actually, my mother doesn't think it's respectable at all. In fact, she told me when I was sixteen that she couldn't imagine anything more vulgar than standing up in front of people to sing some moony poetry. But Tex, the photographer, he encouraged me to try. And our neighbor, Gerhard Nussbaum. He's been a good friend."

"Nussbaum?" Bitsy gasped. "My family's publishing house has been pursuing him unsuccessfully for years. You say he's a neighbor?"

"Yes. We have, or rather *had*, a house on Formentera, where I've been living. Gerhard's property was next door."

"Is he working on anything new?" She sat forward, her attention piqued.

"I don't think so." I shook my head. "He says there's nothing left to say."

"Millions of readers would probably disagree. But then, what do I know? I was muscled out of the business years ago." She picked up her newspaper again, snapping the fold in frustration.

"Have you ever considered going back to work? Now that Dickie's grown and probably starting a family of his own soon?"

Bitsy's lips set in a thin line. "Mr. Waddlestone, my husband, prefers that I devote myself to more philanthropic efforts. But just between us . . ." She paused, lowering her head to stare at me over the rim of her sunglasses. "I think about it every day. Editing—that's what I wanted to do when I was your age."

"Wow, that's . . . surprising. I'm sorry, I can't think of a better word."

"No, that's the sign of a good writer. Why use a ten-dollar word when a nickel will do?"

A lawn mower started up in the distance, and I smiled to myself, thinking back to my father's unwavering belief that people were a lot like paintings—they both consisted of a thousand layers, only a few of which were visible to the naked eye.

✳

Walking into the Breakers later that night, I spotted Billy camped out at the end of the bar. Low lighting enveloped the cavernous space, and coffered, frescoed ceilings evoked a Venetian palazzo. Tuxedoed bartenders shook and stirred cocktails with a focused intensity, adding to the impression that the hotel existed in a vacuum of time. No matter the century, this was a place for gloves to be worn, cocktails to be sipped, and secrets to be whispered.

Planting myself on the stool next to Billy, I signaled the barkeep for another round of whatever my friend was drinking.

"Well, aren't you a sight for sore eyes," Billy exhaled, turning to me. "I was about to go trolling for a date so I wouldn't have to sit here alone."

"In this room?" I lifted an eyebrow.

"You'd be surprised."

"Sorry I was late. Daphne needed last-minute help with the floral arrangements for the reception. Or rather, she needed a referee between her and Bitsy."

"Ugh, that sourpuss. Wouldn't know style if it bit her on the butt. And would it kill her to smile once in a while?"

"She's not so bad."

Billy looked at me as if I'd grown two heads.

"No, really, she's not," I insisted. "We had a chat by the pool this morning. She's not the stodgy old society maven everyone makes her out to be."

"Then who is she?" he asked, still skeptical.

"A woman with limited choices. It takes one to know one."

"Care to elaborate?"

I sighed. "Henry proposed last night."

Billy lowered his daiquiri in shock. "You're kidding!"

"No." I shook my head. "I wish I was."

"But you two broke up! This guy wants to skip dating again and go sprinting down the aisle—the balls! Does he know about Formentera?"

"Yes, and he doesn't care. Or maybe he cares too much. I suspect the whole thing is more about saving face than building a life with me."

"And is that what you want? A life with Henry?"

I shook my head in frustration. "No. Obviously I want to be with Tex. But things are complicated."

"When two people are in love, what else matters? Not that I really *know*, but I've heard . . ." A melancholy expression flickered across his face; gone before I had the chance to read into it.

"Love isn't always enough. Particularly when it means giving up everything you've ever known and betraying someone in the process."

"Bullshit. What would you really have to give up? Your father left you money; just use it to buy an extra seat for Tex wherever you jet off to."

I took a long pull of my drink. Even though Billy wasn't the first person I'd discussed my new financial reality with, it wasn't getting any easier to talk about. "Listen, I'm about to tell you something you cannot repeat. To anyone. Swear?"

"Cross my heart, princess." He swiped his hand across his chest.

"Okay, here goes. My mother spent most of the money from my trust fund trying to save her business, which is now bankrupt. Henry's father offered her a hundred thousand dollars if she'd convince me to reconcile with Henry. Two hundred thousand if there's a wedding." Billy's eyes widened further, but I wasn't finished. "And then there's Tex. He says he can support us, but we certainly wouldn't be staying in places like this ever again." I gestured to our surroundings. "Plus, choosing him means turning my back on Mother, and although she and I don't have the best relationship, the damage could be permanent. I can't lose another parent—even a bad one."

Billy was silent for a moment, then shook his head. "I'm sorry that happened, sweetie, and I'm ready to throttle Emanuela on your behalf, but as someone who came from nothing, I can tell you *this*"—he pointed to the lavish lobby—"isn't all it's cracked up to be. Think about it—were you happier in a five-star hotel before you met Tex, or with him in a shitty little cottage shagging like rabbits?"

"Obviously the cottage. And it wasn't shitty. The rabbit thing, though . . ."

"Was there room service?"

"Does Tex bringing me water he pumped from the well count?"

"I rest my case."

I rubbed the stem of my glass between my fingertips, contemplating his words. "So, love. Is that really all we need?"

"You tell me." He raised an eyebrow.

"You know Henry never once used the word *love* in his proposal? He made this big speech about how we belong together, how it's always been expected, and how he wants to take care of me. Yet he never said he loved me. Meanwhile, Tex and I say it freely to one another, but I've started to realize love doesn't necessarily equal a future. I try to imagine myself fitting into his life in New York, but for some reason I can't see it. And not because of the money, but because it feels like I'm stepping into someone else's future instead of my own. At that point, I may as well just say yes to Henry. At least Mother would be happy with me, for once."

We both stared down at the bar, my words echoing in my head. Billy took another sip of his drink before harshly slamming it down in frustration.

"Princess, I adore you, but I can't listen to another episode of your crazy version of *The Dating Game*. You have doubts about Bachelor #1 and Bachelor #2? Then pick Bachelor #3."

"What do you mean?" I asked, my forehead wrinkling in confusion.

"Me. Pick me."

I laughed. "I didn't think I was your type."

He shook his head. "Look, this isn't public knowledge yet, but I'm moving to Los Angeles full-time. Jay Sebring offered me a job at his salon on Fairfax, and I've accepted."

I felt like I'd had the wind knocked out of me. Billy, not traveling? Not fluffing Taffy's wig everywhere from Vegas to Lisbon?

What was the world coming to? "Wow, that's fantastic!" I choked out. "He handles all the big stars!"

"I know. I accepted because it's a great opportunity, and I'm ready to settle down in one place." He hesitated. "But here's the thing—you could come with me."

"What? What would I do in LA?"

"Make a demo. Play clubs. Network. Meet other musicians, work on your songwriting. You could make a life for yourself beyond all this. Figure out what it is that *you* want. Not what other people want for you. I don't know what my life's gonna look like out there, or yours if you come, but isn't that the point?"

"It sounds amazing," I admitted. "It could be just the push I need to get going, plus I'd love to be closer to you. Do you think Tex would come with me?"

"I think that's a question for him, not me. Though if you wanted to split the rent three ways on a place together, I wouldn't object. When's he supposed to arrive? This seems like a conversation to have in person."

"Friday, in time for the rehearsal dinner. Daphne's mother got him a room here."

"If he knows what's good for him, he'll get on board. But even if he doesn't, you've still got one guy who'll gladly come to all your gigs."

I smiled with gratitude. "Billy, what would I do without you?"

"Sweetie, the feeling is mutual. You and Daphne make life interesting."

"Who would have thought that between her and me, I'd be the one with two men on a string, and she'd be the one headed to the altar?"

"At this rate, I'm expecting Rock Hudson to walk in and tell me he's always had a thing for skinny Jews who smell like Aqua Net."

I shrugged. "Anything's possible."

TWENTY-TWO

ON THE MORNING of Daphne's rehearsal dinner, the Wentworth-Waddlestone mansion hummed with activity. Caterers and florists scurried like geckos while Bitsy barked orders and Mabel huddled on the sidelines in terror. Fifty members of the upper echelons of society were set to arrive that evening for a dinner party at the most beautiful private property in Palm Beach. It would be a small preview of tomorrow's event for three hundred guests.

Seeing that Bitsy had things under control, Daphne and I retreated to the Breakers to wait for Dickie and Henry while they finished a round of golf. I still hadn't mentioned Henry's proposal to her, and it didn't appear as though he'd told Dickie. Not that this was surprising—he'd learned from his father to never announce a sale until the money was in the bank.

As Daphne flipped through a magazine and I tried not to think about the ring box burning a hole through my purse, she said, "So, Dickie told me this morning that one of the guests tomorrow will be Lou Adler. Do you know that name?"

My eyes widened in shock. "Of course! He's the producer who discovered the Mamas & the Papas!"

"Well, right now he's in talks with WBS about a variety special with several of his artists, but I also know from Dickie that he's selling his stake in Dunhill Records to start another label." My ears perked up at that. "Anyway, it got me wondering if he might be in the market for a new act for this new label. A girl who writes her own songs and has a voice like nothing else the world has ever heard."

I tried to stop myself from getting too excited, but couldn't discount the possibility that this could be one of those lucky breaks a person only gets once in their life. "What are you saying?"

"I'm saying, maybe you'd want to perform a song at the ceremony tomorrow. That way, he'll be forced to listen, and so will all the other narrow-minded people in our parents' circle who think girls like us should stay in the background as window dressing. You can show them. Show them we're more than our gowns and diamonds and husbands."

Although I was grateful for her generous offer, the prospect made my pulse race. Would it be a repeat of the Café Sirena disaster? Would my hands shake as I stumbled through forgotten lyrics? This wasn't a café full of strangers; it would be a church filled with people who knew me and were all just waiting to see me fail. They would repeat the story for years: *Oh, remember when David Kimball's daughter made a fool of herself singing at that wedding? Darling, you would have just* died.

Just then, the familiar click of a camera shutter startled me from my mental spiral. I turned, and a happy shriek burst from my lips the second I spotted Tex. Not caring that several dozen

sets of eyes were now curiously watching, I raced across the
lobby, crashing into him.

Laughing, he pushed his camera aside and wrapped me in a
hug. "Hey, Al, what's shakin'?"

"I missed you so much," I cried into his neck. In an instant, I
knew I could never give him up for good. Not for all the money
in the world. I still had problems, and my and Mother's futures
were anything but certain, but losing him would only make everything worse. We'd figure out a way forward, together.

"I wish I could say three weeks without you was no big deal,
but damn if it didn't feel like three years." Tex pulled back, pushing a strand of hair off his forehead. He was even more handsome
than I remembered, though I was a little disappointed to see he'd
shaved—the bearded cowboy of Formentera was no more.

"Welcome, welcome, Mr. Fairchild. Took you long enough,"
Daphne greeted him, rising from her seat.

"Daphne!" He leaned down to give her a hug. "Congratulations
to you and Dickie. And thanks for the gig."

"No, thank *you* for agreeing to shoot this silly old thing. It's not
every bride who gets a talented artist to cover her wedding."

"Not sure this will require much talent. With you and Al in the
frame, it'd be impossible to end up with ugly prints. Easiest job
I've ever had." He turned to me. "Speaking of, you won't believe
how incredible the shots from the island turned out. The travel
editors at *Life* want to do a big spread in the June issue."

"That's fantastic! I can't wait to see them!"

"I saved the private ones of us and Gerhard for your eyes only.
They really kept me goin' during the weeks without you."

"Ooh, Caroline, you didn't tell me you spent the winter posing
for naughty pictures," Daphne teased, winking.

My face turned beet red, remembering the moonlit night by the pool. "No comment. Tex, have you checked in yet?"

"I was just about to. Do you have time to come up to the room with me?" He ran his thumb over the back of my hand, and just that one simple touch was enough to make my blood churn with desire. But while my body demanded he take me upstairs, my brain told me to slow down. We had a lot to talk about, and not nearly enough time right then.

"I *really* wish I could, but we've got lunch plans. I would cancel, but we're going straight from there to the church to walk through tomorrow's ceremony." Plus, I needed to work out a plan for my performance. I didn't want anything to outshine Daphne and Dickie's ceremony tomorrow, but maybe I could make it even more memorable. "I'll see you tonight, though, right? I know you'll be working, taking photos, but maybe we can sneak away for a bit. Or after the rehearsal dinner . . . ?"

"Of course. I understand." He was as easygoing as always, but his eyes betrayed his disappointment. "You should be with your friend. We'll find time for us later. I've got something I want to talk to you about."

"Me too—"

"Caroline, darling, I just spotted Dickie," Daphne interrupted, pointing to the courtyard. "We should probably go."

I sighed. "Get settled in here," I said to Tex. "Later, you're mine." Kissing his neck, I inhaled his familiar pine and citrus cologne. Tonight we'd make up for precious lost time.

※

Bitsy's backyard was already bustling by the time I made my
entrance to the party on Billy's arm. He'd prepped Daphne first
so she could begin greeting guests with Dickie, then afterward
set my hair into a high chignon. My makeup included dark Yardley
eyeliner, long fake lashes, and pale lips. I wore a dress Daphne had
purchased for me, a black figure-hugging sheath with cutouts at
my hip. Billy said I looked like a mod version of Holly Golightly,
but I doubted many people would even notice. Tonight belonged
to Daphne, who, in her iridescent gold minidress, was already the
center of attention.

I spotted Tex right away, snapping photos of guests by the
pool. The sunset bathed the patio in soft pink tones, and I already
knew his pictures would be stunning.

"Caroline!" Henry waved to me across the lawn. Shooting an
apologetic glance over to Tex, I walked with Billy to meet the best
man halfway.

"Henry." I leaned in to greet him. "Have you been here long?"

"No, just long enough to see Bitsy's head explode at the sight
of Daphne in that dress. What was she thinking?" He shook his
head in disgust.

"She looks beautiful," I argued.

"Yes, but it's not appropriate for this type of event. At a disco, sure.
But at a semi-formal dinner at your mother-in-law's house? No."

Fortunately, Billy cut in before I could tell him off.

"So, Henry, what did you decide to get the happy couple as a
wedding gift? I tried to get Caroline to go in on a lifetime supply
of Tab with me, but she wasn't interested."

Henry cleared his throat. "A David Hockney painting. His pool series has been getting a lot of attention among collectors. Not sure where they'll hang it, but even if it's just on Dick's yacht, it should be a good investment. Very LA modern."

"Did you know Billy's moving to Los Angeles?" I blurted.

"No, I didn't! Permanently, or . . ."

"Yes. I've been offered a position at Jay Sebring's salon," he announced proudly.

"Ah, Sebring. A little too trendy for my taste, but he certainly has a lot of fans. Shame about Sharon Tate leaving him for that little Polack."

"Yes, well . . . the heart wants what it wants." Billy searched the patio for a reprieve. "Caroline, should we go find a drink?"

"Don't be silly, you two stay here. I'll be back with gin and tonics for both of you!" Henry flashed his perfect smile.

After he'd gone, Billy leaned down to whisper in my ear, "Has he always been like that?"

"Like what?"

"Like, insulting and nice all at the same time? I have whiplash."

I shrugged. "That's Henry. He means well, but sometimes that much money can cloud the brain."

"Smile, you two," Tex directed, sneaking up on us from the side. I clutched Billy's arm tighter as I searched the patio for Henry, who had his back to us at the bar. I just needed to get through Daphne's big day before officially turning down his proposal.

"Say cheese," Billy hissed through his teeth, clutching my waist to move us in front of the camera. I smiled because it was my friend's party, and I knew she'd want to look back on these pictures with fond memories. Inside, I was a ball of nerves.

After he took the photo, Tex leaned over to whisper, "You look so sexy tonight." His breath ghosted across the sensitive skin of my ear.

Beside me, Billy pretended to be occupied by the cuff of his sleeve.

"Are you staying through the meal?" I asked Tex.

"Yeah, but I have to eat inside with the caterers."

"That's terrible! Does Daphne know?"

He shrugged. "It's fine. Really. Besides, things might get awkward with the best man." He jutted his chin out to indicate Henry, headed back from the bar.

"Tex, I swear I didn't know until I got to Florida that he was in the wedding party. I'll explain everything later." I pleaded with my eyes for him to trust me, to give me the chance to prove that my heart had never stopped being his.

Henry returned to us with three glasses balanced in his hands. "Here we are, gin and tonics, lots of ice. It's gonna be a late night." Passing our drinks off, he surveyed Tex with cool disdain. "Hello, again. Jack, isn't it?"

"Good memory." The muscle in Tex's jaw tensed.

"Oh, I never forget a face. Say, it's a good thing you're here. You can get a photo of me and my girl." Henry put his arm around me, drawing me closer to his side. I shot another apologetic grimace at Tex.

"Smile!" Henry directed, arranging his features into a generic grin. I knew we made an attractive couple, and that anyone who saw this photo would think we belonged in a frame together, with our shared dark hair and similar builds. But what they wouldn't see was my urgent need to pull away from him, or Henry's boiling jealousy over watching me with the man I'd spent the winter with. To be fair, if one of Tex's old girlfriends wanted to take our picture, I would have clawed her eyes out.

As soon as the shutter clicked, I relaxed my face and eased back toward Billy. "I should go say hello to Daphne and Dickie." I craned my neck to find them in the crowd, searching for a life raft in this sea of sharks.

"I'll join you, sweetie." Henry placed his hand on the small of my back, claiming me. Never once in the last decade had he used that term of endearment, so this was clearly an attempt to needle Tex. I let him lead me away, mouthing the word *later* silently over my shoulder.

Bitsy's dinner was impeccable, from the crisp Chardonnay in Waterford goblets to the poached salmon and lemony rice plated on fine china. Between the entrée and dessert courses, Dickie gave a heartfelt speech about how fortunate he and Daphne were to have found each other, as my friend beamed up at him, radiant with love. Even Bitsy looked happy, her fingers intertwined with her husband's atop the tablecloth.

After the dishes were cleared, a band gathered under the pavilion where Henry had proposed just a few nights prior. They began the evening with standard jazz covers before transitioning to rock 'n' roll songs for the younger crowd. Daphne and Dickie were in their own euphoric bubble, giggling as they did the Twist, the Mashed Potato, and the Swim.

Grinning at them from a column next to the dance floor, I soon sensed a presence. I turned to find Tex watching me intently.

"It's good to see you smile." He brushed his thumb across my lips, and I shivered, starved for his touch.

"They make a great pair. I like that Dickie makes her so happy. She deserves it."

He stared at me a moment longer, his expression solemn. "Listen, there's something we need to talk about. Can we—can we go somewhere?"

I surveyed the patio. Dickie and Daphne were still going strong on the dance floor, Billy was speaking to a waiter near the ocean balustrade, and Henry stood in a crowd of other men, sipping scotch and puffing on a cigarette.

"Okay. Things will probably wind down soon anyway. Did you get all the photos you needed?"

"I think so." He nodded. "Should we go back to my room at the Breakers?"

"No, let's just go upstairs. It's closer." I motioned for him to follow, weaving my way past small clusters of people, then through the glass doors into the house. I felt Tex's gaze behind me as we walked, the anticipation becoming stronger as the noise of the party faded. Reaching the upstairs hallway, I led him to my bedroom, closing the door behind us.

In the empty room, we stood silent and still as the sexual tension crackled, each of us daring the other to make the first move. With desire blazing in his eyes, Tex broke first and lunged for me. I dropped my purse and smashed my mouth against his. Like a sudden squall, the kiss was violent and intense, saying everything we felt without words.

With his lips still on mine, Tex gripped my shoulders and walked us in halting steps until the bed hit the back of my calves. We fell onto the soft mattress while I clutched his shoulders, pulling him on top of me. He kicked off his shoes as I lifted a leg to wrap it around his body.

"I've missed you so much. So goddamn much," he rasped.

I nodded frantically, unable to string together words.

He touched my bare hip through the open panels of my gown, and I jolted as if singed by a lit match.

"More," I panted, sliding my pelvis against his. "I need more."

Tex started to lower his mouth to my neck, then abruptly stopped and pulled back with a groan. "I can't," he said, catching his breath. "Not without telling you my news first." He rolled off me and sat up, brushing his hair back from his forehead.

I took a few deep breaths, trying to get myself under control. I had news of my own to share with him, not the least of which was Billy's offer to help us move to LA. Henry's proposal was second on the list, and something I thoroughly dreaded.

He looked up to the ceiling before meeting my eyes again. "I applied for a staff job at *Life*, one that would have guaranteed I could take care of you, provide for you. Thing is, it ended up going to someone else. They said I need more experience, more 'real' subjects."

"What does that mean? What's not real about the pictures you take?"

"It's just, they want photos that tell a story of what's actually happening in the world. Not some fairy-tale dream of the rich and famous. They want real people, real struggles, real problems. And the thing is, I agree with their decision. It's what I'd been thinking about on the island, and I see now my instincts were right. It's time to grow. There's no easy way to say this, so I'm just going to be straight with you—I've decided to go to Vietnam."

"What?" My heart stopped beating. Surely I'd misheard.

"Before you panic, know that I'll be there as a photographer, not a soldier. Southeast Asia is where the important stories are. I get that it sounds crazy and dangerous, and I've already had all the same thoughts you're having right now. But I keep coming back to the same conclusion—I have to take this risk if I ever want to be taken seriously. If I ever want to have a shot at giving us a good life. And maybe, if I'm lucky, my work could make a difference. I've got a Pan Am flight to Saigon booked for tomorrow night, and I aim to be on that plane."

I stared at him, my emotions shifting between anger and shock. "How could you do something like this? And without discussing it with me first? Did you ever stop to consider I might have my own thoughts about where we go next?"

"I didn't want to risk you talking me out of it. I know we made promises on Formentera, and I intend to keep them. I want to take care of you, but I can't do it on a freelancer's wages, never knowing when the next gig will come up." I started to speak, but he silenced me with a finger against my lips. "And it's not only about that. I can't just lie next to you on expensive sheets while guys my age and younger are dying by the thousands in Vietnam. I have to do my part."

"What the hell does thread count have to do with anything?!" I sat up straighter, insulted. "You think you're going to end the war by shooting pictures of burned fields and rice paddies?"

"We talked about this. I thought you'd understand. People here, they don't give a damn. The war is just some confusing fight in a far-off country they'd never heard of ten years ago. All they know is that their sons and brothers and boyfriends are flying over there and coming home in body bags. They don't know why. I want to show them what's really going on. I need to see it for myself."

"Tex, Vietnam is not Nazi Germany. This isn't our fight."

"When *is* it our fight?" He was getting louder, color rising up his neck. "When the communists come to our shores? When they bomb your country clubs and polo fields? Will you care then?"

"Oh, don't give me that patriotic bullshit," I said, glaring. "We both know this is about you wanting to play hero. You listened to Gerhard talk about how nobody paid attention to what was happening in his country until it was too late, and now you think this is your chance to ride in on a white steed. Well, let me tell you—the war is already happening whether we want it to or not, and your photos won't change that."

He scrubbed his hands over his face in frustration. "Al, listen to me. This is done. I'm going. And it would be really nice if you would support me, just like I've supported your singing."

"I would if I thought this was a legitimate dream of yours. But it sounds to me like you didn't get what you wanted, and now you're grasping at anything that might salvage your ego, even if it means throwing yourself into a dangerous situation. But if you'd just sit down and listen to me, you'd see there are other ways. Other stories to tell."

"You don't get it. You're not in the journalism world; you don't understand how things are done. Taking big risks for big payoffs.

Creating your own opportunities." He stood up and started looking for his shoes.

"Where are you going? You're leaving? We're not done!"

He reached down to get the one near the door, and from my vantage point I could see it lying next to the tiny velvet box that had spilled out of my evening bag.

"What's this?" He picked it up.

"Nothing. Just put it on the dresser." I tried to sound casual, hoping he'd think it was just an old pair of earrings.

To my horror, he opened it. "Why do you have an engagement ring? That's what this is, isn't it?" His face filled with confusion and hurt.

"Henry gave it to me earlier this week," I explained. "He . . . he wants to marry me."

Tex snapped the lid shut and threw the box onto the bed, where it landed with a soft *plop*.

"So that's why he acted like he owned you tonight. He does."

I shook my head. "No. I haven't given him an answer yet. But I'd already decided to decline before you showed up. I'm in love with you, and I can't walk away from that, no matter how uncertain the future looks."

"But you considered it?"

"Yes. But you don't know why."

He huffed. "Oh, I can guess. I think there are a few million reasons sitting in a bank account somewhere."

It stung that he would think so little of me, but also that he wasn't entirely wrong. "I admit, that's part of it. But not the whole story. Mother told me the day you left that we're broke. She lost most of my inheritance, and her company is bankrupt. We only have a few thousand dollars to our name."

"*And?*"

"And what? Isn't that enough? Whatever life I once had, that's all over. Thank god Bitsy gave me this room and Daphne bought my clothes for the wedding. I couldn't afford to be here otherwise."

Tex let out a laugh of incredulity. "Am I supposed to feel sorry for you? You 'only' have a few thousand dollars? When I arrived in New York, I had fifty bucks in my back pocket. That's it. I was going to help you get on your feet, offering up my apartment while I'm gone, but I can see why that'd be detestable when you have Henry and the Ritz at your disposal."

"It isn't just about me. Henry's father offered to bail out Mother's business if I took him back. She may have lied to me and made me doubt myself, but she's still my mother. Turning down this proposal means betraying her."

"You can pretend this is about Emanuela, but we both know it's really about the fact that you're a scared little girl. You say you want your life to mean something, but here you are in this mansion, sipping champagne and laughing along with the rest of these rich assholes. You sit around writing letters to a dead man as if he can answer back. You have a valuable painting in a bank vault in Paris, but god forbid you sell it, take the money, and tell your mother to clean up her own mess. You spend your days living in the past, and now here I am, talking about a way to give us a future, but because it doesn't fit inside some perfect box you've imagined, you're too fucking scared to accept it."

Stone-faced, I just looked at him, not even recognizing the person who could say such cruel things to me. "You need to leave now." I was too afraid of responding with something I couldn't take back. Like *Go to hell.*

"Yeah, I think I'd better," he muttered, grabbing his other shoe and slamming the door on his way out.

I stared at the spot where he'd stood until the dam burst and tears flooded my cheeks. In the blink of an eye, our love had turned into a weapon—one that cut both ways.

March 25th, 1967
Wentworth-Waddlestone Mansion
Palm Beach, Florida

Dear Daddy,

I couldn't sleep at all last night, knowing today could be the most important day of my life, and I don't even have the support of the one person I need it from.

But I can't let what happened with Tex distract me. Daphne has given me an opportunity, and I'm not going to waste it. It's time to start kicking.

Love,
Caroline

TWENTY-THREE

WITH BLOND HAIR loose around her shoulders, flower crown, and long, ethereal veil, Daphne looked like something out of a dream. Satin lining hugged her bombshell figure, while a lace overlay covered her arms and upper chest. The gown was time-less and sexy all at once. Standing in the vestibule of Bethesda-by-the-Sea, I turned to my beautiful friend one last time and whispered, "You're perfect."

She blew me a kiss and I smiled, pretending to put it in my pocket.

A string quartet started to play a soft classical melody as we moved to the top of the aisle. Dickie beamed from the other end, with Henry standing proudly by his side. Heads turned as I walked forward, my toes pinching in the yellow satin shoes dyed to match my dress. Underneath, I carried my broken heart like a lead balloon.

When I reached the altar, my grip tightened on the bouquet of yellow and white daisies, and I allowed myself a few calming breaths before turning to face the guests. As the opening notes of the bride's processional song sounded, the congregation rose to welcome Daphne and her father. I spied my mother and Maria a few rows back, Mother understanding better than anyone what we'd both lost five years ago. It wasn't just a person; it was a lifetime of memories that would never have the chance to be made. Daddy would never be walking me down the aisle, and my throat constricted at the unfairness of it all.

As they finally reached us, Daphne's father presented her to Dickie, and they took their place in front of the minister. I still found it hard to believe she was ready to settle into the type of domestic life she'd rebelled against for so many years, but if I knew Daphne, her marriage was sure to be anything but dull.

The ceremony proceeded as planned until right before the exchanging of rings, when the minister cleared his throat and glanced at me. We'd arranged this with him early this morning, just he and Daphne and I, but it hadn't felt real then. Now, with my pulse pounding in my throat and my skin clammy, it was very, very real.

"Ladies and gentlemen, the bride has requested we pause a moment to enjoy a musical performance by her dear friend Caroline Kimball, who has prepared something special for today."

Dickie, at first startled by the interruption, looked at me over Daphne's shoulder and broke out into a huge grin. Beyond him, I could see Bitsy seething as her perfectly choreographed event went down the drain. And Henry, poor Henry, just looked confused.

Retrieving my guitar from where I'd placed it before the ceremony, I stepped up to the lectern, taking my seat on the stool. I glanced down at Daphne, who winked at me, giving a little nod.

"Hello, everyone. If you'll indulge me, I'd like to play a song for Daphne and Dickie, and anyone else who knows what it's like to be young and in love."

And then I began to sing. It was the song I'd started beside Bitsy's pool, worked and reworked during frantic hours last night. No longer about drowning, it was about being saved, and saving someone in return.

Picture us floating
Water cold against our skin
The sky above is crystal clear
Are you ready to begin?

Down beneath the surface
Lose my breath, you give it back
Fight the anchors of the past
Until the rope goes slack

Legs, keep on kicking
Arms, keep on reaching
Eyes, what do you see
Is it the sun, or is it me?

Pull you up
You push me further
Take my hand
Please, hold on tight

Legs, keep on kicking
Arms, keep on reaching
We follow the sun
Till we find free

We follow the sun
Till we find free.

As the song unspooled, I risked a glance at Mother. To my shock, she wore a proud smile, so different from the expression I'd imagined in the Café Sirena. And although I couldn't find him among the crowd, I knew a tall man stood alone in the shadows, watching. Listening to my words, to the song about us. I closed my eyes and let the music wash through me.

But as the final motion of my hand against the strings resonated and the vibration in my throat faded, I opened them again, looking back out to the pews. There was a nervous pause before Mother and Maria began to clap loudly, with more people following until it became full-on applause. I stuffed down the lump in my throat and smiled. Later I would allow myself to take this moment in, to unpack it and examine it from all angles. But for now, all I could do was set my guitar back in its stand and reclaim my place next to Daphne. My body hummed with the excitement of knowing there was no turning back now, no denying that I was on my way toward becoming Carolina at last. And when the couple finally kissed, sealing their union, a hot tear escaped down my cheek. New lives were beginning, for us all.

As Daphne and Dickie headed back down the aisle, Henry held out his arm to me, discreetly slipping me a handkerchief. I dried my eyes, plastering on a smile for our exit. There would be family photos outside prior to leaving for the reception at the Breakers. Before all that, though, I needed to take care of unfinished business.

"Will you come with me while I get my bag?" I whispered to Henry as we waved to various guests.

"Of course."

I steered us to the right of the nave, back to the room Daphne and I had gotten ready in earlier. Curlers, nylons, and makeup tubes lay scattered, waiting for Bitsy's staff to organize it all for transport back to the mansion. Closing the door behind us, I released Henry's arm and retrieved my clutch from the dressing table. I opened it and pulled out the ring he'd given me.

From behind me, he said, "You were beautiful up there today. So was Daphne, but I already know who the prettier bride will be."

"I don't think you do." I turned to him, concealing the ring box against my stomach. Steeling myself, I took a breath and dove into the deep end. "Henry, I can't marry you." I held out the ring box, raising my chin in determination.

Confusion drew his brows together. "I don't understand. Is there something else you want to negotiate? Father hasn't drawn up the official paperwork yet, but I'm sure we can all come to a happy arrangement. However you want to handle this, in regards to your mother and the money."

I shook my head. "This isn't about money. It's about the fact that we don't love each other."

"But I *do* love you! I wouldn't have proposed if I didn't."

"No, you love the idea of me. Or someone like me, who looks the way I do, and has all the right connections, and has never given any indication that she wants to be more than just a pretty face beside you in a *Town & Country* spread."

"But what's wrong with that?" He seemed baffled, clearly not used to hearing the word *no*. "You can't give all this up. I know you—you'd miss it too much. I'm offering to take care of your needs, and your mother's, for the rest of your lives."

"What I need is freedom. I can't be tied to a man I don't love in that way. We both deserve better. Please, take this ring back." I held it out to him again.

Confusion turned to anger, before eventually landing on defeat. Finally, he said, "I already told you, that's yours. Never let it be said that a Halliday goes back on his word."

"Oh, Henry," I sighed. "I hope one day you find a girl you're able to see as a person and not as a business deal." It was the truth—I wanted him to meet someone who'd make him see that love should be more than a transaction. Deep down, I wanted to believe the boy I'd laughed and cried with was still in there; I just didn't have the energy to chip away at the arrogant man he'd become.

"So I guess this means you'll go back to the photographer," he said, straightening his cuffs. Trying to shake off the blow I'd dealt to his ego.

"It's complicated. But just know that even if Jack had never entered my life, it still would have been a mistake to accept your proposal. We want different things. You're happy in this world, but I can't stay in the cage, no matter how nice it might look from the outside."

He nodded tersely. "I hope you know what you're doing. There are lots of cages out there, and not all of them have gold bars."

"I know. I'll be careful."

Henry frowned, glancing at the door. "We should get back out there. They're probably ready to start taking pictures."

"You go ahead. I have to fix my makeup."

He turned and walked quietly out the door, and out of my life.

With a sigh, I placed the ring back in my bag. I didn't know what I'd do with it, but it was a relief to know it wouldn't be sitting on my finger, weighing me down with impossible expectations. My limbs were still free to kick.

I existed in a fog through the rest of the afternoon, my cheeks aching from so many fake smiles. The portrait photographer snapped picture after picture while I focused on his lens instead of my problems. Afterward, I caught a ride back to the Breakers with Daphne's mother and her date, a young Argentinian she'd probably rented for the occasion. I threw myself into the role of happy bridesmaid, knowing I'd be stuck with it for several more hours.

Arriving at the hotel, we followed a crowd of guests to the central courtyard, which had been transformed by Bitsy's minions. White fabric–topped tables lined the perimeter, and giant urns of yellow and white flowers spilled out from every corner. Soft lights sparkled among the palm trees and foliage, while the fountain in the middle bubbled and splashed. Dinner would happen in the adjoining ballroom, its frescoed ceiling an opulent crown on the occasion. I grabbed a glass of champagne off a waiter's tray, eager to numb myself.

"*Principessa!*"

Turning, I saw Mother and Maria climbing the steps to me. *Here we go—happy bridesmaid.*

"You were wonderful at the church, Caroline," Maria greeted, kissing my cheek. "A true poet."

Mother appraised me. "Yes, the song was quite accomplished."

"Thanks, but the bride was the real star of the show. Didn't she look beautiful?"

"A bit traditional for my taste, but still stunning."

"And Bitsy-approved." I spotted Dickie's mother, busy greeting guests around the courtyard. I recognized foreign dignitaries, film actors, socialites, and politicians—the crème de la crème of guest lists. But so far, no famous record producer. Had he not come after all?

"Henry was rather dashing as well," Maria said. "That boy was born to wear a tuxedo."

I frowned at the mention of him. "About Henry, I need to tell you both—I turned his proposal down."

Maria reached out and squeezed my arm. "We thought you might."

Mother simply nodded, her expression unreadable.

"I'm sorry, but I had to. I couldn't marry a man I didn't love. I'm not you."

I watched Mother flinch, my words hitting a sensitive nerve. But then she said something that surprised me. "I'm proud of you."

I looked at her in confusion, certain I'd heard wrong.

"You did what I was never brave enough to do. You defied your family to follow your heart. This Tex—is he your heart?"

I nodded. "Yes. But not just him. Singing too. I know I've got a long way to go before I can say I've made it, but I need to at least try. I owe it to myself, and to Daddy."

She took my hand in hers. "I'm just so scared for you, my darling. A woman doesn't have the same hallway of open doors that a man does. I don't want to see you struggle and regret the choices you've made. And now I'm not even in a position to help you."

"But don't you see? If I'm really going to do this, I need to do it on my own. Without the safety net of money. If losing it is what it takes for me to finally grow up and be part of a bigger world, then maybe this was all for the best."

Mother stared at me, aghast. "Caroline. Forgive me, but to Maria and me, the loss of Leoni is not 'for the best.'"

"About that—Tex said something last night that made me think. He reminded me I've still got *Ojos Verdes* in the safe in Paris."

Mother shook her head. "No. I was silly to mention it before. I can't let you sell that to pay for my mistakes."

"That's the thing—I wouldn't have to. There's another way."

Maria looked at me with questioning eyes. "What do you mean?"

"There's another painting. One you haven't seen yet. We found it in the rafters of the shed, with the note I gave you. Daddy had covered it in an old blanket. It's got the hallmarks of his style, but there's something new and exciting about it too. A hint of where he could have gone as an artist if he'd lived longer."

"Did you leave it in the shed?" Mother asked, shocked.

"No, Gerhard has it. I sent him a telegram this morning before the wedding and told him you and Maria would be back for it. I want you to sell it and use the money to save the business. You see, the painting is of a man who's given up; he's gone under the water and let himself drown. I'm not going to let that happen to me, or to you."

Maria reached out to pull me into her arms. "Oh, *principessa*, this heart of yours." When she finally released me, there were tears in her eyes. "I haven't had the courage to say this to you yet, but please know I never wanted to keep the truth from you. Ema and I had gotten so used to hiding, just to survive. But we shouldn't have hidden from the one we love most." Her face twisted with regret.

"I'm still angry," I admitted. "But I think I understand. I just need time to get used to it all. It's hard knowing the picture you had of your life was manipulated for so long."

"There was no manipulation. Not where it matters," Mother asserted. "Maria adored you from the instant you came into this world. Even before. She stepped in to give you affection when I could not, read you bedtime stories, brushed your hair, and gave me hell when she saw me making mistakes. Just as recently as a few weeks ago, in fact. So don't ever think the relationship you had with her was a lie. Her love for you was always genuine. And though I'm not the best at showing it, so was mine."

My mouth trembling, I leaned in and hugged her tightly. Mother rubbed my back, sniffing like she was holding back her own tears. She'd had to be strong to survive the challenges of her life, but maybe now, I could finally begin to know the real Emanuela Leoni.

"I know there's more to say, but now's probably not the best time." I stepped back and wiped my eyes, glancing around the courtyard. "I need to start circulating."

"Yes, my martini is getting warm. Maria, fetch me another," Mother directed, extending her almost-empty glass.

Maria rolled her eyes. "Oh, fetch it yourself. She knows I'm not *la cameriera.*"

"*Merda*, look what you've done." Mother grimaced in my direction.

The three of us linked arms as we headed to the bar. "Will you be coming with us after Daphne leaves on her honeymoon?" Maria asked.

"Actually, I'm going to Los Angeles with Billy. He asked me to move in with him, and sunny California seems like a good place for reinvention."

Mother looked at me with surprise before smiling. "Well, when you start to miss the rain, you are welcome to stay with two penny-pinching Italian-American Parisians any time you want. We would love the chance to fuss over you."

"Mother, you'll never be truly cheap."

"Why do you say that?"

"Because I know you. You'd sooner rob a bank than fly coach."

Maria laughed, a great big bark of delight. "I love this idea!"

I sighed, shaking my head. "Oh god, now I'm worried."

TWENTY-FOUR

THE FAMILIAR NOTES of "Cherish" played over the sound system as Dickie and Daphne walked to the center of the ballroom. Under painted ceilings of blue skies and puffy clouds, the two lovers smiled at each other as they danced, while a crowd of happy, inebriated guests looked on.

Beside me, Billy made jokes about the Waddlestone family tree, but even he couldn't distract me from my anxiety over Tex. I tried to avoid Henry's bitter face across the room, though I noticed him chatting with Patricia Carrington, a socialite with a healthy trust fund from her maternal grandfather's pharmaceutical company. If he couldn't land a date, perhaps he could make a sale.

As I stood half listening to my friend, I felt a tap on my shoulder. Turning around, I came face-to-face with a California star-maker.

"Lou Adler," he said, extending a hand.

My throat went dry. "Caroline Kimball," I replied, shaking it. "My stage name is Carolina. Daphne mentioned you were on the guest list. I'm a fan."

He assessed me carefully. "Carolina. The mysterious, green-eyed beauty. I like it. People wouldn't expect a talented guitar player in such pretty packaging. Where'd you learn open tuning?"

I was surprised he'd noticed, but I guess I shouldn't have been. "My father taught me to play, but the last few months I've been working on a different sound."

"I've only heard a few boys do it before. You write all your own songs?"

"I started out with folk, but I like coming up with my own music and lyrics." I tried to sound confident in my abilities, though I was anything but.

"That song you performed at the wedding—it wasn't bad. Made me almost uncomfortable, like you were confessing something. I think I liked that about it, though. What stages have you been on?"

"The Café Sirena, in Formentera, Spain. And, well, Bethesda-by-the-Sea," I said sheepishly.

He laughed, and I exhaled in relief. "So your eyes aren't the only thing green about you. That's okay, green's one of my favorite colors. Tell you what, you ever find yourself in LA, I want you to give me a call. We'll set up a meeting to talk about getting more experience."

"Absolutely! I've already got plans to move there, so don't be surprised if that call comes sooner than you think. Thank you so much for this chance, Mr. Adler!"

"Lou. And don't thank me yet. You've still got a long way to go before there's an album with your name on the shelf. But you've got something."

I nodded, aware that my privilege and connections could only get me so far. The rest would require hard work and determination.

After he left, Billy and I hugged each other in excitement.

"This is it, princess! Soon I'll be saying I knew you when."

"Let's not get ahead of ourselves."

"Don't you dare stop me from celebrating tonight; you know I use any and all excuses for more champagne. I'll grab us a fresh bottle."

After he left, I walked to the windows, staring distractedly at the glass. I didn't know how long I stood there before a familiar reflection appeared like a ghost. I turned to find Tex looking pensive, his camera at his side.

"Did you save me a dance?" he asked, his voice low and intimate.

"Do you still want one?"

He took my hand and led me outside to the palm-lined lanai, where the ocean breeze swept across my flushed skin. Setting his camera on a bench, Tex faced me, holding out his arms. Reluctantly, I stepped into them and rested my head on his shoulder. The opening melody of "God Only Knows" by the Beach Boys floated out to us as my body relaxed against him. We swayed to the music, my mind replaying the horrible things we'd said to each other last night.

Tex spoke first. "You look beautiful. Prettier than the bride."

"That's what Henry said too."

He tensed at the mention of my former friend and almost fiancé. "So you talked to Henry? Did you accept his proposal?"

I shook my head. "No. I meant what I told you last night. There's no way I could have said yes. Not now that I know what real love is."

He exhaled, his shoulders loosening. "What did your mother have to say about that?"

"Does it matter?"

"No. Not to me. All that matters is that there's still a chance for us."

I hesitated. "I hate to sound like a broken record tonight, but is that what you still want?"

He cupped the back of my neck with one hand, urging me to look up. "Of course," he said roughly against my lips. "I said some stupid things last night, and I'm sorry. It's been tearing me up all day, thinking about it. I love you; that'll never change."

"You might love me, but you didn't have enough faith in me to talk about our future together before you made plans and bought tickets."

"No." He shook his head. "I knew that one look at your face and I'd chicken out. Because how could I get on another plane once I've held you in my arms again?" As if to prove his point, he squeezed me even tighter. "But how could I live with myself, knowing I wasn't brave enough to take the big chance? It's not the dangers of war I'm most afraid of; it's saying goodbye to you."

A lump formed in my throat at the thought of him coming home in one of those cheap aluminum coffins they showed on the evening news. "Before you told me about Vietnam, I was going to tell you I wanted to do the same thing: take the big chance." I swallowed, continuing. "Billy got a job at Jay Sebring's salon, and he's offered to help me get on my feet in Los Angeles. I hoped you would come with us, but I suppose LA and I will still be there when you're ready."

Tex looked at me, stunned, before giving a low whistle. "Look at you, kickin' up a storm. I'm proud of you." I knew he meant it too—he'd always believed I was capable of leaving the shelter of the jet set. "And don't you worry—I'll be ready sooner than you think. In the meantime, will you write to me? Tell me what you're up to in California?"

I shook my head. "I've got a better idea: I'll send you songs. But only if you send me pictures in return. I want to see what's in your heart."

He kissed me then, searing his lips to mine. Trying to imprint himself. "You. You're my heart. But sure, I'll send you pictures. As many as you want," he promised. "And someday, I'll be back to give you everything else. Anything you want from me, it'll be yours."

My mouth flattened in an attempt to hold back the sob threatening to spill out. I knew our time was running out, and I had no idea how long I'd have to live without him. "Right now, can you just hold me? At least until the song is over."

"Yeah, Al. I can hold on for a little while longer."

And so we swayed, not even hearing the music anymore, or the deep call of the sea across the night air. The only noise that registered was that of two hearts, fracturing and bending, mixing and mending, until neither of us could leave without taking a piece of the other. Tethered across oceans and hours, I could already feel a part of him beating inside me, just as part of me was already in him. Calling him back, like a siren on the rocks.

I would be waiting.

LOS ANGELES

June 12th, 1967
Laurel Canyon
Los Angeles, California

Dear Daddy,

Time moves so fast when you're not staring at the clock. I blinked, and suddenly I have a new name, a new city, and a new life. Air, light, water, and time—it turns out California is an excellent greenhouse.

There's just one piece still missing, and gosh I miss him something fierce. Watch out for him, will you?

Love,
Carolina

TWENTY-FIVE

THE FLASH WENT off with a startling *pop* as nebulous dots filled my vision. A gray backdrop hung behind me, surrounded by hot, oppressive lights. Large resin earrings pulled at my lobes, and the orange tights I wore under my tunic had begun to stick to my thighs. A makeup artist scurried over to touch up my powder, and I flinched against the brush bristles. The product they had me hawking was presumed to be somewhere on my body, though I could have just as easily been selling lipstick as hairspray.

It was my fifth modeling job since moving to LA, and while I detested all the poking and prodding and hours spent waiting in a chair, at least it paid enough to help Billy with rent. I didn't get the high-profile editorial jobs on offer in New York, but Mother's agency contacts had set me up with some decent ad work on this coast. Not my dream occupation, but it enabled me to live in the city of stars until I could become one myself.

"One more shot, luv, and I think we got it," called a voice from the darkness. With all the lights pointed at me, it was difficult to see the photographer. "Twist your head to the left, shoulders back, show off the earrings."

I did as instructed, my face a blank canvas of arched eyebrows and sucked-in cheeks. Concentrating on tiny movements like inhaling and exhaling helped distract me from a constant loop of worries: Tex and Vietnam, auditions, gigs, and the nagging fear that I was just another girl with a guitar and grandiose dreams.

Flash, pop! "Beautiful, beautiful, luv. That was the one."

Relaxing, I massaged the back of my neck. The photographer approached me, setting his camera to the side. It was larger than the one Tex used, more cumbersome than the little black and silver Leica that had been like a permanent appendage to his hands. God, how I missed him.

"You're a natural at this. Been modeling long?" He had a cockney accent that American women probably went gaga over. I was unmoved.

"Just a few weeks," I replied, eager to beg off.

"Yeah, you're the spittin' image of that Ali MacGraw. Bet you hear that all the time."

"Who?" I unclipped the earrings from my aching lobes, passing them off to a wardrobe assistant.

"That model, worked at *Vogue, Harper's Bazaar*. Heard she's getting into pictures now. You better hurry up if you want to get there first."

"Oh, I'm not an actress. I'm actually a musician." It still felt foreign to use that word when describing myself, but I'd played enough sets by now to know that the girl onstage in the spotlight was allowed to call herself that, even if she didn't have a record on the shelf yet.

"I knew you seemed a little more intere$
ditzy birds comin' through here. Say, you f
drink after you get changed? There's a bar
sometimes Jimmy Morrison pops in."

I pursed my lips to keep from laughing. Did
for this? Also, I knew for a fact that the Doors   .... ᴜɪ ᴛᴏwn.
"Sorry, can't. I'm doing an amateur night at the Troubadour and
have plans to meet a friend there."

Daphne, back from her lengthy honeymoon with Dickie, was
in town for a meeting with the new head of Paramount, Robert
Evans.

"Ah. 'Nother time, then. Those advertising blokes knew what
they was doing when they cast you. I bet you could sell a bikini in
a blizzard." He winked, flashing a crooked grin.

I smiled politely and stood up to leave. I knew modeling was a
means to an end, but brother, that end couldn't come soon enough.

Warm wind tousled my hair as I drove past the dive bars and car
rental lots on the Sunset Strip. Signs for go-go dancers and live
comedy whizzed by, promising cheap drinks, no cover, and a
night of bad decisions. My little blue Chevy Corvair propelled me
around the turn onto Santa Monica Boulevard, guitar nestled
safely in the back seat. After deciding to let Mother keep most of
the proceeds from the sale of Daddy's final painting, to help get
House of Leoni back on its feet, I'd pawned Henry's engagement
ring to buy the car. Although a small part of me was tempted to
call and thank him, I still didn't feel particularly grateful for anything that had happened between us last spring.

inally spotting the medieval sign *Doug Weston's Troubadour* among a string of businesses, I found a spot and parallel parked. I'd only just opened the door when a familiar squeal hit my eardrums.

"DAAAARRLINNGGGG!" Daphne's shriek echoed across the pavement. As she reached my car, our bodies collided in a dizzying cloud of perfume. We squeezed our arms tightly around one other as I laughed, giddy from seeing my best friend for the first time in months.

"Look at you!" I exclaimed, stepping back to get the full picture. "My god, you're so tanned!"

She twirled, showing off her Pucci minidress, white go-go boots, and newlywed sheen. "Between sailing the Caspian Sea, sunbathing in Sardinia, and camel rides outside Marrakesh, I've got a golden glow to last through August." Daphne ran her hands over her bare arms. "Isn't it marvelous? Poor Dickie got so sunburned. Good thing his sexy nurse was able to take the sting out at night."

"No details, please." I grimaced, grabbing my guitar case. "You sure you're okay waiting in line with me? I don't know what kind of spot I'll get, if I get one at all." By now I'd become used to the sting of disappointment that came with being told I was "good, but not good enough." My songs "interesting, but not quite there yet." Wherever *there* was . . .

Lou Adler had been kind but firm when I'd met with him shortly after my arrival here, saying I needed to play the clubs before we could talk seriously about recording a single. So here I was, on the streets of LA, waiting for a break just like everyone else.

She waved me off. "Oh please, I don't care about that. I just want to spend time with you. How else will I get to be your number one groupie?"

Still smiling, I linked arms with her as we walked to the entrance of the club, toward the sign on the front door advertising this evening's event: Hoot Night, as it was called among locals. We got in line behind a few other people waiting for the booking agent to emerge at four o'clock. All of us—musicians, comedians, poets, magicians—showed up hoping for a chance to grace the stage for a brief fifteen minutes later that night.

"Now, tell me everything you've been up to," Daphne commanded once I'd set my case down.

I shrugged, knowing my new reality would probably sound tedious to her. "Not much to tell, honestly. Billy found us a cute little house in the Canyon. He spends most of his days at the salon, which gives me time alone to write and practice." Mother had been right when she said it would take more work than I could ever imagine to succeed at this. My fingers were calloused and sore, my ego bruised, but I couldn't abandon this dream, or the feeling I got from playing songs on the back deck of our house or in a dark, smoky club. Like I was home.

Behind us, the line started to grow, and I scooted closer to Daphne. "How was your meeting with Evans today? Billy said he comes into the salon sometimes—a real ballbuster."

She frowned. "Could have gone better. I think he's looking for more flower child, less bombshell. Probably somebody like you, actually. Want his number?"

I shook my head in bewilderment. "What is it with this town? Everybody just assumes that if a girl my age lives here, she wants to be in movies. I tolerate the modeling jobs so I can afford to eat and buy gas, but that's only until I start making real money with my music. I've never wanted to be in the frame."

"Well, you wanted to be in *someone's* frame . . ." She winked.

I frowned, leaning against the building. Although I thought about Tex at least ten times a day, it was still a sore subject.

"Oh, I'm sorry, darling, did I put my foot in it?"

I shrugged off my initial reaction. "No, it's okay. Really, I'm fine. I miss Tex like crazy, but I know he's doing something that matters to him."

"Has there been any word from Vietnam?"

"Sort of. Communication's been complicated. Before Tex left Florida, I gave him Mother's address in Paris. He sent his mailing information in Saigon to her, and she passed it on to me. Since then, I've sent him tapes of my new songs, just reel-to-reel recordings I make at home, along with my address here. And he sends me photographs. One or two were of him, but most are shots of the people he's met over there, or places he's gone. Never phone calls—we decided it was far too expensive and difficult—and the notes with our packages just give the barest information. We agreed to let our art speak for us, but now I'm not so sure it was the brightest idea. I'm fixated on him, and it's hard to think about anything else. I just miss him so much, and it scares me that I've nearly forgotten what his voice sounds like."

Daphne squeezed my arm in sympathy. "You know, I bet he's over there feeling exactly the same. I saw the way he stared at you in Palm Beach, like you were the bloody moon and stars. And in Acapulco, before being rudely interrupted by *moi*, you were about five seconds away from taking a spin around the maypole. A very thick, long maypole."

I blushed as my eyes widened. "You mean that night in the pool? You looked?!"

"Naturally. And all I can say is, well done, you. Of course, I've got no complaints in that department now either. Dickie's bank account isn't the only thing that's well-endowed."

"Oh god, I am not having this conversation with you." I shook my head, laughing.

"Don't be such a prude, darling, it's unbecoming. Oh, I almost forgot—do you and Billy have plans this weekend? Dickie and I have two extra tickets to the Monterey Pop Festival."

The festival was all anyone had been talking about in the clubs, and I'd been hoping to catch a ride up there with someone. "We're in! I have no idea what Billy's doing, but whatever it is can be cancelled."

"Wonderful! Oh look, they're opening the door." She pointed at the entrance, where a man with a clipboard had just come out.

"If I make it onto the list, do you want to go next door to Dan Tana's for an early supper?"

"Perfect! I'll call Dickie from the restaurant and tell him where we are. He was hoping to catch your set after he's done with his meetings today. Big things brewing at WBS, apparently. But before he joins us, you absolutely must tell me more about Billy's new boyfriend. He's being annoyingly tight-lipped."

I looked over my shoulder to make sure the people behind us were otherwise occupied, before leaning in to whisper, "You didn't hear it from me, but you know that show *Bewitched*?"

Several hours later, after a successful audition and one celebratory plate of spaghetti, I was finally called down to the stage. Taking a deep breath and rolling my shoulders back, I grabbed my guitar and walked toward the spotlight. A sudden rush swept through my body the minute my eyes locked onto the club's patrons, knowing we were in this moment together. Knowing that I wasn't alone, if only for the length of a few songs.

"Hi, I'm Carolina. This is my first time playing a Hoot, so be nice, okay?" I smirked. "Just kidding—this town isn't known for being nice."

Then my fingers took their places on the frets, and I hummed the first few bars of "Blues Rushed In" as my other hand found the notes. Tossing my head back, my hair falling against my shoulder, I began to sing, my voice traveling all the way up to the wooden rafters. In other venues, I'd gotten adept at drowning out the clinking of glasses and whispered conversations by concentrating on my lyrics and the feelings behind each song. But here it seemed that I didn't need to resort to my mental tricks—the room got quieter the longer I played.

Though I only had time for three songs, I could tell by the final round of applause, and one errant whistle, that the performance had gone well. Returning to the audience afterward, I noticed a man with a mustache pointing toward me, excitedly saying something into the ear of his friend.

"Darling, you were amazing!" Daphne said as I reached our table. "The crowd was absolutely *mad* for you."

Beside her, Dickie stood up to kiss me on the cheek. "Really fantastic, Caroline. Or, sorry, *Carolina* . . ." he said theatrically. "I still can't believe you can write songs like that. I can barely string four words together."

"But the only four words you need to know are 'Daphne, you

are magnificent,'" my friend said, blinking her doe eyes up at him.

"Well, you *are* magnificent. And beautiful, and funny, and sexy, and—"

"*Okay*," I cut in before things got more awkward. "I'll leave you two lovebirds here while I grab us another round. I have no idea what happened to our waitress."

"Making out in a corner with that cute comedian and his banjo."

"Who can blame her?" I shrugged. "Be right back. Dickie? Whiskey sour, right?"

He gave me a thumbs-up as Daphne started to nuzzle his neck. Turning away, I shook my head. I hoped Tex and I wouldn't be that annoying when we reunited. *If we reunited.*

Sidling up to the bar in the adjoining room, I stood next to two men who had their backs to me. The bartender looked busy, and despite my little wave, I struggled to catch his attention.

"What'd you think of 'legs' in there?" I heard one of the men say to his friend.

"The brunette with the guitar?"

My pulse quickened as I realized they were talking about me. I didn't know whether to run or make myself invisible, but curiosity won out and my feet stayed rooted to the beer-stained floor.

"Kind of a small rack, but I'd still do her."

"Hey, you think her voice is that loud and high-pitched everywhere?"

"Good point. It's always the hippie chicks that make the worst screamers in bed. It's like, baby, I get it—you want to be a star. But my neighbor doesn't give a shit about your dreams. Neither does my dick."

They laughed as my face filled with heat. I wanted to crawl into a hole and die of humiliation. That was all I was to them, all I'd ever be—just a pretty face and a pair of legs. Good for only one thing, and it sure as hell wasn't music. I glanced around, seeing the room in a new light. Was that what the rest of the men here thought too? That I was just a prop? A foolish girl play-acting at being a real artist?

"Hey, what'll it be?" the bartender asked, startling me.

Before the men next to me had a chance to turn around, I shook my head in apology. "Nothing, sorry." I scurried away, my heart pounding. I just needed to go.

Back at the table, Daphne and Dickie were still making cooing noises at each other. I reached for my guitar case, making sure everything was secure before snapping the lid shut.

"Listen, sorry, the line was long at the bar, and I couldn't wait. I really need to get going."

Daphne looked up. "Oh, that's no problem, we'll go with you! Up for a nightcap at El Coyote? I'm in the mood for margaritas."

I shook my head. "No, really, it's been a long day. I had a modeling shoot earlier, then this show, and I didn't realize how exhausted I am. You two should go have fun; you don't need me. Besides, we'll be spending the whole weekend together at Monterey Pop."

"Oh, are you coming too?" Dickie asked eagerly.

"Yes, darling, I invited Caroline and Billy to join us. There's room in the car, right?"

"Of course! The more the merrier!" He stood up to kiss me on the cheek, always the gentleman. "Drive safe, we'll call you tomorrow. You were great tonight—I really mean that."

I smiled sadly. "Thanks, Dickie. I know you do."

Problem was, he was the one nice guy in a room of assholes, and outside this club, the world was *full* of assholes.

Arriving at our house in the Canyon, I pulled my car into the driveway, noting the empty spot where Billy's red Mustang was usually parked. I was eager to get inside and try to put my feelings of dejection and embarrassment into a song, if only to prevent them from drowning me from the inside out. *Keep kicking,* my brain repeated, again and again.

Entering through the kitchen door, I set my things down on our small Formica table and picked up a message from Billy:

> *Princess,*
> *Out with Paul. Don't wait up . . .*
> *B.L.*

Next to his note was the box I'd received from Gerhard yesterday, containing his thoughts on the latest tape I'd sent him and a bottle of his olive oil. So much had changed for me this year, but thinking about Gerhard pruning his olive trees and drinking his favorite brandy gave me some comfort. Like maybe Tex and I really would walk hand in hand down his road again. Now that Henry's father had sold the final painting for an exorbitant price, and Tex's *Vogue* pictures from last winter had generated renewed interest in Leoni, the house on Formentera was saved for another day. A better day.

Back in my bedroom, I discarded my dress and undergarments in favor of a silk robe. As I tied the sash, my attention snagged on the framed painting over my bed. *Ojos Verdes*. Beneath the dark shapes and symbols, green slashes glowed iridescent, even in the dimmest light. My eyes, and Daddy's.

On the opposite wall was a collection of framed photographs, all shot by Tex. Some were of Formentera, cut out from the magazine spread that had appeared in *Life* at the beginning of the month. Others were shots he'd sent me from Vietnam—a little girl in a conical hat holding a soda bottle; a man with a wrinkled, weathered face selling fish at a market; a couple embracing in an alleyway; even one of an antique watch. That was my favorite. Time had always been the third wheel in our relationship, our love happening either too late or too early. But maybe eventually, we would be right on time.

Walking into the adjacent bathroom, I dipped my finger in the jar of cold cream on the sink, ready to leave the dress-up-doll version of myself back in the club. I smeared it over my face, eyeliner and lipstick becoming a muddy oil slick before vanishing with the pressure of a damp rag. Wiping the last traces of residue off, I stared at the freckles gleaming back at me. *Don't hide them.*

Lighting a joint, I strolled through the house and slid open the patio door. Summer in Los Angeles was hot and dry, and we suffocated daily under the candy-colored smog. I stepped into the moonlight, walking to one of the potted orange trees, savoring the warm burn of smoke in my lungs. "Ruby Tuesday" drifted through the air, a gift from the Stones fan next door. I touched a branch, feeling the thin, waxy leaves between my fingertips. I could barely make out the small green fruit just beginning to form, but I picked one anyway. Rolling the hard lump back and forth in my palm, I imagined the possibility of what it might turn into if given enough time and care. The vibrancy, the sweetness, the taste of sunshine.

Tossing it onto the ground with the other discards, I glanced up at the moon and exhaled, remembering all those nights ago when Tex and I had swum under this same sky, feeling like anything was possible. Music, art, love—they weren't just abstract dreams. They were real, and we had touched them for the briefest of seconds. Smoke billowed and dispersed as insects chirped in the distance. Funny how men tried so hard to reach that barren desert out in space. Maybe the astronauts just wanted a chance to look back at Earth, to see this brilliant blue marble full of life, and say, *Sorry for leaving. I'll come back now.*

TWENTY-SIX

"IF I GET one more request for a mop top, I swear someone's gonna lose an ear." Billy dunked his scissors and comb into the blue jar of Barbicide next to my shoulder. "Twenty-five dollars for a haircut, and this guy wants to look like he just stepped off the cover of *Tiger Beat*. Hell, even the Beatles are over it."

I laughed, setting my *Cosmopolitan* aside. I'd stopped by his salon early so he could blow-dry my hair before a go-see this afternoon. And who was I kidding—it was always fun to spy on the celebrities coming through. People like Paul Newman, Steve McQueen, and Warren Beatty, sitting there in bright smocks, waiting for their turn with the maestro. I'd done a double take the day Clint Eastwood emerged from a private room in the back. For a second, I thought it was Tex, so similar were their builds and facial features. I couldn't wait to tell him about meeting his slightly inferior doppelgänger.

"I thought you were a 'hair architect.' Can't you make anything look good?" I ran my fingers through the wet strands around my face, smoothing out the tangles.

"Princess, there are *limits*." Removing the short scarf from his neck, he tucked it into the back pocket of his pants and pushed up the sleeves of his weathered chambray shirt. It was the unofficial uniform of Sebring employees, purchased from the Fred Segal shop around the corner. Hip, casual, and very California.

He assessed me in the mirror. "So, what are we doing today? Teased, flipped, curled, or ironed?"

"They want something natural. I think it's for a Volkswagen ad."

He burst out laughing. "YOU, in a VW bus, feelin' groovy? That's the most far-out thing I've heard all year."

"Listen, one nibble from a guy who wanted to record a version of "Blues Rushed In" does not automatically mean I get paid to play music. The key is to find a manager who'll take me on. Until then, I grit my teeth, say cheese, and smile."

It turned out the Troubadour Hoot wasn't as big a disaster as I'd originally thought. The man with the mustache tracked down my number from the booking agent and called soon after about an opportunity on his upcoming album. For a while, I thought this might finally be my ticket out of the pit of despair, but the bubble burst two weeks later with the news that the song wasn't going to work for him after all. However, that brief confidence boost sparked a fire to find someone who could get me more opportunities. If Scott McKenzie thought I deserved a shot, maybe I really did.

Billy's face turned apologetic. "Sorry the demo isn't getting much traction."

"It's okay—I just have to find the right person at the right time. Cass said she's having a party tomorrow night when she gets back from New York, so I might stop by and see if there's anyone

there who'll give it a listen. She tends to attract all kinds of indus-
try people."

"And dealers . . ." Billy smirked, well versed in the Canyon scene.

As he turned on one of the handheld blow-dryers, a shampoo
girl approached and tapped him on the shoulder. She held her
fingers to her ear and mouth, indicating he had a phone call. He
passed off the dryer and she took over, waving it back and forth
around my ears, blasting my scalp with hot air. I picked up my
Cosmo again, intrigued by the article about computer-arranged
marriages. I wondered how long it would take Taffy to set a date
with IBM for her daughter.

Just then, movement in the mirror caught my attention. Billy
was waving frantically to me, his eyes wild. I couldn't hear over
the buzz of the dryer, but his lips kept forming a word over and
over. *Ties? Tax?* No, *TEX!*

I jumped up, abandoning the magazine. Racing to the front
of the salon, I caught Billy saying something into the phone. It
sounded like, "Hold on, she's coming now."

"Is it him?" I blurted. "Is it Tex?"

Billy nodded. "It's him. He's okay."

I took the handset from him, my palm trembling. "Tex? Are
you there?"

"Hey, Al, what's shakin'?"

At the sound of his voice, my knees gave out, and Billy caught
me around my waist. Tears filled my eyes, and my heart felt like it
could burst out of my chest.

"Oh my god, how did you find me?!"

"I remembered you said Billy would be workin' at Jay Sebring's
salon, so I had a friend at the AP track down the number. Figured

I might get lucky and catch him there, then get him to tell me your home number. I know we said we wouldn't waste money on phone calls, but anniversaries are an exception."

I shook my head, wiping my cheeks. Billy got me a chair, and I smiled at him in gratitude. He tapped me under the chin, then went back to his station.

"Wait, anniversary?" I searched the wall for a calendar, and there it was, in bold type under the Monday column—September twenty-fifth. I'd met him a year ago today.

"You forgot, didn't you," he teased.

"No, I . . . Okay, I did. Forgive me?"

"I reckon it's all right you forgot the date, as long as you didn't forget me?" I detected uncertainty in his voice, and I wanted to kiss it away in person.

"That's the dumbest thing you've ever said." I shook my head. "Of course I haven't forgotten you. I've got your pictures tacked up all over my bedroom walls."

"I like knowin' you go to sleep looking at them. That's why I only send you the prettiest ones. There're others that . . . well, let's just say they're not so pretty."

I'd seen plenty of horrific imagery on the news, and that was just the stuff fit for television. "Can you tell me anything? Are you still in Saigon?"

"Yep. I found a small apartment and steady work in the AP darkroom. Sometimes I explore the countryside when I can find someone headed out on a transport, but I'm discovering plenty of stories here in the city too. How the Vietnamese are dealing with all the new foreigners, what everyday life is like, that kind of thing."

"What about the food? Are you eating well?"

He grunted. "Ugh, don't ask. This Texan wasn't meant to live on what they call cuisine over here. 'Fish guts' is not my favorite soup flavor."

I grimaced. "All the more reason to come home sooner."

"Between the bugs and the monsoons, I don't know how anyone can stay longer than a year. You got me used to clean sheets and low humidity; I'm ruined now."

Hope bloomed at his words. "So, when do you think you might leave? I don't want to pressure you, but god, I miss you. It's great you went after something that mattered to you, but when is it enough?" The sound of his voice had ignited a long-simmering ember; I needed him here with me.

"Soon. I got a plan, but first I want to hear what you've been up to in LA. Hangin' around Billy, by the sounds of things?"

"I just came to his salon today so he can do my hair before a modeling audition. I've gotten some print ads, nothing too exciting—mostly beauty products and cars."

"So I don't have to worry about you turnin' into a Playboy Bunny?"

I laughed at the idea of me naked on the pages of Hef's magazine. "Definitely not. Although from what I've seen here, sex sells, unfortunately."

"Don't think that's the kind of market you want, Al," he joked. "But speakin' of, how's the singing going? I know your songs are only getting better and better, but how about the gigs?"

I frowned, disappointed I didn't have better news for him. "So-so. I've made some good connections, and I finally saved enough money to record a demo, but I'm still waiting on that one big break. I've been playing small clubs when I can, and the Troubadour a couple times. Things would be a lot better if I could find a manager who wants to take me on. Luckily, Billy's a one-man publicity machine—with scissors."

"I'm glad he's steppin' up while I'm away. Only he's probably missing the most important thing."

"Really? What's that?" I plugged a finger in my other ear, trying to drown out the noise of the salon. I didn't want to miss a word.

"If you want to promote yourself, you're gonna need some good photos, right?"

"Well, it's not like I don't have things to choose from. I *am* a model, after all."

"I don't much like the idea of some other guy taking your picture for this. For cars and hairspray fine, but not for your music. So how's about meetin' me halfway, in Honolulu for Valentine's Day, and I'll take your picture. How does the Royal Hawaiian grab you?"

I wanted to jump up and down, but I also needed to set him straight. "The Royal Hawaiian is swell, but I don't need anything that fancy. I just need you."

"The Royal Hawaiian, Al," he insisted. "It's gotta be that. When our kids look back at the wedding photos, I don't want them to ask me why I took their mom to some dump three miles from the beach."

My breath caught in my throat. Had I heard him right? Wedding photos? "Wait, what are you saying?" All the blood rushed to my ears. "I need you to spell it out."

"All right, if you insist," he laughed. "M-A-R-R-Y M-E. Question mark. And I don't mean just a pretend marriage to fool angry old cleaning ladies in Spain. A real one this time."

An immediate acceptance was on the tip of my tongue, but I had to make one thing clear first. "If I agree, then this has to be it. No more goodbyes. That's all we've ever done, one after another. From now on, we make choices that'll keep us together." I held my breath, waiting for his response.

"No more goodbyes, Al. After Hawaii, I'll come back to LA with you. You get booked on a tour? I'll sit next to you on the bus. Vietnam has taught me a lot, but the biggest thing is that I don't need to be in a war zone to get the best shot. I thought this was where I'd find 'real,' but nothing about this war is real to me. It's just this bizarre movie where men follow the orders of other men who have no idea what it's like to watch their friend die right in front of them. Americans were sold a pack of lies, and now it's too late to do anything about it. The train has already crashed and burned. I can take pictures of the wreckage, or I can take pictures of a girl on the cusp of changing the music scene forever. Both subjects are important, but only one of them means anything to me, and that's you. You're the realest thing I know."

My smile grew so big that Billy, spying on me from across the salon, must have thought I'd cracked up. "Okay, then. My answer's yes. Yes to meeting you in Hawaii. Yes to marrying you!"

He exhaled over the line's static, and it made me happy to know my acceptance wasn't a foregone conclusion. "All right, then. Now that's settled, and you've made me the happiest guy on the planet, I better get off this call. It's costin' me a fortune at the telegraph office, and I still need to buy you a ring."

I shook my head, still grinning. "I don't need one. I promise, I just need you. February fourteenth, I'll be at the Royal Hawaiian. And wait, let me give you my home number. This not talking thing—it's for the birds."

He laughed. "Yeah, I guess you're right. What were we thinking?"

"We were thinking it's expensive and inconvenient, and it is. But don't worry, I'll be a big star soon. I'll pay you back."

"I know you will, darlin'. I know you will."

November 14th, 1967
Laurel Canyon
Los Angeles, California

Dear Daddy,

Imagine the shock when I turned on the radio and my voice was coming out of the speaker! I thought it would take a lot longer for anyone to hear "Follow the Sun," the single Lou recorded, but I should have known Jerry White was a miracle worker. When he signed me as a client at the beginning of October, he said he'd get me on the radio in less than six weeks. We made it just under the wire! It's funny: you wait and wait for luck to strike, and when it finally does, everything starts to happen so fast.

When I heard my song in the car, I pulled over and cried. Just sat there and cried. I'd fantasized about this a thousand times, never imagining I'd feel such a strange mix of panic and relief when it finally happened. And in the next moment, sadness. The sadness that always comes when something amazing happens and you're not there to experience it too. I can't call you and tell you to turn on the radio. I can't hold the phone up to my ear and listen to you telling me you're proud of me. But I know, Daddy. I know.

I mailed a copy of the single to Mother in Paris, and can you believe what she said when she heard it? "My daughter, the star. The brave shooting star."

Love always,
Carolina

TWENTY-SEVEN

I WALKED THROUGH the doors of Musso & Frank and spotted my manager, Jerry, already seated in a red leather booth. A sweating martini rested in front of him, the remainder in a tiny decanter on ice. He'd already ordered another for me.

"You do realize it's only two in the afternoon," I said, sliding in next to him.

"Yeah, but it's five o'clock in New York." He tapped his glass against mine before taking a sip. I laughed and joined him. Icy-cold perfection.

"Isn't Musso & Frank a little upscale for musicians?"

"Not when they've got your pedigree. But don't worry, I won't tell anyone."

I smiled, reminded of why I was grateful to have Jerry representing me. From our first meeting at Cass's house, it was clear he understood not only my past, but my potential future too. And it had taken him only twenty-four hours to call me after I'd slipped him my demo. I liked a man who moved quickly when he found something he wanted.

"So, what deals are we making today?" I asked, taking another sip.

"How does a full LP sound to you?"

I almost choked on my olive. "Are you serious? The single just came out!"

"And it's doing very well. Lou called yesterday and said he wants to get you back in the studio immediately. Said to tell you 'Green has turned to gold,' whatever that means."

I thought back to our first meeting in Palm Beach, when I'd wanted so badly to impress him. How different my life was, just a short time ago.

"Anyway, he wants this to be a story you're telling about places from your jet set days. Your Acapulco song is a good start, but he wants more. The hippie trail is big right now—people want to hear about freedom in a far-off land. He's thinking of calling it *Passports*. Maybe do a combination of guitar and ukulele. Lou can give you the details."

I couldn't believe what I was hearing. A real, full-length album of my own songs, by one of the best producers in the business. It was almost too good to be true.

"Are you sure? I thought we'd agreed to play down my past. You said, 'Nobody wants the musings of a poor little rich girl.'"

Jerry laughed. "Just to clarify, you can talk about sunsets and sailboats all you want. Maybe leave out the diamonds and fully staffed yachts."

Fair enough. "So when do we start?"

"As soon as we're done here. Lou wants to record right after the holidays. Think you can be ready?"

"Absolutely. This is so exciting!" I was buzzing, and not just from the midday alcohol.

"Another thing we need to talk about is promotion," Jerry continued. "Now that your single's getting airtime, I think I can get you opening gigs for some of the bigger bands. The Byrds are playing the Whisky in December. We'll get you in there, then after Christmas you do the album, and we'll line up more dates for February."

I hesitated, realizing it was finally time to divulge my plans with Tex. Initially, I hadn't wanted to tell anyone but Billy and Daphne, for fear I'd jinx it. But now that we were looking ahead to 1968, the time had come. "February's going to be tricky. You see, I'm getting married that month."

Jerry's eyes bulged out of their sockets. "Excuse me? Married? To whom? You don't even have groupies yet!"

"You remember the photographer? Tex? I told you about him when we met."

He nodded.

"He called at the end of September and asked me to marry him on Valentine's Day. I haven't told many people because the date was so far away it almost didn't seem real. Now we're making plans, and February will be here before we know it. But don't worry about the album or touring—Tex already said he'd follow me anywhere. He can take pictures for the label! Or maybe that new magazine they just started in San Francisco—*Rolling Stone*, I think it's called?" I was tossing out ideas as fast as they came to me, but I desperately wanted Jerry to be on board with this plan. Nothing would work if Tex wasn't a part of my life next year.

"Look, I'm happy for you, doll. Really, I am." Jerry hesitated, obviously nervous about what he wanted to say next. "I'm just looking at this from a business perspective. I think you realize

that part of the Carolina package is your looks. You can be as indignant and offended as you want and say it should only be about
your music, but we both know that's a crock of shit. If the only
thing you cared about was writing songs, I'd introduce you to
some of the Brill Building alums. But that's not what you want. *You*
want to be the one singing those songs, not someone else. You
want it to be *your* face on the cover of the album. That's not a bad
thing, and you shouldn't apologize for it. But you just gotta accept
that when people see that album on the shelf, men will want you
and women will want to be you. That's how stars are made. Only
now I'm worried once the world knows you're officially off the
market, the male fantasy part of the equation will be kaput."

"That's ridiculous!" I sputtered, not knowing which point to
argue first. "What about Michelle Phillips? She's married."

He shrugged. "Well, they're not exactly puritans in that house.
The fantasy still exists as a genuine possibility in her case, if you
know what I mean."

I shook my head. "I'm sorry, but this is the way it is. Tex is going
with me wherever I'm headed. These songs that everyone loves
so much? They wouldn't exist without him. He's my muse and I'm
his. I can't do this without him anymore, and I don't want to."

Jerry drained his drink, looking up to the soft lighting overhead. "I guess this is what I get for signing a girl after the Summer
of Love. Naturally, she's in love."

"Naturally." I smiled.

"So the husband is a part of this," he conceded. "What about
your parents? At this point, you're known only as Carolina. Once
people start writing articles, the world is going to find out who
your mother and father are. Are you okay with that?"

My lips thinned. As much as I wanted it to be otherwise, there was no escaping my family name. "I guess I'll have to be. I just hope people get the chance to hear my music without thinking of what happened to Daddy. I have my own life, my own experiences—I don't want them to think all the songs are about his. And as for Mother, I'm going to be wearing her clothes because she's talented and her business needs the publicity right now. But that's the end of it. Her personal life doesn't factor into my career."

The world still didn't know the truth about Mother and Maria, and I planned to keep it that way. It wasn't my story to tell—it was theirs, if they ever felt comfortable.

"Fair enough," he said, raising his hands. "So, any other surprises I need to know about before we go full steam ahead? You're not hiding a kid somewhere, are you? Or a long-lost twin?"

I laughed. "I'm the daughter of David Kimball and Emanuela Leoni, soon-to-be-wife of Jack 'Tex' Fairchild. I'm a water sign, and I prefer gin to vodka—anything but Kipling's." I shuddered. "I like dogs, but not cats, and I've never broken a bone. Now you know everything."

"I doubt it, but maybe we need another round to make sure. Waiter." Jerry lifted his finger to signal.

I knew I chose this guy for a reason.

January 31st, 1968
Laurel Canyon
Los Angeles, California

Dear Daddy,

*It's been a mad rush trying to finish recording
my album before Hawaii. I'm proud of the music. I
think you would be too.*

*Funny, I spent so much time waiting for my "big
break" that I failed to see it was already happening
in tiny, invisible increments. Tex, Formentera,
trying, failing, trying again, Lou, the Troubadour,
Jerry . . . kicking—always kicking. I was waiting
on a tidal wave, never noticing I was already
caught in the current.*

*Yours pulled you under, but mine pushed me
forward.*

Into the sun.

Love,
Carolina

TWENTY-EIGHT

WITH A GRUNT, I heaved my large Samsonite onto the bed and flipped open the latches. I couldn't wait any longer to pack; my anxious energy needed an outlet. The flight to Hawaii was still two weeks away, but it felt like two years. Why the hell hadn't I insisted we meet sooner? Would Christmas in the South Pacific have been so terrible?

Instead, I'd spent the holiday in Palm Springs with Mother, Maria, and Billy at our friend Nelda's house. It was strange not seeing the snow-capped mountains of Gstaad outside the window, but we'd all agreed it was time for something different. On our last night, Mother had surprised me with a simple white dress for my wedding. A-line and hemmed just above the knee, it was constructed of interlocking flowers over crisp cotton lining. She'd designed it for the woman she met on Formentera, not the one who whiled the nights away in Acapulco villas or Gstaad ballrooms. It wasn't as fancy or opulent as Daphne's, but it was right for me. And as she'd pointed out, she would sooner die than risk her daughter getting married in a hula skirt.

Turning back to the closet, I'd just reached up to a high shelf for my sandals when I heard Billy coming down the hall. He knocked on the door and poked his head in. "Five minutes. What'll it be tonight? Stinger? Tom Collins? Manhattan?" It had become a ritual of ours to share cocktails in front of the evening news while we waited for Tex to call. Those brief chats on the last day of every month kept me going until I could be in his arms again.

"Collins, please. I'll be there in a sec," I replied, glancing back at him. He'd gone through a rough breakup last month but seemed to be doing better now. At least he wasn't haunting the kitchen in his raggedy plaid bathrobe anymore.

I strolled into the living room just as he was topping off our drinks with soda water. "Will you do a braid crown for me?" I leaned down to twist the knob on the television, hearing the tubes in the back whirr to life.

Billy stepped back from the bamboo bar cart, passing me a chilled highball glass. "Take a seat on the floor." He moved the pillows around on the sofa and plopped down in the middle, taking a comb out of his front pocket. Always prepared, my friend.

I pushed out the coffee table and sat between his legs, leaning forward so he could work. The WBS logo flashed across the screen, camera focusing on the solemn face of the newscaster. Billy started to gather hair on the side of my face, his long, nimble fingers idly working. I loved when we did this; it felt like I got the real Bartholomew Lipschitz while the rest of the world had to make do with his flashy double.

A mention of Vietnam caught my attention, alongside the words *Special News Bulletin*. As images of gunfire, people running, and the American embassy under siege flashed across the television screen, a sickening dread settled in my chest. I set my glass down, not daring to blink. They called it an uprising of the North Vietnamese, on a night that was supposed to be a holiday. Sneak attacks on unsuspecting villages and cities, including Saigon. Billy put down his comb, eyes glued to the footage.

"I don't understand. I thought Saigon was safe," I said, my voice wavering.

He squeezed my shoulder. "It's probably nothing. Just another day over there, right?"

I shook my head. "No. This is different. This is big." Acid rose in my throat as the footage cut to bodies in the streets, lying like discarded sacks of grain. Only a tennis shoe or wristwatch to prove they'd once been alive.

"I'm sure he's okay. It's not like he had any kind of business at the embassy, right? And he's smart enough to hide if it comes to that."

I could tell Billy was trying to comfort me, but I barely heard anything over the roaring in my ears.

Just then the phone rang, startling me out of my trance. I ran to it, knowing it was too early to be Tex but irrationally hoping it was. "Hello?" I answered, clinging to the impossible.

"Caroline." Mother's voice was both a relief and a disappointment. "Are you watching the news? We're still at Nelda and Joe's; they had the television on. It's Saigon."

"Yes, Billy and I are watching too. I didn't see him, Mother. I didn't see him in the street." Tears formed as my shaking hand struggled to hold the phone. Most of the time I could turn a blind eye to the dangers Tex faced over there, but now I was forced to look.

"Do you have any way to contact him?"

The pragmatism in her words gave me strength. Mother was always good in a crisis.

"No, he's the one who calls me. In fact, we're supposed to talk later tonight at our normal time."

"If he doesn't get through, don't panic yet. The phone lines are probably jammed," she reminded me.

"What should I do?"

"Maria and I will make a list of everyone we know in government. Or anybody who's married to someone in government. Just in case. Wait for him to call, and keep Billy with you. I'll telephone again in the morning."

I sniffed. "Okay. And thank you, Mother. Thank Maria for me too."

"Be strong, my brave girl."

We said our goodbyes, and I put the handset down, turning back to the television. They'd already moved on to a story about the space program, and I wanted to scream at the anchor to go back. Who cared about the damn moon when people were dying?

We spent the next two hours pacing the living room, alternately watching the television and the phone, willing it to ring. I picked up my guitar at one point, hoping music might calm me down, but I could barely get my fingers to remember the simplest chords. Billy called and woke Daphne in London to see if Dickie might have WBS connections who could tell us something, but we knew even if he did, it wouldn't happen tonight.

God, why didn't I make him come home sooner?

Finally, just after ten o'clock, the shrill sound of the phone startled me awake from where I'd collapsed against Billy's shoulder.

I raced to the receiver, but when I picked it up, all I heard was crackling static. I could just make out a faint voice saying "Caroline."

"Tex? Tex, is that you? Are you okay?" I shouted. I felt like I'd fallen down an elevator shaft and hadn't yet hit bottom. He had to be okay—he just had to be.

The static eased a bit, and I thought I heard "safe" and "don't worry."

My shoulders sagged with relief. "Come home now!" I pleaded. "You don't have to wait and meet me in Hawaii. Come to Los Angeles first and we'll figure it out."

". . . no flights . . ." More static. And then he said something that terrified me anew. ". . . need to stay . . . finally . . . work . . . important."

"What does that mean?" I wailed. "Jack, this is crazy. Just fly to LA as soon as you can. It's too dangerous now."

"Two weeks . . . Honolulu . . ."

And with that, the line went dead in my hands. I pressed the switch in rapid succession, as if I could magically call him back to me.

Billy stepped closer to my side. "What's going on?"

"He's staying. The connection was bad, but I think that's what he was trying to tell me. He said 'Honolulu,' but he also said he's doing something important."

"That could just mean he needs time to wrap things up. You know, you really should give proper notice when you leave a job. If you'll recall, that's how I ended up in a safari tent outside of Mombasa with Taffy at the end of April. Lord, how the mosquitos loved Shalimar."

My lips attempted a smile at his joke, but couldn't quite hit the mark. I was too worried about the words I might have missed over the faulty lines connecting us from halfway across the globe. Was Tex trying to tell me he needed *more* than two weeks? That I shouldn't go to Honolulu because he couldn't marry me now? And if that was the case, and he wanted to delay, was I prepared to give him more time? I'd sacrificed so much already and didn't want to waste another second on someone who couldn't make our relationship a priority.

"I can see that brain of yours spinning out, and you need to stop it right now," Billy commanded. "He loves you and he wants to marry you. He wouldn't have gone through the trouble of getting a call out to you, in the middle of a goddamn war zone, no less, if he didn't."

"But does he love me enough to marry me in two weeks like we'd planned?"

My friend frowned like he was disappointed in me. "You know he does. And if I'm wrong, and it turns out he's actually a chicken-shit piece of garbage, then I'll fly out and join you in Honolulu myself. I can't give you a wedding, but I can give you love. Unconditional, princess. Always."

He wrapped me in his arms, and I squeezed him back tightly. "I don't deserve you," I mumbled into his chest.

"No, but you'll write a hit song about me one day that sexually confused teenagers will play alone in their bedrooms while weeping, and we'll call it even. Speaking of, have I told you yet how proud I am of you? Album on the way, standing on your own two feet, ready to conquer the world. Two years ago, would you have believed all this would be possible?"

"Definitely not."

"See, there you go. Sure, it would be great to ride off into the sunset with your cowboy, but that horse'll still move with only you in the saddle. You're going to be okay because you *are* okay. You've been okay for a long time now."

A single tear tracked down my cheek at my friend's words. He was right—I didn't need Tex to make a life for myself. But lord, how much better that life would be with him beside me.

Honolulu

February 14th, 1968
Somewhere over the Pacific

Dear Tex,

Soon we'll be reunited, which potentially makes this letter overkill. But I couldn't resist one last chance before we're bound together in marriage to write the words I LOVE YOU.

I can't predict the future or know whether we'll have the happily ever after of movies and fairy tales. I can't even be sure you'll make it back to me. But what I do know is that everything that's passed has led me here, sitting on an airplane, flying to you. My funny valentine, my white rabbit, my tall drink of tequila. I wouldn't have changed a single thing to end at this beginning.

I love you always,
Al

TWENTY-NINE

"ALOHA, AND WELCOME to Honolulu," the stewardess's honey-sweet voice crackled over the intercom. I let out the breath I'd been holding, glancing out the window next to me. Palm trees raced by as the plane taxied, a rainbow shining off in the distance. Hawaii always knew how to make a good first impression.

Running my finger over the envelope seal, I flipped it over and wrote *To My Husband*. The plane came to a stop, and I unbuckled my seat belt, gathering my handbag and ukulele case from the overhead bin. Stepping into the warm sunshine, I climbed down the steps toward the long-haired island girl, her arms laden with flower leis. She slipped one over my head, smiling with quiet serenity. I thanked her, then walked quickly toward the terminal to collect my suitcase. While others might be seduced by the perfect weather and colorful orchids, I didn't have time to take a breath and slow down. Not when the love of my life was waiting for me.

✳

When we pulled up to the Royal Hawaiian, I paid the taxi driver and motioned for a bellhop to collect my bag. As my heels clicked against the marble entryway of the Pink Palace, I looked left and right in search of Tex. Disappointed not to find him waiting in the lobby, I approached the front desk.

"Welcome to the Royal Hawaiian, miss. Checking in?"

"Yes. The reservation is under Jack Fairchild, I think."

"Yes, I see here, one double room under Mr. and Mrs. Jack Fairchild, two people, for six nights." She turned to get a key from the rack behind her.

At least she'd confirmed that this was all real: he'd actually called to make these plans.

I cleared my throat. "Can you tell me if Mr. Fairchild has already checked in? We were supposed to meet here."

She scanned her book again. "No, it looks like you're the first. Should I send him up when he arrives?"

I refused to imagine the worst yet. "Yes, that's fine. Thank you." I accepted the key and turned to the elevators. He would be here; his flight was just arriving after mine. *Stay calm.*

The bellhop escorted me upstairs, opening the curtains and setting my suitcase on the luggage rack, accepting my tip before abandoning me to the empty room. And god, was it *empty*. I glanced out the window at the glistening sea, and the bodies spread up and down Waikiki. Little catamarans bobbed in the water, and farther down the beach, Diamond Head towered like a slumbering giant. The perfect place for a honeymoon; the only thing missing was the groom.

Shrugging off my suit jacket, I unbuttoned the top two buttons of my blouse and unzipped my skirt. I let it fall to the floor in a heap, then sat on the edge of the bed and reached for the telephone. Checking my watch, I saw it was already six o'clock in California—Billy would be home from the salon by now.

The line rang twice before connecting. "I made it," I said in greeting.

"Good. And? Is he there?"

"No, not yet. But he reserved the room under Mr. and Mrs. Jack Fairchild. So that's something, I guess. He definitely planned to be here."

I heard him take a drag of his cigarette. "Don't panic yet. We don't know what the flight schedules are. Or who's getting in and out of the country right now. Just because he's late doesn't mean he changed his mind."

"No, I know. He booked the room for six nights, so I've got time to wait." I stared at the ocean and the colorful umbrellas lining the beach. "I feel like a girl who got stood up for a date. Pathetic. Except I can't be mad at him, because I have no idea what's happened to him!"

"You're not pathetic. Why don't you go down to the bar for a mai tai? Or shopping for a muumuu?"

"I already brought a beach dress."

"Who said it was for you?"

I smiled and twisted the phone cord around my finger, crossing and recrossing my legs. My nervous energy needed somewhere to go. "I think I should stay put for a while, just in case he arrives tonight. I don't want him to walk into an empty room. Trust me, it's kind of the worst. Plus, it's Valentine's Day. The hotel is probably crawling with happy couples."

"Ugh, tell me about it. Even the gays are nauseating today. I wish you were here to watch old monster movies with me."

"Next year," I promised.

"Nah, you'll be a married woman then. You won't have time for your sad single friends anymore."

I shook my head. "I'll make time. For you, always."

He took another puff, silent for a moment. "All right, princess, you go get ready for your man. And if he still isn't there by tomorrow, call me, and I'll be on the first plane out. We'll find matching surfers."

Laughing, I replied, "I promise. 'Night, Billy. I love you."

"Love you too."

Replacing the phone in its cradle, I stood and walked to my suitcase. Reaching into one of the pockets, I pulled out the box containing my wedding gift to Tex: my father's watch. It was stopped now, as it had been on the island, but I wanted us to wind it together. I wanted us both to see the second hand start to tick forward, knowing we were stepping into our future. Knowing that, finally, we were right on time.

I set the box on the dresser and began to unpack my clothes, grinning as I pulled out my wedding dress and the little veil Billy had insisted on buying me. My suggestion for a simple flower in my hair had fallen on deaf ears. *Leave the flowers to the hippies. Real brides wear a veil.*

Eventually running out of things to put away, I gave in and called for supper to be sent up, adding a mai tai to the order. Curious, I glanced out the window at the surfers bobbing in the water. Billy might like the looks of them, but I definitely preferred cowboys.

※

Morning rays assaulted my face, forcing my attention to the clock on the nightstand. Blinking the numbers into focus, I saw it was only seven a.m. I'd stayed awake until ten last night, reading and rereading the same chapter in my book, unable to concentrate. I kept waiting for the doorknob to twist, but it never did.

Brushing a palm across the cool sheet next to me, I frowned at the barren space where Tex should have been. I'd dreamed last night that he and I were standing on a beach, blue water crashing against the shore. My father stood beside him, Mother and Maria on my other side. Daddy looked at Tex, then me, before holding up his watch with a wink. I couldn't remember more, but just that brief image felt like a sign that everything would be okay. Like maybe our time was almost here.

Realizing I couldn't stay in the room forever, I hauled myself up and opened the curtains wider. Through the palm trees beneath my window, I could almost make out the pink umbrellas down by the circular pool. The water called to me, as it always had when I wanted to jump out of my skin. I grabbed my red bikini and ukulele, eager for a change of scenery.

Stopping by the front desk on my way outside, I instructed the concierge to direct any calls for me to the pool bar. He promised he would, calling me Mrs. Fairchild. The name should have sounded foreign or jarring, but somehow it didn't. Like Kimball had only ever been a placeholder.

The lanai was empty, with no rowdy children or couples to ruin the tranquility. Piling my things on a chaise, I shrugged out of my loose caftan and walked to the deep end, lungs heaving in a breath as I raised my arms into a diving stance. Feet springing off the ledge, I plunged into the cool water, silencing my thoughts. After long, lazy strokes, my body transitioned to a float as my eyes blinked up at the sky. The scents of plumeria and coconut were faint in the air, and beyond the overhead foliage, the pink hotel loomed, rising like a grand empress in the jungle. Rose-colored luxury, indeed.

Relaxed, I started to hum the notes to a song I'd been thinking about on the plane. A vision of lyrics streaked above me in white cursive handwriting.

Fly over the hills
White peaks of marshmallow clouds
You said, Come to me, bird
Flap your wings over blue seas and sycamore trees

And when we meet
Will you remember my voice
Or was it changed by the wind
And the seas and the sycamore trees?

My arms waved gently, legs kicking every so often to stay afloat. As the sun rose higher, slowly bathing the shaded patio with golden light, a prickling sensation hit me—a feeling of being watched. Lifting my head out of the water, I heard that faint sound my ears could have detected across a thousand crowded rooms, through a thousand crystal glasses meeting in celebration or a thousand notes pulsing through a stereo. In the quiet of a sleepy Honolulu morning, it hit me like a shot.

Click.

Spinning in the water, I searched among the umbrellas for a set of smiling eyes and that magnificent crooked nose. And there, next to a wrought-iron table, stood a tall man with a camera. Returned to me once more. Returned to me forever.

"Oh my god," I breathed, arms and legs paddling furiously toward his end of the pool. Inhaling a mouthful of water, I began coughing as I approached the concrete edge.

Laughing, he crouched down, holding his camera lazily over one knee. "Now don't go drownin' on me, Al. I've traveled an awful long way to get to you."

"Is this real? You're actually here?" I stared up at Tex in a daze, reacquainting myself with the lines of his face, the length of his beard, and the flop of hair against his forehead. Sideburns new, lips the same. I catalogued every square inch in a fraction of a second.

"My plane just landed. I'm sorry I couldn't get word to you last night—mechanical issues in Saigon. I hightailed it over here as fast as I could from the airport, and when I stopped to pick up the key, the desk clerk told me 'Mrs. Fairchild' was currently enjoying a morning dip. Gotta say, Al, I know your set doesn't go for last names, but I like the sound of that one."

Gripping the ledge, I pulled myself closer as he kneeled on the ground. He lifted a hand to cup my cheek, thumb brushing my lips, tracing their outline.

"And wouldn't you know I'd find you in the water. Still kickin'. Calling me toward you."

"You always did like chasing after pretty girls in swimming pools."

"Just the one."

Grinning, he held up his camera, focusing the lens on my face. Before he could stop me, I tugged on his shirt, pulling hard. As his body started to fall, seconds before his head hit the water and the camera collided with the pool deck, I heard that perfect sound once more. A shutter capturing a moment in time; a beginning and an end. A turquoise pool and a green-eyed siren, lit by the rising sun.

Click.

AUTHOR'S NOTE

While the main characters of *Follow the Sun* are entirely fictional, they inhabit a world that was very real. Much of this world was captured by photographer Slim Aarons (1916-2006), and it's because of his prolific coverage of the international jet set that this book exists.

I will never forget standing in a tiny bookshop in Amsterdam during the summer of 2013, flipping through the pages of *Poolside with Slim Aarons*, feeling like I'd entered an alternate reality. Lucious Kodachrome photos of attractive people in attractive places, each frame telling a story about this glamorous era that existed at a very specific point in the twentieth century. Was it *really* as fabulous as it looked? It was a question I couldn't stop asking, and my curiosity grew into the book you now hold in your hands.

Much of Aarons' iconic imagery has found its way into *Follow the Sun*, along with other anecdotes and interesting details I found in my research on both the jet set and the early days of the Laurel Canyon music scene. Artistic liberties have been taken with some of the historical figures and locations; however, I've tried to stay as accurate as possible in terms of key dates and pop culture milestones. Rather than a textbook account, it is my greater hope that this novel conveys the feeling one gets when looking at a Slim Aarons photograph: like you're a voyeur to a dream; a time traveler to a place in the sun.

ACKNOWLEDGEMENTS

The fact that this book exists beyond my hard drive is a testament to the many, many generous people I've met on the long and winding road to publication. I didn't think I'd ever be given the chance to thank them publicly, so having the opportunity to do so now is the cherry on top of the sundae (or the twist on the rim of a cocktail, if that's your preference).

First and foremost, I'm eternally grateful to my agent Jess Dallow, and the entire Brower Literary team. Jess, I came to you in the middle of a pandemic, arms full of baggage, with a manuscript that still needed work. Miraculously, you welcomed me in. I cannot imagine a better champion for my words, or a better partner in this business. Thank you for believing in this story, and all the stories yet to come. To Kimberly Brower, thank you for making me feel like a success before a single book was ever sold. I'm lucky to have found an agency that takes such good care of its authors, at every stage of the journey.

To my brilliant editor Amanda Ferreira, who immediately understood what this book is (and perhaps more importantly:

what it is not), always staying true to my original vision at every stage of the editing and publication process. Maybe it's cheesy, and maybe I watch too many romantic comedies, but after our first conversation, I couldn't help but think of that famous line from *Bridget Jones's Diary*: "You like me just the way I am." Amanda, you are this book's Mark Darcy. I am so lucky I get to work with you.

To everyone at Random House Canada, thank you for making this nervous debut author feel incredibly welcome and supported. Sue Kuruvilla, your early enthusiasm for this story meant the world, and to my copyeditor Sue Sumeraj and proofreader Eleanor Gasparik, you both saved me a thousand times over, making this manuscript sparkle like one of Daphne's diamonds. Talia Abramson, you made my dreams come true with your gorgeous cover design!! I felt like the luckiest author in the world when this hit my inbox.

I'm scared to admit how many rewrites this manuscript went through in its decade-long journey to the bookstore; let's just say, it was more than one, less than a hundred. So many talented authors were generous with their time and feedback, which is even more incredible when you realize how good their work is. Seriously, how did you find the time to help an unknown aspiring writer *and* finish your own books? Kelly Siskind, Gwynne Jackson, Shelby Riley, Rosie Danan, and Mae Thorn—thank you for pulling me along when I was exhausted and couldn't see a way forward. This novel exists in its current form because of you all.

There are some very wonderful friends who propped me up in my dark moments and acted as sounding boards when I needed it most. Maureen Lee Lenker, Rosalie Leonard, Brooke

Burroughs—I'm so grateful to have you in my corner. You inspire me every day with your creativity and kindness.

To Mel, who read my terrible first draft and was very, very careful with my fragile ego—your generosity knows no bounds. Can you believe this is finally real??? I sure can't.

To Nadine, who offered space to share my words, advice I gratefully accepted, and her artistic talent when it came time to take my dreaded author photos—thank you for always guiding me to the best light.

Kathy and Kim—there's nobody I'd rather toast the big moments with. I'm lucky to call you my sisters, and it has meant the world to have your support.

To everyone who has followed me on Cinema Sips, thank you for helping me create this community I'm so incredibly proud of. The blog kept me motivated through all the failed drafts, all the waiting, and all the rejections. It also enabled me to connect with a lot of fantastic people over the years, and it's been one of the great pleasures of my life to bond over our shared love of movies and cocktails.

To my *Moviejawn* crew, I could not ask for a better cheering section. You've given me the types of friendships I always wished I had as a shy teenager of the late-1990s who wanted nothing more than to have deep conversations about the filmographies of John Waters and Richard Linklater. Finally, I found my clique. It's been amazing to watch the zine grow into something truly special, and I'm honored to have my articles in the vicinity of so many talented writers and creators.

To Len, who told me the most difficult thing I'd ever have to do is figure out what I *want* to do with my life. In many ways, this book is a direct result of that advice. Gosh, I wish you'd been able to see it on your bookshelf.

To Grandma Jo, my target audience, forever and always.

And now the hardest part...

I had no idea when I started writing *Follow the Sun* that Caroline's grief would one day become my own, but sadly, it has. The luckiest of us grow up with a loving father who tells their kid to dream big; I was fortunate enough to have two of them. Dad, Jim—even though I can't call either you on the phone and hear your voices anymore, I know you're both proud of me.

One person I *can* still call is my mom, who if you ask her, will probably say she had nothing to do with my becoming a writer. However, I'd say that the woman who read me *Make Way for Ducklings* and *Berenstain Bears* books until her voice was hoarse, who let me check out more *Baby-Sitters Club* and *Sweet Valley High* paperbacks than either of us could safely carry out of the Indiana Free Library, who allowed me to watch soap operas and Danielle Steel miniseries as a small child, has everything to do with it. Melinda exposed me to good storytelling and showed me how important it is in our lives. I would be nowhere without her love and encouragement.

And finally, the biggest acknowledgement goes to my husband, Chris, and our girls, Pickles and Peaches. Anyone who follows my social media knows I'm pretty much obsessed with our family. Chris, I'll never forget the time I felt so defeated about publishing that I soaked one of your shoulders with tears. "Don't worry," you said. "I have two." I decided to write a love story about artists who inspire and strengthen each other because they say it's better to write what you know. I may not live in the 1960s or be a member of the international jet set, but I know a good deal about finding your soulmate and making an incredible life filled with art, books, music, and joy. No offense to Caroline and Tex, but ours is still the greatest romance I could imagine.

LIZ LOCKE is the founder of CinemaSips.com, a weekly guide to cocktail and movie pairings, as well as a frequent contributor to *Moviejawn*. Originally from western Pennsylvania, she now lives in Austin, Texas, with her husband and very adorable rescue dog. When not writing or watching her favorite classic films, she can usually be found with a cocktail in one hand and a book in the other.